HER WARRIORS' THREE WISHES

A DANTE'S CIRCLE NOVEL

CARRIE ANN RYAN

Her Warriors' Three Wishes
A Dante's Circle Novel
By: Carrie Ann Ryan
© 2013 Carrie Ann Ryan
ISBN: 978-1-947007-65-9
Cover Art by Charity Hendry

For more information, please join Carrie Ann Ryan's MAILING LIST.
To interact with Carrie Ann Ryan, you can join her FAN CLUB.

HER WARRIORS' THREE WISHES

Jamie Bennett knew that warrior angel Ambrose Griffin was hers from the moment she learned that the things that go bump in the night are real. She, along with her friends, was forever changed the night the lightning struck and altered her fate. But what she doesn't know is that while Ambrose might be hers, she's missing someone else.

Ambrose always holds himself back because he can't afford to lose anyone else. He's lived and lost lifetimes over as he's fought for his people, and though he knows that Jamie could be his if he takes that risk, there's something missing. Or, more accurately, *someone*.

When Jamie is kidnapped and sent to hell, Ambrose will not only risk a war between the realms to find her, he'll find his heart in the process—in Jamie and Bailin. When Bailin, a demon from hell, meets the two people who could fill his heart and his soul, he'll need to fight for something he hasn't felt in over a century—hope.

DEDICATION

To my Street Pack who wanted to know more about the Dante's Circle world.

ACKNOWLEDGMENTS

Thank you to my Pack who make what I do worth it. You guys are always right there helping out when I need it. And of course my hubby who when I said I'd be writing a ménage story about an angel, a demon, and a not-so-human, you said, "Of course."

Also, thank you to my readers. You guys are amazing and make everything I do that much better.

CHAPTER 1

It's odd how a strike of lightning can change a person's destiny, but it takes the decisions and strength of others to make it happen. The wind brushed against his wings and he brought them closer to his body, needing that ounce of control.

Ambrose Griffin looked out along the angelic enclave as he stood high on the cliff's edge and inhaled the fresh, open scent. This was his home, or at least it should have been. It was more of a resting place for him now. He didn't even know when the loss of home had come to him. Changes were coming, he felt them in every fiber of his being, yet he couldn't see their outcomes. To be honest, he really didn't want to. He might have been older than dirt, but he wasn't a seer. He didn't envy those who held that so-called gift.

Ambrose didn't want the world like it was. He'd seen countless civilizations rise and fall, people live and die faster than the sand that drifted away with their ashes along the wind.

Frankly, he was tired, the aches in his bones not from old age, but from time itself—he was an angel, he *didn't* age —but from the weight of his past.

He was a warrior angel. One designed, trained, and delegated to hand out the justice of the angelic council. His blade was the final cut of judgment. His sword was that of law and order. He lived and breathed the duties set forth by the council, the same council that beckoned him to join their ranks each time he saw them—at their request, not his.

Each time they summoned him and begged him to take a place within them, he'd declined. He'd seen the depravity of power and wanted nothing of it. The council had changed in the past year, a short time for an angel, but the change had been needed.

After the Angelic Wars—the centuries' long battles between two factions of angels—had ended, their council had been poisoned from within by Striker. The treasonous, brown-winged angel had started the Wars himself and had not stopped when the final blade had been lowered. No, he'd continued on in secret, almost killing Shade, Ambrose's brother-in-arms, and Shade's true-half, Lily.

They had persevered, and now Striker was no more— killed at the hands of Shade himself. Yet, with Striker's death, the empty seat on the council beckoned him, or rather the other council members had. He wanted nothing to do with it. He had all the power he wanted and desired nothing more. He didn't want to sit idly by and make declarations and decisions for others. No, he'd rather feel a blade warm in his hand as he fought for all that was right.

It was all he had done for his five-thousand-year existence and all he could see in his future. He needed nothing else.

Not even *her*.

No, it wasn't the time to think of her. It was never the time to think of her.

He'd seen the worst in man and angel alike far more often than not. Angels weren't the godly and holy beings people thought. Though those might exist—he wasn't so sure—they did not enter this realm or any of the other supernatural realms.

Humans weren't exactly as human as others would like to think. No, they were diluted versions of all things inhuman. Centuries of breeding with other supernaturals had created a supernatural without magic. Though, at first, the humans had known of magic and all it entailed, over time their true beginnings had been lost to them. Science and religion had warred with each other, erasing the true keystone to their humanity.

Now it was just as well. Humans weren't ready for the existences of angels, shifters, brownies, demons, and so many others to become common knowledge. They feared what they did not understand, and a war to end all wars would be an inevitable outcome. Seerers had foretold it, and Ambrose knew it to be truth deep down in his bones.

The gods, or whatever others called them, had other things in store however. A year before they'd struck seven women, seven close-knit friends, with a lightning strike that had unleashed the supernatural DNA within their genetic makeup. Each woman might or might not unleash the most prominent supernatural strain of DNA in their own code, though for their sakes, Ambrose hoped the latter. A change such as that would be a shock—no pun intended.

Lily, the first to change, had made it through and was now a brownie because of the lightning and the fact that she was stronger than she thought and had Shade by her side. Of course, it was also Shade's fault that her powers had been unearthed to begin with. Even with the lightning, it had taken their bonding and making love for her powers to be fully unleashed. A simple meeting with Shade had brought her powers to the surface, even though they had not been fully realized. It took that mating of a true half for the change to be complete.

It would be like that for the other six of them—if they met their true halves.

Any one of the other girls could be going through that pain that unsettled feeling that came with finding their true half but not completing the mating.

Ambrose gave a long sigh, one filled with an eternal memory that seemed to bear down on him with each passing day. With a swift intake of breath, he leapt off the edge of the cliff, his wings spreading wide, catching a wind current. He flew down to the ravine, following the river's path, the wind lashing through his hair. He never felt as alive as he did when he flew amongst the clouds and then again with nature. This was why he loved being an angel, even though the weight of the years felt heavier as time moved on.

He landed on the edge of a cliff that gave way to a marketplace. He'd told Shade and Lily he'd meet them on the other side of it, and he didn't want to be late. We walked past a grouping of younger female angels, and they each gave tentative smiles in his direction.

Well, they were younger to him. By the taste of their powers as they seeped off them, he knew them to be at least a few hundred years old. Babies to an ancient like him.

And if they were considered babies, then she—

No, he couldn't think about her. Not if he wanted to remain sane. He'd spent the past year in the angelic realm dealing with the aftermath of Striker's betrayal—away from her.

The girls—no, women—flexed their wings, each a painting of beauty and fragile elegance. Cool in their portrayal, iced in their immortally.

Not for him. No one was. Not even her.

Ambrose knew what the others saw. White wings, not as plain as those in the drawings by humans, but almost crystalline in nature, gleaming in the sunlight. He had the body of a warrior, one strengthened over eons of war and dispensing justice. His white hair ran straight down to the middle of his back, slightly mussed from his flight. He usually wore it tied back with a leather band but had opted to let it go free to feel like a younger man, a freer one.

What had he been thinking?

From the women's stares, he may have made a mistake.

He didn't want their attention. He'd had his angel a lifetime ago and didn't want another. He knew what *could* be his fate, and the angels fluttering their eyelashes and wings were not it. He gave a regal nod and a cool stare. Their smiles vanished, but their gazes didn't waver.

Apparently, they liked the challenge?

No thanks. He didn't desire their attention, didn't deserve it. He was just a warrior angel, not a man to be admired.

He left them where they stood, their discontent clear, but he let it wash over him. The market was filled with the hustle and bustle of activity. Mothers held their babies close because a child was a prized gift in their culture. Children played in the street as there were no cars needed in their lands. Merchants sold goods as though it were a long-ago time in the human realm. The angels moved at a slower pace, though they held the technology to do anything. They were a mismatch of cultures and times. Some wore robes, while others, like him, wore jeans and other items of the modern movement.

He'd hated the robes anyway. The wind would always leave him feeling a bit breezy and exposed. He bit his lip to hold back a smile at the thought of what others would wear under those robes, didn't want to scare anyone today.

Ambrose walked past a group of young males play-fighting with wooden swords. Although a bullet could pierce a body, angelic or not, most angels preferred the more elegant weapon to fight, and for a warrior, it was a must. These young boys had their sights on the warrior class, one that would take much effort, but he'd help them when it came time for their mentoring—if they made it that far. Wordlessly, he walked up to one boy and adjusted the grip of his sword before moving on. He stopped abruptly when he noticed they were all frozen in place, their mouths open in shock.

"You need to be sure you handle your weapons with care," he advised, his voice deep and rough with lack of use. He only spoke if needed; there was no use in wasting words when actions would prove just as useful, if not more so. "Your opponent will be stronger than you in some cases, and you need to rely on your skill, as well as what's ingrained in you. Be aware."

With a nod, he left them in silence. Behind him, he heard murmurs of his name, whispers in reverence. He'd done that boy a favor, something the boy's father should have done. Though Ambrose was a warrior, he was also a mentor and a weapons enthusiast. Weapons were his passion.

His only passion these days.

His collection rivaled those of the best museums, if not surpassed them. Scholars would envy it had they known it existed, but his life was shrouded in secret from the humans, as it should be.

"Scaring young children, are you?" Shade Griffin said as he walked toward him with his arm around his true half and wife, Lily. Shade was his brother-in-arms, his partner in justice, brother by choice and not blood.

He was also the brother of his late wife, though that had been long ago.

Lily laughed, a sweet trill that made Ambrose think of family. She was now his sister, someone he'd die to protect, and her beauty surpassed most: ivory skin, large green eyes, and chestnut hair. He could easily see why Shade had fallen in love the moment he'd seen her.

"Shade, stop making fun of Ambrose," Lily scolded and elbowed him in the ribs.

"You still laughed, my dear," Shade said and kissed her temple.

She blushed and ducked her head. Ambrose lifted a corner of his lip and rubbed her cheek with his knuckle. Shade raised a brow, and Ambrose moved back, not caring in the slightest that Shade was territorial. He didn't fault the other angel for his attitude, but Shade should know Ambrose had another on his mind and didn't want Lily that way. It was still fun to needle him, even though the world thought he wasn't the most humorous of men.

"You're fine, Lily," he soothed. "I know you only laugh with him to humor him. He needs the help with his fragile ego."

Shade threw his head back and laughed. "Ambrose just told a joke and almost smiled." He clutched his chest and staggered back, bringing Lily with him. "I think I need to sit down."

"You're a riot, oh-wise-one," Ambrose said dryly. "Was there a reason you wanted to meet here?"

Lily looked around, her face radiant, glowing even. Was she…? Perhaps, but he'd let her tell him the news. Women seemed to like that.

"I've never been here before, so I thought it would be a nice change," Lily said, practically bouncing on her feet.

In the past year since their meeting, she'd been to the angelic realm a few times, but only to Shade's home or his own. She and Shade spent most of their time in the human realm, protecting her six friends in case the other supernaturals found out exactly what was going on and it turned dangerous. Ambrose had said he would help but had taken the coward's way out and gone back to the angels to help deal with Striker's betrayal.

He knew his break from the humans was almost at an end. The angels didn't need him anymore to oversee the change, and he knew the human women needed him more. Shade, and the girls' dragon friend, Dante, were on watch, but Ambrose should have helped more.

He still had time though. Maybe he could make amends.

"Ambrose?" Shade asked, worry in his features.

Ambrose shook away his thoughts and guilt and looked back to his two best friends. "Sorry, I was lost in thought. What is it you needed to tell me?"

Lily and Shade shared a worried glance that transformed to pure bliss, and a little stress on Shade's side.

"We're pregnant!" Lily explained, her cheeks rosy and her eyes bright.

Ambrose smiled, full out, a rarity, he knew. He pulled Lily into a tight hug and twirled her around. "Congratulations, Lily, my dear, you will be a wonderful mother."

Images of his own children's faces flashed in a fading

memory, but he didn't feel any pain, only that hollowness of a long-lost future.

He put Lily down and gave her a chaste kiss on the mouth. "I will be there for you if you need me."

He clapped Shade on the back, and Shade gave him a look that said the other angel knew what Ambrose had been thinking about. They'd been friends and brothers too long to hide those things.

"I'm very happy for the both of you," Ambrose said. He pulled back and held his arm across his chest. "I will do all in my power to ensure your child, and your future children, are safe and happy," he vowed.

Shade mirrored his movement, and they both bowed. Tears stained Lily's cheeks, but she still held her smile.

"You'll be godfather, Ambrose, right?" she asked.

As if he could say no. He nodded, pleasure at the thought of their trust running through him.

"Of course," he said, his voice choked with emotion.

"We've already told the others in the human realm," Lily continued. "Sorry we didn't tell you first, but it didn't make any sense to come here before telling them."

"I don't mind, Lily."

"Jamie will be godmother; is that okay?" Lily asked. He knew she'd sensed something off between him and her friend, but thankfully, she hadn't broached the subject.

Jamie.

The name he'd fought so hard to forget.

The woman who haunted his dreams, more so than his dead wife.

Jamie, the woman who could have been his true half if he'd let it happen—who *was* his true half.

"Of course," he said again, this time a new emotion threatening to choke him. "Let's celebrate with a good meal, shall we?" He led them to a small eatery, his thoughts not on their conversation, but on the woman he'd avoided.

Jamie deserved more, a future. Not the broken shell of a man. He wasn't selfish enough to think he would make her happy, though he desperately wanted to be that man. Sometimes he thought he could be—could see their future.

No, he couldn't. She was too young for him. Too full of life. She'd be happier without him.

He closed his eyes while Shade and Lily talked to each other. He tugged on the cord that connected him and Jamie, the one she didn't know existed because she hadn't made the change to supernatural yet, even though he knew she was feeling the effects of the need to change. Luckily, it hadn't been as bad as Lily's, so he could leave her. She might feel only slightly weak, but she hadn't had the seizures or other side effects that Lily had endured, thankfully.

Unlike Lily though, Jamie had been feeling the weakness for almost a year.

And, it was his fault.

He'd left her, and they hadn't made love.

Hadn't even kissed.

He hadn't wanted to tie her to a man too old to be what she needed. In his heart, he'd known there was another for her. He'd felt it. The world consisted of just one true half per person, and some triads, Ambrose felt for certain there was another for Jamie, one that would be her true half. He knew in his heart that she would be happy with that other man, whoever he may be.

He sighed. Now he was just kidding himself. There wasn't potentially several mates out there for any one person. If he could feel like something was missing, like there was another for her, then that meant there had to be someone for him, as well.

He shook his head. No, he couldn't think about that.

Not yet.

Jamie was not the one for him, despite the cord that tethered them. Despite the lightning that had caused it all to begin with.

Her body was weakening because she'd met him and he'd started that change—or, in his opinion, that curse. He couldn't let her go through it any longer. No, he wouldn't be with her. She deserved better, but he *could* find that other man. The one he knew existed as sure as he felt the cord that connected him and Jamie. He would do what he must to find that man for her. He couldn't bear to think of her in any more pain.

Or any pain at all to think of it.

Nevertheless, he knew more pain was coming. She'd been living too easily for too long, and fate was a bitch when she wanted to be. Their connection might have allowed him to heal her physically, just like the night of Striker's death when he'd first felt the cord, but he couldn't heal this. He knew he would have to find this other man for her to be whole. That way she could find for her the one who could help her find her supernatural half and live in peace.

He would find him so Jaime could feel alive again.

Ambrose wasn't for her. No, he was for no one.

He wouldn't wallow, but he would live like he always had, hollow but with a purpose.

Jamie.

PYRO PACED THE LENGTH OF HIS FOYER, ANGER ROLLING through him with each step. His son was dying, but not fast enough for his taste. The bastard had forsaken their oaths and refused to take souls into the hells realm. Why couldn't the little twit die already?

Soon though, Pyro felt Balin begin to fade more with each day and relished it. Within days, Pyro wouldn't have to deal with the chain that shackled him to this realm. Although Balin didn't force him to remain in hell, if Pyro left, he was afraid of the damage Balin would do in his absence.

Like free the slaves and gladiators.

No, that wouldn't do.

Pyro went to his throne, an ornate chair made of the bones of his enemies, and plopped down, his body weary with boredom, something that could never do for a demon such as he.

He needed something to pass the time waiting for Balin to die. He couldn't kill his son in hell. No, ever since Lucifer had killed his own son in hell, they'd put a curse on the ability to kill one's loved ones. Damn that demon for ruining everything like always.

Maybe it was time to put his other plan in place. With Balin about to die, Pyro could use his men and powers to hurt the enemy who'd given him the scar that ran down the side of his body. The scar that revolted the women he took to his bed. Though they had to deal with it anyway, he wouldn't let them leave once he found them. That was not a demon's way.

Yes, it was time to pay Ambrose a visit.

He couldn't go to the angelic realm to find him. No, that would start a war, a war he would relish, but he was not in the mood to deal with the politics. However, he *could* go to the human realm and *not* start a war—it was in his blood. No one cared about the humans anyway. They were just the piss and backwater of the purebloods.

And, if his sources here correct, there was a woman who'd peaked the old angel's interest. A woman who'd been struck by lightning and lived to tell the tale. No, the two angels and that dragon where not as secretive as they thought. All of the realms knew something was amiss with those women, but no one cared enough to deal with it unless it affected them.

One of them had turned into a brownie.

He wondered what the woman who Ambrose had set his gaze on would turn into.

Maybe Pyro could cut it out of her.

Oh yes, that sounded like a plan. He'd take the girl and

bring Ambrose to him. Though the angel wouldn't want an all-out war by stepping on hell's land, he could find a way to make it happen. The old bastard was crafty like that.

Pyro smiled, his teeth lengthening, his talons curling.

Yes, this would work. He'd send his men to get the girl, play with her to his heart's content, and the old winged bastard would come to him.

And, while all of this was happening, Balin would die from his own stubbornness, his own failure to do what was meant to be a demon.

Perfect.

A scream tore from the woman he'd pinned to the wall earlier and he sighed.

Fuck, he'd forgotten about her in all his planning. Well, it was of no use wasting a human since they were so hard to come by these days. Fools were forgetting the magic and not summoning the demons as often.

Pity to those who did.

Pyro took out his blade, sharp and deadly, just the right size of blade to extract the most pain and smiled again. He stood then walked to his captive.

"You really should know not to summon things stronger than you," he warned as he slowly sliced away at her flesh. The human's eyes turned a brassy dull, the life fading out of her as she screamed, and he let the terror wash over him in pure bliss.

"Sadly, I'm bored with you now, so I'm going to give you to my men. I was going to kill you, but now I have another human in mind."

Her blood spattered on his bare arms and he turned away, licking the rivulets as he did so. With a nod to his men who had come into the room at the final scream, two of them went to her, grins on their faces.

Pyro had to find this human woman and lure Ambrose to him. That was his goal. The other humans could wait until later. A scream filled with insurmountable pain echoed along the walls behind him, and he took a deep breath, letting the horror seep into his pores.

It would be a good day.

Finally, Ambrose would pay.

Jamie Bennett cursed as a car sped by her through a puddle, splashing her with muddy water. The asshole obviously meant to compensate for a shortage of *something.* Dirty water and mud dripped from her hair and rain jacket, only adding to her already dreary, exhausted state.

Oh, yes, the mud accentuated her look, right?

With a growl, or at least what she thought was a growl but was more like a whimper, she pulled the muddy locks of hair from her face. Her chestnut hair now had lively gray and puke-brown streaks in it. Thankfully, she'd worn her raincoat since the weather patterns seemed to be stuck on rain. They'd been living in a gray world for months now, even though summer was just around the corner.

With one last shake of her head to remove what mud she could, she walked into Dante's Circle, her favorite bar and sanctuary. Dante's wasn't a normal bar. No, it was owned and operated by a dragon.

Yes, a real dragon.

Not that she and her friends had known that when they'd stumbled upon it a couple of years ago. One of them, Becca, had even gotten a job as a bartender there to pay for school. Before, it had been a way for her and her six friends to let go of the worries of the day and connect the way none of them could with others outside their circle.

Then the night of the storm had changed everything.

Jamie and her friends had been struck by lightning, and now they weren't humans anymore. Not that they'd ever been *truly* as human as they'd thought, but Jamie didn't quite understand the science of it all. Lily, the chemist of the group, knew all about that.

Now Lily had turned into a brownie because she'd met Shade, and Jamie had turned into a…well, a nothing. She just hurt.

A lot.

She felt as though she was ready to change—her skin too tight, her body too active—yet nothing had happened.

Apparently, she needed to have sex with her true half.

The man—or angel—she thought just might fill that role wanted nothing to do with her.

Yay for her.

Jamie took another step into Dante's, removed her jacket, and hung it up on one of the numerous pegs on the wall. She loved the feel of the bar, the way it felt like home with its hand-carved wood paneling and shelves. There was a pool table in the corner, but it didn't add a sense of a pool hall to the bar. It just made it a place to have fun. Tables with mismatched chairs covered the room, making it feel warm to her. Pictures of the town and its inhabitants and paintings from local artists covered the walls.

Dante's Circle could have held every aspect of the history of the town, especially with a dragon–who was god knows how old–as the owner, if Dante had desired it.

No, he preferred it to be his own little corner of the world.

Perfect for Jamie and her friends.

"Jamie! What on earth happened to you?" Becca asked. She put down the tray she'd been holding on the bar and grabbed a handful of paper towels, running toward Jamie. Her curly red hair bounced on her shoulders.

Jamie took the towels out of Becca's hand before her friend could mother her. As she wiped her face, she rolled her eyes.

"Some asshat with a small penis drove by too fast and splashed me."

Becca's eyes widened. "I assume you know the size of his penis because of his car, not from personal experience."

"Fuck off."

"He must have pissed you off because you *never* cuss like that."

Jamie's skin tightened, and weakness spread through her. She fought off the shakes that normally came with it and she knew she must look pale. "Yeah, that's it." Not the fact that she'd felt out of sorts for a freaking year because a certain angel had left her alone in the human realm.

A flash of white caught her eye, and Jamie barely held back a gasp.

Oh, that just figured.

Ambrose, the man she'd tried to forget, walked toward her, a frown on his face. The man—no, angel—seemed to always be frowning, never smiling. His face would probably crack if he ever did show a happier emotion.

"Is everything all right?" he asked, his voice deep. The rough sound shot straight through her system. She was helpless to defend herself against it.

She knew she resembled one of the heroines in the romance novels she loved to read, standing there doe-eyed, falling in love…

Damn the man.

No, she'd be one of those newer characters, the ones who stood tall and acted as if they didn't care before they took up their sword and battled demons of their own.

Yeah, she'd be one of them.

Jamie squared her shoulders and nodded. "I'm fine thanks, Ambrose." His name on her tongue caused a little rush of something she'd rather not think about to flow through her.

Damn the man again.

He looked good. Too good. He'd put his white-blond hair in a ponytail, and it only accentuated the masculinity of his features. He was built, sexy—a warrior god. Those gray eyes…she could lose herself in them if she would let herself.

He nodded, his gaze traveling over her, whether to check for wounds or because he liked to look at her she didn't know, and she tried not to care. He didn't have his normal aura of being a stoic man who knew all and could do all. No, something was off.

"Good to hear," he said and then cleared his throat. Why did he look nervous? "It's good to see you, Jamie."

She held back the pleasure at those words. *He's just being friendly, remember?* "It's been a long time."

"Yes, it has."

"Are you done flirting over there?" Faith yelled from the table. "Come on and sit so we can order. What took you so long?"

Jamie held back a wince at her friend's not-so-subtle tone. Crap, talk about awkward. She looked up into Ambrose's face, and he lifted the corner of his lip. Her stomach fluttered at the sight of his smile—or at least a partial one.

God, talk about pathetic. It had been a year since she'd seen him, and she wanted to throw herself at him. The image of her doing so filled her mind and she held back a groan. She wasn't a desperate woman; she could handle the temptation.

The laughter echoing in her head, which sounded suspiciously like Faith, could easily be ignored.

Becca went back behind the bar while Ambrose stood back and gestured for her to walk first. That was good, that way she wouldn't be caught staring at him like a starving dog clamoring after a bone.

A meaty, delicious, mouth-watering bone.

She blinked. That was enough of that.

Her six girlfriends and Lily's husband, Shade, were now sitting at the table waiting for her to join them. She must have been deep in thought, and looking idiotic, if Becca had made it back to the table before she had.

She gave Faith a long look. "Thanks for that," she said dryly.

"Anytime, doll," Faith said, not a single glimpse of remorse in her eyes.

Jamie took her seat at the table while Ambrose took the last empty one—the one directly next to her.

Oh, that wasn't subtle at all, guys.

She shifted in her chair as awareness of his presence slid over her body. Why did she want him so much? It made no sense; she hadn't even seen the man in a year.

Why couldn't she just get over him? Maybe she'd been wrong and he wasn't really her true half. After all, she didn't really know exactly what it meant to have one. She'd only learned about it through Shade and Lily. They were the only paranormals she knew.

Well, there was always Dante, but he was tightlipped about the whole mating-power thing. He'd always been quiet and reserved with her and her friends when he wasn't barking out orders like a normal barkeep. Plus, the man had a weird connection to her friend, Nadie, the virginal blonde of the group. She snorted at the thought. Yep, that was Nadie all right.

"Where's your head?" the man in question asked. Dante

truly was a beautiful man, his dark hair holding midnight-blue streaks that flowed down his back. He was ripped like a cover model with tattoos and piercings making him look sexy and dangerous.

And, totally not who she wanted.

Dante sat down on a stool next to their table and cocked his head.

"Sorry, I'm just still pissed at the puddle man," she lied.

Yeah, like she'd tell them she'd been thinking about true mates and the sexy angel sitting next to her taking up entirely too much space.

"Hopefully he'll get a ticket later," Nadie said as she brushed a lock of long blonde hair behind her ear. Nadie was beautiful woman, but she never did anything about it.

Yeah, not so much.

"You know that won't happen," Lily said as she leaned into Shade's hold. They really were a gorgeous couple. His darker skin tone was like caramel to her ivory. While her eyes were big and green, his were a fractured ice-blue, uniquely amazing. While his black hair was tied back, Lily had let hers fall around her shoulders, and Shade absent-mindedly played with it.

"Of course not. Asshats like that get away with every-thing," Amara said before taking a drink of her beer. She ran a hand through her curly auburn hair then smiled.

"Oh, yes, the asshats of the earth," Faith said. "Why can't we just kill them all? Don't you boys know something that can help?"

Shade threw a pretzel at her, and she ducked, her chin-length black hair going into disarray.

"Stop throwing food in my bar," Dante ordered.

Eliana threw a pretzel in his direction, and he caught it without even looking. Her brown eyes widened, and everyone froze.

"What? Should I continue to hide what I am? Maybe act like a klutzy human?" He narrowed his gaze at Becca then winked. "No, dear, that's not all humans, just you."

Becca glowered at the dragon. "Okay, I think we have an asshat at our table."

Jamie laughed then took a sip of her drink Dante had delivered without an order. If it weren't for the fact that none of them ever had more than one drink at any time, she'd be worried that the bartender knew tastes so well.

Honestly, she was really boring. She owned a failing bookstore that she'd tried to perk up with countless signings, recommendations, book clubs, and food, but it was no use. The indie bookstore was a dying breed, and she'd have to find something else to do or she'd lose everything.

She took another gulp of her drink and tried not to think about it. Everything hurt as it was. She didn't need to think about one more thing to add to her pain.

"So, Ambrose, why are you back?" Faith asked, a blunt curiosity in her tone.

Jamie's attention narrowed to the angel of her thoughts. Yes, why *was* he back after all this time? Was he here to help her though her change?

She felt a blush cover her face at the thought. Uh, yeah,

"helping" her through the change would require sex. So not happening.

Ambrose took a drink of his beer and settled back into his chair. He wouldn't meet her gaze, even though she wanted it.

Hell, she needed to get over him.

"I've done what I've needed at home," he said, his rough voice hitting her in all the right places. "Now I'm here to fulfill my promise."

Hurt assaulted her, sharp pains that wouldn't fade away. Why did she have to feel bad about that? It wasn't as if she'd had the romantic notion he'd come back to her. So, she'd thought it. That hadn't meant it could actually happen…right?

She bit her lip and closed her eyes before taking a deep breath. She'd be okay. She'd survived before; she would now.

The conversation turned over to their various day jobs, though Jamie was only half listening. Between her body feeling weak, her bookstore failing, and the angel beside her who didn't want her, it was all too much.

"I'm feeling a bit tired," she said during a lull in conversation. "I'm going to head home."

"Be careful, Jamie," Ambrose warned.

She faced him, determined not to let her feelings show. "Always am."

"I'm serious. We don't know what the world thinks of your predicament. I want you to be careful. Would you like me to accompany you?"

Oh, God, how she'd want that. She could invite him in, have a drink, get naked…no. That wouldn't be happening.

She shook her head and stood. "No, I'll be fine. It's been a year and we're fine. If you were so worried, why haven't you been here? The warning's a bit late." She turned to her friends who were watching them with curious glances. Great, she'd have to answer for the tension in the air. Not now, no, now she needed to leave. "I'll call Lily when I get home." If she'd just said she'd call any of them, then they'd all worry until she'd call *all* of them.

By the time she'd gotten to her car and driven home, her body was ready to shut down for the night. God, she was tired. She was *always* tired these days.

Jamie sank into the cushions of her couch and sighed. Maybe she wouldn't have to see Ambrose much while he was here. As much as she wanted to see him, she couldn't, not if she wanted to stay sane.

The window above her head shattered, sending glass all over her body, slicing into her skin as pain radiated through her. What the hell?

Instinctively, she lowered her body, but something pulled her by the hair and threw her into her wall. She crashed into pictures, bringing them to the floor with her. She raised her head, trying to see her attacker, but he kicked her in the face. She screamed as her cheekbone broke, her body growing heavy.

Oh, God, whoever he was, he was going to kill her.

"Don't fucking kill her," a voice said.

She didn't recognize it, but maybe they'd help her since he didn't want her dead.

"Right," another voice said, this one closer to her. "The master wants her alive for his plans. We can heal this bitch up later."

Fear, unadulterated fear, slid over her.

She wasn't going to die here, but it would come soon.

Jamie tried to lift herself up off the floor so she'd be able to fight back, but hands grabbed her again. She twisted and struggled, but he slapped her on her broken cheek. Tears burst from her as she fought not to vomit from the pain.

"Oh, Master's going to like you. You're a fighter," the one who'd hurt her said.

As the world blackened, all she could think of was Ambrose. He'd come when she didn't call, right? He'd come.

Metal clashed against metal as Balin Drake's sword came down across his opponent's blade. The sound rang out through the cavern, deep in the pits of hell. The stalagmites reached down like claws, grasping for their victims. Balin swung again, the other demon staggering back with the force of the blow. Balin gritted his teeth, his body weakening at the lack of energy, but fought on.

This may have been just a training exercise for the other demon, but for Balin, it was a way of life. In the hell realm, war, famine, loss, and torture were a norm, the only way to live as a demon. Fighting against another demon, training, killing, maiming was all part of their lives—their memories.

The other demon, Fawkes, came at Balin again, his sword too high, not protecting his mid-section. If Balin had been any other demon—the kind who relished killing and death—he would have sliced the younger demon through the belly. The flesh would slide around the blade like butter then Balin would twist, damaging and cutting every internal organ he could with just one hit.

However, Balin wasn't any ordinary demon. No, he was a pure-blood demon who had a conscience and was sick of death and blood—a rarity if not a complete unknown in the realms of hell. So, Balin wouldn't kill Fawkes today, maybe another day if Fawkes turned on their fragile alliance, but not today.

Balin elbowed Fawkes in the gut and cursed. "Watch your body, idiot. You're likely to make yourself a kabob and be roasted on a spit if you continue to fight like that."

Fawkes grinned like the teenager he was and lowered his sword. "A spit? Do you really think they still do that? We aren't barbaric."

Balin put down his sword on a nearby rock since he hadn't bothered with a scabbard for the day, then threw his head back and laughed, even as a weariness slid through him. "Barbaric? Oh, son, we are. You just spend your time chasing girls with tails and horns without a scratch on them. Once you see your first war, you'll understand. Your own father was known as the demon who picked the bones of enemies from his teeth."

Not to mention other things, but Balin didn't want to mention those things to Lucifer's youngest "late in life" son. He didn't want to deal with the bastard's wrath. Lucifer's, not Fawkes'.

"That's not really true, is it?" Fawkes asked, his face scrunching up. "I know my dad's not the greatest guy in the world." *That was the understatement of the millennium.* "He couldn't really have done everything they say, right?"

Balin took a deep breath and winced when his side ached. Damn, he was getting too weak to even do a small form of training. He'd have to stop soon.

He'd have to stop everything soon.

"You know most of what anyone says about a legend is invented or exaggerated, but some of it is likely based in truth." He couldn't lie to the kid, not if Fawkes wanted to live past twenty—when a demon was considered fully adult and ready be indoctrinated in war.

Fawkes blinked hard then looked down at his sword. "It's tough being the son of the Devil."

At least the Devil had calmed some in his old age. Balin's dad was still a bastard and sadist in every sense of the word. Pyro needed to die, yet Balin couldn't do it, not if he wanted to live. Damn Lucifer. Because of Lucifer, fathers could not kill sons and sons could not kill fathers, not in the realms of hell.

And, because of his sickness, Balin couldn't go to the human realm and deal with the problem there. He was literally stuck in hell, shriveling away while Pyro lived and flourished.

Yeah, being the son of the Devil sucked, but being the son of Pyro wasn't a fucking picnic.

"You'll be fine, Fawkes," Balin said. "You'll learn what you need to and thrive. You don't have to be like your father. You can be better than that."

Fawkes gave him a long look. "Yeah, I could, but then I'd die, right?"

Ah, the reality of being a demon. *You try to be good, and you die.*

Just like me.

"True, but there's a way out of that."

"Yeah, but you never found it and now look at you." Fawkes' eyes widened, and he ducked his head. "I'm sorry."

"You're not yet twenty, Fawkes. When you turn twenty and you have to take your first soul, you'll understand. I resisted. I've resisted for so long that I'm dying."

"You have until your three hundredth birthday before you die, right? You can still find that loophole."

Balin let out a breath that shook, showing too much of his age. "I'll turn three hundred in five days, Fawkes. I'm pretty sure my time is up."

Fawkes' eyes widened, and shame exuded from him, mixing with the sorrow-laden air.

"I..."

Balin held up his hand. "Don't worry about it. I know what's coming. I've *known* what's coming. I chose my fate."

"But..."

"Let's fight again. This time, be sure to keep your guard lower so you can cover your belly. Those wounds are hard to heal, even for a demon."

They fought again, swords clashing, sweat running down both their faces. They each were tanned from the fires in the pits of hell. Balin was larger, stronger looking, though weakening from within. Fawkes had red horns on his upper forehead that stuck straight out to a point about a foot from his head, just like his father. Balin's horns were black and curled back over his head so they appeared to flow with his hair. Both sets of horns were extremely sensitive, but hard as bone.

Yet one still had to make his choice—to take the souls of innocents or to live a half-life, one of retribution.

The other had made his choice long ago and was suffering the consequences, but it was worth it. Balin might have been dying, but it would be worth his own soul and those he'd saved.

They ventured farther along the cave, the heat from an uncontrolled fire raging out of control behind them. They'd have to quit soon, or they'd burn.

Sweat ran down his face as his muscles strained under the strength of his opponent. If Balin weren't careful in his weakened state, Fawkes would win.

Fawkes seemed to realize this and pulled back. Balin cursed and gave the man a nod.

"Tomorrow?" Fawkes asked, his tone eager.

Balin shook his head, his chest heaving. "No, I think I'm done, Fawkes."

"No, you still have time. Don't give up."

Balin lifted a corner of his mouth and shook his head. "I'm not, but I don't want to waste my energy." He winced as hurt crossed Fawkes' features. "Fuck, that's not what I meant. I'm just tired, Fawkes. I need to make sure I can still walk on my own two feet."

Fawkes took a deep breath and held out his hand. Balin grasped his forearm and squeezed.

"You'll let me know if I can help, right?" Fawkes asked.

Balin nodded. "I don't think I'll need it, but yes, I will. There's nothing you can do, Fawkes, but I'm glad to know you as a friend."

They parted ways at the mouth of the cavern, and Balin walked to his home, a modest home on the outskirts of his father's territory. Such was the life a demon who refused to eat souls. He made his way inside and stripped off his boots and leather pants as he walked toward the shower. He was covered in blood, sweat, grime, and desperation, a little more than he cared for.

As a demon, it became his need at the age of twenty to take the souls of innocents to ingest for energy. Demons ate and drank like humans but needed souls to live past the age of three hundred.

It had always been that way and would always be. It was in their genetic makeup.

Few had ever fought that destiny, and even fewer had lived, because, for that to happen, they needed the life energy of more than one person. Once a demon found their true half, they'd connect on a soul level that surpassed all connections and not only would they have a relationship with the one, or in some cases two people, who were meant for them, but that connection would thrive on a loop of energy, resulting in the life of the demon.

The only problem was that demons did not have true halves with demons. It just wasn't done. In order for a demon to find their true half, they needed to go to the human realm—or any of the other realms—to find them. What made it worse, in order to go to the other realms, a demon needed to have a large supply of energy—meaning they had to be young.

Between wars and being trapped in his father's basement, Balin had lost all that time, and now he was stuck in hell, dying.

If he hadn't had pride, he'd have killed himself long ago.

He turned on the hot water and stepped under the spray. He sighed as it hit his muscles, helping the aches and pains. Damn, if he hadn't known he had only five days left, he'd install one of those seats for the elderly. He felt eons older than his two hundred and ninety-nine years.

He soaped up his body, cursing as he hit some of the small cuts from the rocks and the tip of Fawkes' blade. Fuck, the boy had gotten close. The sad thing was Fawkes still had years left in his training, and Balin was just too tired to fight as hard as he had his whole life.

The temptation to just take a taste of a soul as it passed through the veil swept through him, but as always, he resisted. He always had, and soon, he'd die following his own morals.

As a human thought about giving it all up, or because of their own evil, the veil between hell and the human realm thinned and demons could see the souls, eager and ready to pluck the ripened.

Balin had never succumbed.

It had been close years ago, but he was stronger in that respect at least.

He ran his hands through his hair and over his horns. He'd never been the kind to jack off that way, though he knew others loved it. There were clubs dedicated to horn fetishes, licking, touching, and things he didn't even want to think about. A demon's horns were as sensitive as their dicks, yet Balin had never come that way.

He'd always had the notion his mate would do that for the first time.

He gave out a dry laugh. What a fucking crock.

Balin turned in the shower and soaped up the rest of his body then wrapped a hand around his cock and squeezed. He'd had sex over the years with random demons—male and female—but he'd given up the practice years ago. No use when he'd just die anyway.

And, now, he sounded like a whiny fucking bastard.

He ran his hand up the length of himself, bracing his back against the shower wall, and stroked harder. An image of a laughing woman with chestnut hair and a man with gray eyes flashed across his mind, and he came fast and hard.

Fuck.

Whoever the people in that image were, though most likely it was just a dream, he wanted them.

Too bad he'd never find them.

He didn't want to die, but it looked like an inevitability. He'd do what he could to find a way out of hell, but it didn't seem likely. The only way it looked even remotely possible was if his true half came to him.

Balin laughed as he turned off the water and stepped out of his shower. Right, like that would ever happen.

His phone rang, and he sighed. Damn it, he was too tired to deal with whatever bullshit was on the other end, but if he didn't deal with it, it would probably bite him on the ass —literally.

He pulled on his leather pants, leaving them untied, and walked to answer the phone.

"Yes?"

"Get over here, I have a treat for you." Pyro hung up once he finished speaking, and Balin rolled his eyes.

That wasn't a request. No, that had been a summons, and Balin wasn't strong enough to fight back. Fuck, he hated being weak, and that was exactly what he was.

He put on his boots then found a button-down shirt so he wouldn't have to go out shirtless. Although most did since it as so hot, he wasn't in the mood to show his scars to his father. The ones on his back, his father's handiwork, only made the bastard smile.

When he made it to his father's sprawling mansion, Balin held back the bile that rose in his throat. Damn, Pyro sure liked his opulence. The man had a fucking moat, filled with lava.

"Balin! Get your ass in here," Pyro yelled from the front door.

Balin gave his father a cool look; he never let the man

see anything but a lack of emotion. That set the bastard off but kept Balin sane.

"What took you so long?"

It had taken less than ten minutes, but whatever.

"I'm here now," he said.

Pyro waved his hand and rolled his eyes. It was like looking into a mirror, but where Balin's eyes were black with flecks of red, Pyro's were full-out red. They'd always been that way, so Balin didn't think it was because he lacked souls in his own system.

"I have a new toy from the human realm and wanted to show it to you before it got damaged."

Revulsion slid through him at the thought of what awaited the poor human. Once humans made it to hell, they rarely made it out alive.

Pyro was known to leave the carcass or bones in the streets of the human realm to scare the police force, and any human he could. The games some demons played sickened Balin.

"Why would I want to see that?" he asked.

Pyro narrowed his gaze. "I'm giving you one last shot, boy. Take her soul while she still lives and quit being an embarrassment to me."

"I'm not going to take her soul."

"Fine," Pyro spat. "Die like the flaccid failure you are. You're still going to have to watch me play with her. Once I'm done, if she still lives, I'll put her in the games to see how quickly the games tear her limb from limb."

Balin held back a shudder. The demon games were

versions of the fights between human gladiators, where demons and other species fought against each other to the death. Putting a human in there would be a brutal deal for sure.

There was nothing he could do. He could try and take her away, but he had nowhere he could hide her, not when he would be dead within the week and he couldn't get out of hell.

Fuck.

They walked through the decadent foyer to the torture chamber on the first floor. At least Pyro hadn't taken her to any of the lower basements. The first-floor chamber was, relatively, the least deadly of the bunch.

Death hung in the air, but the stench was too old to be from the human woman. Pyro had killed recently, probably that morning. Balin clenched his fists even as his body weakened that much more, his energy draining, his knees shaking. Damn, he couldn't save anyone, not in his state.

When Pyro opened the door, Balin held back a gasp.

Fuck.

This human had to be the most beautiful woman he'd ever seen, even with the bruises, cuts, and broken cheekbone. It wasn't her beauty that drew him, no, it was something about her…something that could be his.

He took a step forward, but Pyro held him back.

His father raised a brow and smirked. "A beautiful specimen, isn't she? I'll have a healer take care of that cheekbone before I have a go at her. I don't like fucking my women when they look like shit. My men were idiots and hurt her, but I killed them, so it made me feel a bit better."

The woman was chained to the wall, her body lax in an unconscious state. Who was she? Why had Pyro taken her?

How could Balin help her?

"Once I get through with her body, the demons at the games will like her. They'll probably use her for a whore for a bit before they put her in the games. I'm sure they'll enjoy that. She looks like she could use a good fucking."

Balin clenched his fists at his father's vulgar words. He wouldn't let this happen to her. No, there was something about her…

Could she be…?

"Word is she's Ambrose's true half, but he hasn't claimed her yet. I don't know why, but this will kill the bastard." Pyro slapped Jamie hard across the broken cheek, and she let out an unconscious whimper.

Fuck, she couldn't be Ambrose's true mate because he was pretty sure this human woman was his.

Fate really was a bitch.

WHEN BALIN LEFT, PYRO PACED AGAIN IN HIS FOYER. THAT had been an interesting reaction on his son's part. Almost as if…no, that couldn't be.

Could it?

Had the rumors been wrong and this Jamie wasn't Ambrose's true half but really Balin's?

Fuck, either way, it could do. He'd have to have her killed quickly, but not here. He'd already promised her to the games. Balin couldn't have time to realize there might be a connection between them. He could regain his energy.

He'd have to move up Jamie's torture. There would be no time for fucking and whoring, only her death in the games.

She'd go tomorrow. Pyro would make sure of that. As soon as the healer came to fix her face so she'd be a draw at the games, he'd throw her to the wolves—maybe not so figuratively.

Plus, there was something about her, something that nagged at his senses. Was she truly human? No, the rumored storm must have been real because Jaime was turning into something. What, he didn't know. He needed her dead, quickly.

His plans were moving faster, but he'd still have his revenge either way. He had to.

CHAPTER 4

Ambrose paced in the living room of the home he had rented for his stay. Why hadn't Lily called him to tell him that Jamie had called her? Gods, he sounded like a common teenager, waiting for his school crush to call a friend. The feelings coursing through him were nothing like a teen's. They were feelings he desperately wanted to ignore, but as soon as he'd seen Jamie, he knew he couldn't anymore.

He wanted her.

He had no idea how his old bag of bones would accomplish that, but he would find a way. First, he had to know she was all right.

And, of course, there was the whole other mate thing that bothered him.

Was there another one out there for Jamie?

He had never heard of that, only pairs and triads.

Could that mean…

He froze in mid step and blinked. Could they be a triad? Was that why he felt there was another?

Ambrose didn't know, but no matter what, he needed to make sure Jamie was all right first. He'd give Lily five more minutes, then he'd go to Jamie himself.

He sat down on the stool by the bar, his head in his hands. He'd rented the house so he could figure out what to do. He hadn't planned on staying long, only long enough to find Jamie's other half, or whoever the other man was to them, and to protect the seven women from other supernaturals. He hadn't even unpacked yet, not knowing what his future held. It pissed him off to have his plans on the wind as he was usually the one with everything set in stone, battle plans pored over and every strategic outcome analyzed. Yet, when it came to Jamie, he was out of sorts, lost.

Why had fate decided to let him find her now? He'd been alive for over five thousand years, yet he'd never gazed upon his true half until he was so old he didn't even want one. Who was he to have a woman so young with so many new experiences in front of her?

Jamie was probably at home, snug in her bed, or reading a book. He knew she loved reading romances and anything that had a happy ending. It helped that she owned a bookstore. Maybe he'd show her the collection of books he'd piled up over the centuries.

Great, he sounded like the Beast trying to win Belle's heart with a side of "Would you like to see my etchings?"

How long had it been since he'd tried to woo a woman?

Did he even *want* to woo her?

Yes, he did, but that didn't mean he should. She was way too young for him. That was the whole reason he'd stayed away for so long. He could do nothing for her. Jamie was full of life and laughter—well, at least she had been before she'd met him and the trigger to their mating had started.

This situation wasn't like with most true halves—or triads if that was the case with them, but he didn't want to think about that—where they met, and in their hearts, they recognized each other and knew they were perfect for each other in every way.

No, with the seven lightning-struck women, things seemed to be different. With Lily, the first to meet her true half, once she'd met her mate, it triggered the transformation into her supernatural. Jamie seemed to be reacting slightly different than Lily, not as sick, at least from what Ambrose had seen—thank the gods.

Once they made love, then the transformation into her supernatural half would be complete, and she would become whatever was running in her blood. With Lily, it had been a brownie. Ambrose didn't know what Jamie would turn into, but he knew he'd help her whatever way he could.

Even though he didn't deserve her.

It wasn't because he was still mourning his late wife, Ilianya. No, he had moved on from her long ago. Yes, he still missed her in a way because he'd lost a part of himself when she'd died too tragically. She'd been soft, pleasant, and a wonderful mother to their two children, Nathan and Laura.

She'd been Shade's sister and had brought the two men together in a brotherhood that was stronger than blood. When the wars had claimed Ilianya, his children, and Shade's fiancée, Cora, Ambrose had given up on love.

Love only brought pain and loss.

Then Shade had found Lily, and Jamie had come into Ambrose's life. He'd tried to give her up, tried to run away from the problem like a coward, yet he'd failed.

He still wanted her.

He didn't deserve her.

Why wouldn't she call? Was she okay?

His phone rang, bringing him out of his thoughts. He ran to it, nearly knocking over his side table in the process. He took a deep breath, settling himself. For fuck's sake, he was a five-thousand-year-old warrior angel; he needed to act like it. After all, he was the stoic one, the one people never saw smile. He didn't have to run to the phone like a teenager.

"Yes?" Ah, that sounded more like himself.

"Ambrose?" Lily asked.

He'd forgotten to check the readout on his cell phone; luckily it was Lily. And, hopefully, she was just calling to let him know Jamie had made it home and he didn't have to worry anymore. Yes, that was why she was calling; it couldn't be for more than that. His old heart couldn't take it.

"Yes, Lily, how can I help you?"

"It's Jamie. She never called and isn't answering her phone. I'm getting worried."

Pain clutched his body at her words. No, Jamie had to be okay.

"Maybe she's just in the bath reading like you women like to do." The image of Jamie in the bath with her caramel-latte skin, wet with trails of bubbles leading to places he wanted to taste assaulted him, even as worry gripped him.

Lily let out such a frustrated sigh that Ambrose regretted trying to make light of the situation. He was too worried to try to retain his normal monotone.

"Even if she was in the bath, she's like me and would have her cell phone on her. Plus, she didn't call like she said she would. I'm worried, Ambrose. I'd go over there, but I can't even stand straight. The morning sickness isn't so morning anymore, and Shade won't let me go."

"I'll go right now. Lie down and let Shade take care of you. That's what he's there for, Lily."

She let out a relieved sigh. "I'm sure she's all right, Ambrose, right?"

Ambrose swallowed hard. "I'm sure she is. Let me take care of her."

"I know you've been avoiding her, so I'm sorry to bring you into this."

Ambrose was already out the door and to his car when he answered. "You never have to be sorry about asking me to take care of your friends."

Especially Jamie.

"Let me know what you find."

"Of course," he said as he pulled the car out onto the

road. He lived only ten minutes away from Jamie. A curse and a blessing in some respects.

She had to be okay. Most likely, she'd turned off her phone for peace and forgotten to call. He didn't want to think about another outcome, though he already had one in his mind. He went through his mental checklist of the weapons in his car and on his body—he always had a small arsenal with him wherever he went.

Plus, he had even more in his cache—the magical storage space, for lack of a better word, that held everything close to an angel's body. He never had too much in it because it took energy to keep it full, but he had enough weapons to take out whoever would hurt his Jamie.

His Jamie.

Yes, she was his, even though he'd run from it.

He pulled into her driveway and parked next to her car. Something was off. He felt it in the air, the heaviness that coated his skin, his tongue.

Someone had been here.

He pulled out his sword from his cache as he got out of the car and tucked it to his side to avoid scaring the neighbors if they were watching. Humans were too curious for their own good sometimes. He knocked on the front door, but no one answered. Not wanting to startle her, or whoever might be in there with her, by breaking down the door, he walked around to the back and froze.

"Fuck," he muttered under his breath as blood roared in his ears.

The back window that faced her living room was shattered, leaving her house open to the elements. He reached out with his senses and didn't feel another presence, but he couldn't be sure. Some supernaturals, like him, could shroud their existence in the shadows, and he didn't want any surprises.

He jumped through the broken window, and bile rose in his throat. The glass from the window had shattered into pieces along the floor and onto the couch. Something had broken her coffee table, its wooden shards everywhere. There was a puddle of blood on the floor that weakened him at the knees, but that wasn't what made him want to scream.

No, not that.

There was no need for him to check the rest of the house, not when he knew she wasn't there. He couldn't feel her there, though he knew she was alive.

No, the message written in her blood on the wall was what brought him to his knees, the glass and wood cutting deep into his skin, reminding him he was alive and able to fight to bring her back.

She's mine now, bastard. –Pyro

Ambrose held back the war cry of anguish that threatened to break free of his throat. He didn't want to rouse the neighbors or the police with his pain. No, this wasn't a human issue. A fucking *demon* had taken her to hell.

Not any fucking demon, but Pyro, the demon he hadn't been able to kill because he'd been distracted by Shade's first battle. He'd scarred the demon down his side, but it hadn't been enough.

Not nearly enough if Pyro was still taking revenge.

Taking his Jamie.

Oh, gods, she had to be alive.

He'd fight for her with every ounce of his being.

There were no good demons, only dead demons in his mind. The only demons who didn't take souls died too young and were most often too weak to be of much good to the cause.

It looked as if he were going to hell, though he couldn't go by himself. Not if he wanted to live and not start a war between the angels and demons. The angelic council would never condone a battle over a human—even Ambrose's human.

Fucking elitist bastards.

He clenched his fists, took a deep breath, and ran to his car to head to Dante's Circle. The dragon might be able to help him get into hell or at least have an idea on how to get to a portal. Ambrose didn't know much about Dante, other than he was a dragon who cared for the seven women, especially Nadie. Somewhere, deep down, Ambrose trusted Dante, and he would use that. Anything to save Jamie.

His hands shook as he drove, his body shaking right along with them. He couldn't even imagine the pain Jamie would be enduring at the hands of Pyro, the fear that would overtake her.

He'd save her; he had too.

Ambrose wasn't an idiot though. He knew it was a trap. Pyro wanted payback for that scar, and Ambrose would walk right into it. He didn't care. Jamie was more important than any pain he'd have to endure.

"Dante!" he called as he slammed open the door, scaring some of the patrons at the tables. None of that mattered. Only Jamie did.

Dante strolled from the back, his piercings and tattoos making him stand out, not to mention his blue-streaked black hair that fell to the floor when not braided.

"Yes, Ambrose?" Dante drawled.

Ambrose stormed to the back area so he wouldn't upset the humans more than he already had. He might have started one scene, but he didn't need another.

"I need your help," he said.

Dante's eyes widened ever so slightly, and his body went on alert, no longer the carefree bar owner, but a dragon with the power to kill with a single flick of his wrist.

"What is it?"

"Jamie's gone." He was surprised his voice didn't break when he said it. "A demon by the name of Pyro has her in hell, and I need to go there to help her."

Dante cursed under his breath and walked to his office. Ambrose followed him, his body and everything else on edge.

"I can't go alone, not as an angel; you know that. It would start a war, and the council would filet me, even as a warrior. I can't bring Shade down because he's also an angel, and it wouldn't do any good. Lily's pregnant, and I can't take him away from her. I need your help," he repeated, the words heavy on his tongue. He was not the type of man to ask for help lightly, but Jamie was worth far more than his pride.

"I can't go with you," Dante said as he rummaged through a chest behind his bookshelf. What the hell did the old dragon have back there?

Wait, what?

"You can't or *won't?*" he asked, anger in his tone.

Dante stood and glared, his eyes turning all white. The room cooled dramatically, and the other man's body shimmered and flexed.

Holy shit, he couldn't turn into a dragon here, not in this place. It was too small, and Ambrose was not in the mood to die.

Because no matter how strong of an angel he was, and besides Shade, he was the strongest, he was no match for a dragon with a temper.

"Can't," Dante said through clenched teeth as his body visibly calmed.

Ambrose relaxed slightly, though he was still on alert, being cooped up with a dragon and the fact that Jamie wasn't near him.

"Why not?"

"Because I'm banned from hell."

What the hell? How did one get banned from hell? As an angel, he was *advised* not to enter the hell realm because his presence would immediately be known and he could die and perhaps start a war.

He wasn't *banned.*

One had to do something truly…horrific…or *something* to be banned from a realm.

Wisely, he didn't ask why, but nodded for the dragon to continue.

"Like I said, I can't go with you, but I can get you in."

Ambrose shook his head. "I know of a few portals, so I can get to it, though those portals are hard to get through. I don't have a way of cloaking myself or anything while I'm there. I'm no match for an entire horde of demons on their land."

Dante nodded. "I understand, but I have a portal in the back of this place. You can get in through there."

Ambrose's eyes widened. What kind of secrets did this dragon have? Did he really want to know the answer to that?

"I can also help you cloak yourself," Dante continued.

"How can you do that?"

Dante handed him a gold medallion that was engraved with some kind of writing that Ambrose couldn't decipher. Which was strange itself since Ambrose could speak most languages, dead and alive.

"Wear this around your neck at all times and no one will be able to tell you're an angel unless they fight you and smell your blood," Dante explained.

"Where the hell did you get this?" He winced at his bad pun.

Dante lifted a pierced eyebrow. "In hell, where else? Just wear it and try not to kill too many demons on your way. Also, you say it was Pyro who took her?"

Ambrose nodded. "I'm going to kill him."

"Good, he needs killing. His son, Balin, could be an ally, if he's still alive." A shadow passed over his face, and Ambrose blinked.

"An ally?"

"Balin doesn't take souls, but Pyro has locked him up for so long he's been unable to come to the human realm to find his true half."

"So his body is dying because he doesn't take souls. Why didn't you help him get out if you knew him?"

"I tried." Dante's eyes whitened again before he shook his head.

"So Balin is his son, so he might know where Jamie is." It was a start at least.

Dante nodded. "Yes, and knowing Balin, he's probably already trying to help her. Though his three hundredth birthday is coming up within days, Ambrose. You know what that means." The dragon leveled his gaze at him.

"He's out of time." Sadness washed through him for a demon he had never met. "I'll help him if I can, Dante, but Jamie is my first concern."

For always.

"Understood." Dante led him to a doorway in the back of the building and gestured toward it. "You have weapons in your cache?"

"Of course, as well as a first aid kit and other things that Jamie may need. I'm ready." Anticipation thrummed through him at the thought of what was to come. It wouldn't be an easy journey, but Jamie was more important than the pain he might endure.

"Good. The portal will lead you to the south end of the territory east of Pyro's compound. You probably have a good six-hour hike to Pyro's. That is, of course, if you don't meet any enemies along the way, and we both know the likelihood of that."

Ambrose nodded and pulled his sword from his cache. "I'm ready. Let the others know where I am."

Dante held his arm out, and Ambrose grasped it in a warrior's handshake. "Of course. May you find Jamie and get out safely. Honor and peace be with you."

"Thank you, my friend."

Dante's eyes widened at the use of "friend," but Ambrose knew it was true. They were all connected through the lightning storm and would fight for each other with every breath.

Ambrose opened the door and stepped through the portal, bracing himself. The feel of claws raked at him, fire licked its way up his legs and around his back, choking him. With each step, his legs became heavier, his body became drowsier.

Jamie.

She was his reason for everything.

Jamie.

The heat scorched him, the fires of hell hot with the hatred and pain of eons of generations.

Like the snap of a rubber band, the portal released him, and he crashed to the rocky ground below. The jagged rocks bit into his already sore knees from the glass at Jamie's apartment, but he stood quickly, armed and ready.

The depths of hell resembled a barren dessert. The flowing rivers of lava changed at a moment's notice, catching an unexpected intruder without care.

Ambrose was in hell in every sense of the word, but his Jamie was out there.

He had no choice. He'd die for her. He just hoped he wasn't too late.

CHAPTER 5

Jamie cracked open her eyes and held back a whimper. Oh, God, her body ached something fierce. She tried to move, but something held her in place. Her neck strained as she looked up, and tears slid from her eyes.

Someone had shackled her to a wall so she sat with her legs free, but nowhere to go.

Memories of how two men had broken into her home, beaten her, and taken her away assaulted her. Since her arms were raised above her head, she couldn't check to see what might have been broken, but she rubbed her face against her arm anyway.

Wait, hadn't her cheekbone been broken?

She distinctly remembered the shocking pain and the urge to throw up when it had happened and when the man had slapped her again.

It was fine and only ached a little bit.

Had she imagined it?

No, she didn't think so because she'd never felt that kind of pain before. She knew some supernaturals had healing powers, and Ambrose had once healed her because of the connection they shared—or could have shared—but she didn't have a clue how she'd been healed.

From the sight of the dungeon, or wherever the hell she was, she was certain Ambrose hadn't been there to heal her.

Chains dangled from various heights on the walls and ceiling. Dried blood and something else—Jamie didn't want to even contemplate what that could be—dotted the floors and splashed the walls. Tables with manacles, chains, and other instruments stood in the center of the room, and each had a side table of knives, blades, what looked to be a blow torch, and other things that Jamie wasn't sure the purpose of.

Bile rose in her throat.

A torture chamber. She was in a torture chamber and too weak and human to get out. For a moment, anger spread through her at the thought that that wouldn't be the case if she'd been a supernatural. If Ambrose hadn't run away and if she'd completed the change.

There was no use thinking in "ifs" at the moment. She was surely and dearly screwed.

From what she could see, there was one door for the entire room. If she had a chance to escape, that would be where she'd go. Who knew what was on the other side of it and who would be there? She had no idea who had her and where she was. For all she knew, she could be in another realm.

Jamie gulped then rested her head back on the wall behind her. Ever since the lightning strike, her world had been torn apart and pieced together in a kaleidoscope of supernaturals. Nothing was the same anymore. Everything was bigger, more dangerous, and constantly put her at the bottom of the food chain. She was human—at least for now, and it didn't look like anything was about to change on that front—meaning she could only fight as hard as she could as a human woman.

Not good enough.

The tears tasted salty on her too-dry lips, and she tried to control herself. She'd read enough books in her life to know that freaking out and pitying herself wouldn't accomplish anything. She pulled at her chains and only managed to hurt her wrists.

Unless someone came in and let her go, she was truly stuck.

Well, hell.

Jamie closed her eyes and thought of Ambrose. He'd come for her, right? Or, maybe Shade or Dante would. They were strong and had powers that none of her friends had. Lily might have been a brownie and had enough strength and power to help others, but she was pregnant, and Jamie hoped to God Shade didn't let Lily out of sight.

Wait, what if her friends were here too? Dear Lord, how selfish could she be? She had no idea why they'd taken her.

For all she knew, all her friends were in similar cells, chained to walls and bleeding out.

She pulled at her chains again and cursed when she only managed to bang herself on the head with the metal.

"If you keep doing that, girl, you'll just make it worse for yourself," a voice said from the doorway.

Jamie froze but didn't sink into herself. She didn't want to show the fear that strangled her. A man with red eyes and black horns that followed the curve of his head stepped into the room, a menacing smile on his face.

Red eyes and horns.

Definitely not human then.

Though she and her friends had studied up on most of the supernaturals in existence, and had even met a few since she'd found out about the things that went bump in the night, she'd never seen one like this.

She knew what it was from the texts she'd read.

A demon.

There was no way out of this.

Most demons, like ninety percent, ate souls and liked to kill their prey slowly. And, by the look on this one's face, she was pretty sure he fell in the majority category.

Must not show fear.

Jamie raised her chin and glared at the demon, even though inside she wanted to crawl into a ball and call for her mommy. Either way would have left her in the same situation, but this way, she at least had her pride...whatever shreds she had left.

"Do you know where you are, Jamie dear?" the demon

asked as he walked toward her. He knelt so he was eye level and traced a finger down her newly healed cheek.

Despite herself, she shuddered at the touch.

"Who are you?" she asked. Didn't all the books say to keep your captor talking so he didn't kill you so quickly?

"I guess you don't know where you are." He traced his finger along her lower lip, and she resisted the urge to bite him since he could probably kill her with his pinky. "I'll tell you anyway. It's more fun when humans know the dangers that I've put them in, don't you think?"

Jamie didn't think he actually wanted an answer to his question, nor did she particularly want the answer herself.

"I've brought you to hell, doll. I think you know what I am, don't you?"

Hell.

She was in fucking hell.

Literally and figuratively.

Jamie gave the demon a slight nod, her eyes wide.

"Good, I knew there was more to you than just being Ambrose's bitch."

He knew Ambrose. Did that mean the angel had something to do with this, or did all angels and demons have vendettas against each other? Her thoughts swam as she tried to come up with a reason he would bring her here.

Did it matter?

The demon held the upper hand.

She was only human after all.

"I'm Pyro, by the way."

Pyro? He sounded like a comic book bad guy, not a

demon who held her life in his hand. Jamie held her tongue though so she didn't anger him. She didn't even want to think about what would happen to her if he were truly angry.

First, she had to find something out.

"Why did you take me?" *And, do you have my friends?* She kept that to herself because she didn't want to call attention to them, just in case.

"Didn't you hear me? You're Ambrose's. Anything of his I can take—or maim and kill—is a plus for me. Oh, and when he comes for you, and he will because rumor is he's your true half, he'll die, as well. And, if he doesn't come because he's a fucking coward, then he'll want to die anyway because he let you die. I win either way."

It didn't sound as if he had her friends as well, but, oh, God, he couldn't kill Ambrose. Not that she particularly wanted to die, but she *really* didn't want Ambrose to die. Though the angel hadn't wanted her, she didn't wish him harm.

"I see from your reaction that you knew he was your true half," Pyro said as he walked to one of the tables and picked up a blade, toying with the sharpened edge.

A shiver of fear ran down her spine.

This was going to hurt.

Badly.

"Did you wonder why he didn't want you? So did I, honestly. What could be so wrong with you that he'd forgo a lifelong romance with someone who completes him?" Pyro rolled his eyes at that. "It sounds like a romance novel. One where you don't get your happy ending, dear Jamie."

Ambrose would come for her…but did she want him to? From what she remembered in her reading, angels didn't live very long in the hell realm because of the immense hatred between the two factions. Though Ambrose was a warrior and strong, that didn't mean he could survive in a fight against an entire species.

"What are you going to do to me?" she asked, then mentally slapped herself. Why had she asked that? Did she really want to know what a demon who'd locked her in a torture chamber wanted to do to her?

Pyro threw his head back and laughed. "Oh honey, I'm so glad you asked that. You see, I had plans to have your body in every way possible before I threw you to the other demons so they could have their share. Because of certain… events, I've been forced to change those plans. No matter, you're not my type anyway. I prefer my woman to handle it a little harder. You, my dear, look like you could break with the slightest pressure—even though that sounds like a treat to me too. What I am going to do is cut into you a bit so I can taste the blood in your veins. Because we both know, dear, there's something different about you, isn't there? I want to see if I can taste what you are before I give you to the gladiator games and watch a demon tear you into pieces. They may or may not have their way with your body beforehand as well. It depends on their mood. What do you think of my plans? Sound good to you?" Pyro smiled and walked toward her, malicious intent in his gaze.

Jamie couldn't help it anymore and threw up beside her chains, her stomach revolting at the thought of what was to come and how helpless she was to fight against it. She would fight. She couldn't go down complacent; it wasn't in her.

Pyro released her from her chains, and she instinctively struggled, trying to get her feet on the ground so she could run.

Come on, do it, run. Find a way out.

She got one foot on the ground, and Pyro gripped her by the arms, throwing her into the wall. Her head slammed against the cement with a deafening *thump,* and she closed her eyes so she wouldn't pass out from the dizziness. Jamie twisted in his hold, trying to break free, but he was too strong, and she was too…human.

"Oh, I like the fight in you, Jamie, but stop it before you hurt yourself. I want you awake when I cut into you."

Jamie bit her lip so she wouldn't cry. She had to be strong, but she wasn't an idiot either. The more she fought, the harder he held, and as it was, his hands around her arms were cutting in deep, bound to leave bruises. She'd find a way out of there. He would only cut her a little, right? And, then they'd leave the room, and she'd have a better chance.

She could endure that.

She was strong.

Jamie said it over and over in her head as a mantra, and Pyro chained her to the table and started cutting. The pain ripped through her with each tiny, precise slice. He cut into her leg, her hip, her side, and her arm. Blood ran in rivulets down her side, warm along her cooling body. She closed her eyes and focused on thoughts of her friends and Ambrose, even as her body shook from shock.

She'd survive. She had to.

When something wet licked at her hip, she opened her eyes and gasped. Pyro licked the blood off her, his eyes in ecstasy as she shuddered in revulsion.

"You taste sweet, like candy," Pyro said as he licked his lips. "Not human, no, you have something in you." He furrowed his brows and sucked on his lip. "I can't tell what it is. Whatever happened to you isn't finished yet. Something has to trigger it but hasn't. You're a mystery, Jamie. And I love mysteries, tearing them open so I can see every little piece of them."

Fear weighed on her, heavier than the chains that held her to the table.

"Too bad for me that I have to get you to the games now. Fucking plans getting messed up."

He slapped her hard, her head rolling to the side as she tried to blink to stay awake.

"Like I'd let you stay conscious while I take you to the games," Pyro said as he backhanded her again.

This time she saw only darkness.

When she woke next, she found herself lying on the floor, a metal collar around her neck, attached to a chain. Pyro held the other end. Oh, God, it wasn't over. She looked around, even as her body ached, and didn't recognize anything. Really, what did she know about hell?

Pyro was talking to another man, but she couldn't hear

what he was saying, not with her ears ringing and her head pounding. She looked around some more and held back a gasp. They were at a coliseum of some sort, like the ones in Rome, but not as rundown.

This must be the place for the games Pyro had been talking about.

The games that he must be selling her to now.

With the collar around her neck, there was no way to escape, not with the demons strolling around her, their horns in various shapes, sizes, and colors. Oh, God, it was just too much. Where were her ruby slippers so she could just go home and wake up from this nightmare?

She wasn't Dorothy, and she was definitely not in Kansas anymore.

Pyro tugged on her chain, and she reached up to her collar so he wouldn't choke her any more than he had.

"I'll put her in with the animal. He'll make sure she doesn't escape," the other demon said.

Animal? Oh, God, what was he putting her in with?

"Good, enjoy. She's feisty," Pyro said before turning to her. "Jamie dear, this is where we part. Thank you for doing your part." He bent at the waist and traced a finger along her jaw.

"Go to hell."

"Already there, baby. It's home. Don't forget, you're here too." With that, Pyro handed her off to the other demon and walked away.

The demon didn't say a word but tugged on her chain. It bit into her neck, and she stood on shaky legs so the thing didn't decapitate or choke her. He led her through a doorway then through a maze of tunnels that must have been underground. Not that she really knew, but the stench of old water and mold told her it was the likely option. With each step, her bones ached, and the hallways grew colder.

Jamie wrapped her arms around herself, trying to keep any semblance of warmth she could. The demon didn't talk, just merely grunted as he moved through the hall before he stopped in front of a room that looked like a prison cell, complete with bars. It was almost complete darkness, save for the light from the hall.

He pulled on her chain, opened the door, and threw her in. She crashed into the floor, agony ricocheting up her arm as she hit hard. The demon unchained her and took off her collar. As soon as he did it, she tried to get up and run, but he was too fast. She let out a scream as he threw her against a wall, her body sliding down like a ragdoll.

"No escaping. You'll die soon anyway."

The demon slammed the barred door shut, and Jamie finally let the tears fall.

She was going to die.

There was no question.

She couldn't fight them all, and Ambrose wasn't coming.

Something shifted on the other side of the cell, and she pushed herself back against the wall.

"Who's there?" she said, her voicing cracking, her throat sore from the collar.

"You're human," a deep voice rumbled.

"Yes, what are you?" she asked. She'd just remembered

they said they'd put her in with something called "the animal." Maybe she'd die here instead of in the actual games.

She didn't really want to die. Not now, not anytime soon.

"I'm a wolf shifter," the voice said as a truly feral-looking man stalked out from beneath the shadows.

His hair met his shoulders in a slightly wavy brown. She could see the yellow of his eyes in the light. Definitely not human, even a little bit.

He wore only jeans that looked as if they'd seen better days and had the body of a god. A god that, apparently, wanted to kill her. Not that she knew it for sure, but since that seemed to be the normal turn of thought with the last people she'd seen, she could only think that.

"What is your name?" he asked as he knelt in front of her, curiosity in his gaze.

"Jamie," she whispered as fear coated her tongue.

His nostrils flared, making him look like the wolf he claimed to be. "I'm Hunter."

Hunter. So, now she knew the name of the man who wanted to kill her.

"Why are you here?" he asked.

"What?"

"Why are you here? What did you try to summon? Only stupid humans would dare do such a thing. No wonder you're in this mess."

She shook her head vehemently. "No, I didn't summon anything. I swear. This demon, Pyro, had his goonies or whatever kidnap me from my home so he could kill my… my true half."

Hunter tilted his head again, as if considering what she'd said. "I won't kill you, Jamie. If this demon really did take you away from your home, I'm sorry." His eyes took a faraway look. "I was taken from my home as well."

"I'm sorry," she said. There really wasn't anything more to say.

"You should get some rest. The games will start in the morning, or at least what passes for morning in hell. You'll need all the energy you can get."

"I'm human. I can't fight the way they do."

Hunter shook his head. "If they put us in the same cage, then you'll fight with me against another. It's good for their business to have pairs—it provides more gore and terror." He flexed his fingers, as if looking at something on his hands that wasn't there. "I've never lost a battle, not in all the years I've been here."

Relief spread through her, though she knew it would probably only be short lived.

"Thank you."

"Don't thank me yet, Jamie. I don't know all their plans. I'll do what I can. Maybe your true half will come to save you."

What if she didn't want him to? Not that she didn't want to live. No, she totally wanted to. She just couldn't bear the thought of Ambrose dying because of her.

There really didn't look like there was much choice for

her in any matter. In the morning, she'd wake and she'd fight.

She was strong.

At least, she had to keep telling herself that.

HUNTER BROOKS WATCHED THE HUMAN CURL INTO A BALL and pass out from sheer exhaustion. If she were to fight on her own, she'd die within moments unless the opponent wanted her to suffer. He couldn't have that, not when she looked so small and helpless.

A curse for him, really.

He'd just have to save her too.

He looked down at his hands and swore he could still see the blood that had stained him for so long. He'd killed countless times to save himself, but he'd kill again to save another.

Was it worth it?

How much of his soul did he have left to lose?

CHAPTER 6

Balin slid the knife into its sheath at his waist and sighed. His body had weakened to a frighteningly low amount of energy. Not good if he wanted to save this human woman who may or may not have been his true half.

He ran his hand through his hair, his muscles tightening but tired. His true half? Could it really be that simple? Balin snorted. Okay, not simple, but at least there was a possibility, something that he hadn't thought was possible. He didn't know if he had the strength to survive what was coming, but he'd fight for her…and for himself nonetheless.

He had nothing to lose.

Not anymore.

Pyro had said he'd have Jamie at his home until he was done with her, then he'd sell her to the games for other demons' enjoyment. Balin clenched his teeth at the reminder of what Pyro could be doing to Jamie at this moment, though the idea of what would happen once she reached the games sent a dose of ice down his back.

He quickened his steps, grabbed his pack, threw it over his shoulder, and said one last goodbye to the home that had sheltered him for so many years. No matter what happened tonight, he'd never come back to this place. He'd either be dead or would find a way to get Jamie out of here.

Jamie.

He liked the way her name sounded on his lips, though it had taken placating Pyro to get the name from him in the first place. As Balin made his way to his father's house through the caverns on the other side of his home, he thought about the woman he was going to save or die trying.

She had lustrous brown hair that he wanted to run his finger through, just to see if it was as soft as it looked. Her blunt bangs framed her face, and he knew they'd make her eyes stand out, whatever color they may be. He'd just have to take a closer look when she was conscious. Hell, it sounded weird when he put it like that. Her skin looked as though it was darker through genetics, not from the sun, much like his own. The caramel color practically begged for his tongue, something he'd enjoy testing out one day.

That was, if he made it through whatever came next.

Balin shook his head, pissed with himself. He had to stop thinking about things like that.

He'd save her. He had to.

In his long life, he'd always had the notion of finding his true half, but he'd never put any real thought into who she might be, what she would look like, what she loved. He hadn't wanted to put too much hope in a dream that most likely would never come true.

He'd never thought about what he would do once he found her. Would he woo her? Would she know him on sight?

He wasn't too sure in Jamie's case, as she was human, but he'd always thought that maybe if she were another paranormal being, she'd know him for who he was.

A demon with a heart.

Balin stopped where he was, ignoring the sharp rocks, the lava pools, and the heat from the fires around him.

A demon with a heart?

Really?

That's what he called himself now?

Hades, he sounded like a loon, a freaking weakling who didn't deserve a true half.

And, really, he wasn't sure he did. After all, he'd spent most of his life in his father's dungeons, too drugged and beaten to be of any use. When he hadn't been there, he'd been fighting against the other factions of demons because that's how life prevailed in the deepest pits of hell.

He hadn't had a choice as a younger demon, and much like Fawkes did now, Balin had wanted to prove himself beyond being the son of the infamous Pyro. When Balin had chosen not to take souls, but to live weaker than the rest and depend on the strength of his mind and spirit. Rather than just the strength of his sword-bearing arm, he'd shamed his father to the point he'd almost succumbed to temptation and fed off the lives of the innocent and not-so-innocent.

Balin had lived through it all, weakening but with his morals intact. He'd always known his fate would be death. He'd almost given up and let it take him.

Now he had something to live for.

Jamie.

He had to find her. Had to save her.

Had to sleep with her.

He winced at that last thought.

Though fighting for their lives would take all his energy and just might kill him, the thought of sleeping with his true half scared him more than the former.

He'd had his share of women before, demon and the like, but he'd never slept with his true half. How was he going to explain to a human that he needed her to spread her legs for him to live?

Hades, that sounded like the worst pick-up line in the history of bad pick-up lines.

What about his father's enemy, Ambrose?

Pyro had thought Ambrose was Jamie's true half, meaning Balin could be totally wrong in his thinking and going off to fight for a woman who would be his death anyway.

It didn't matter. He'd find out exactly what she was to him and to Ambrose. He didn't have a choice, not really. He could either die alone in his home, wishing for a better outcome, or he could fight for the woman who could be his savior.

Though the latter sounded like the hell he lived in, it was worth it.

It had to be.

Balin crept through the jagged rocks, aware he was on his father's territory where he could be killed on sight since he hadn't been invited. He slid a knife into his hand, just in case. The heat from the red sky beat down on him, the heat draining whatever energy he had.

He just needed to make it to the entrance to the underground tunnels, and he'd be fine. Once he was out of the direct heat, he'd be able to recharge as much as he could without souls as he made his way to Pyro's and eventually to wherever Jamie was being held.

The crunch of rock beneath a leather boot reached Balin's ears, and he lowered his body behind a boulder, his senses on high alert.

He gripped his knife, ready to take out whoever was there. He might have been weakening due to lack of souls, but that didn't make him any less a fierce fighter.

He swallowed the lie and listened.

An arrow shot past him, missing him by an inch, and he rolled to the side, throwing the knife as he did so. He heard a groan from his assailant, and Balin slid his sword from its scabbard and risked a peek to see who it was and how many there were. He let out a breath at the sight of a lone soldier, squared his shoulders, and ran out from behind the boulder.

The other demon staggered, Balin's knife embedded deep in his chest, but still raised his sword, prepared for battle. Balin ducked at a clumsy blow, shifted to his steady leg, and sliced the bastard's head off with one quick strike.

The look of surprise on the demon's face was priceless.

As if the weakling son of Pyro couldn't have killed the demon in one quick blow.

Balin wiped his sword off on the pants of the dead soldier and did the same to his knife once he took it out of the demon's chest. He didn't want to leave any weapons behind in case the other man had friends, and frankly, Balin had a feeling he'd need all the weapons he had in the upcoming battle for Jamie…and his life.

Pain shot through him, and he coughed. Hell, he'd used up too much energy fighting. Quickly, he surveyed the area and didn't see anyone else there. That didn't mean he was alone, but it was the best he could do. He had only another ten or so minute hike until he made it to the mouth of the cave, and then he could recharge as he made his way to Jamie.

Jamie.

Yes, she was the reason he did this. It was worth it.

It had to be.

He practically stumbled the last few feet but gave a thankful prayer to whatever god would take him as he made it to the cave. The lack of fire, explosive heat, and red sky would help him breathe as he made his way, thankfully.

He could only hope he wasn't too late.

Balin made it through the tunnels with relative ease, the path familiar to him, as he'd taken it numerous times as a kid so he wouldn't be beaten. Pyro had always found him later and hit him harder, but Balin had at least had those few minutes of peace, and he was pretty sure Pyro had never found out how Balin had escaped—something that had angered the man even more.

Balin suppressed a shudder at the phantom feeling of the hot poker Pyro had used to sear his flesh as punishment.

He couldn't let Pyro do that to Jamie.

Reaching the end of the tunnel, Balin pressed his hand along the outwardly invisible seam and twisted the hidden handle. The door popped open with a quiet hiss, and Balin made his way through, closing it firmly behind him. He didn't sense anyone near him, but he couldn't be too careful.

He crept along the halls of the dungeons his father loved to build and made his way to the top floor. There were no guards below, only ones on the first floors. Once someone made it past the dungeon door, they didn't make it out alive so there was no reason for guards below. Well, at least in all cases but Balin's.

According to Pyro, though, he was special.

Lucky him.

Balin had looked through the cells as he made his way up and didn't see Jamie, only dead demons that needed to be cleaned up eventually.

Demons didn't last long in Pyro's care.

Balin made it to the room where he'd last seen Jamie, uneasy that he hadn't seen or heard his father yet. He could only hope the bastard was asleep in his room or out killing something weaker than him.

He slowly opened the door and cursed, a deep disappointment sliding through him.

Fuck.

She wasn't there.

Terror hit him hard, but he buried it. He searched the other two rooms on the ground floor but didn't see her.

Hades, that could only mean one thing if what Pyro had said was true.

He'd taken Jamie to the games early.

Why?

Balin slinked through the house, dodging guards, and made it through the front door so no one would sense him. He hid behind a boulder, trying to catch his breath and gather his strength.

Why had Pyro taken her so early?

His father wouldn't have become bored with her so easily, not when he thought she was Ambrose's. No, he'd have wanted to play with her longer, savor the experience.

Again, he swallowed the bile at that thought.

Shit, could Pyro have noticed the connection between Balin and Jamie?

He'd tried to smother his expression when he'd entered the room, but there had been that split second of surprise and awe at seeing the woman who'd been his dreams—who could save him.

Hell, had it been his fault?

He prayed that Pyro hadn't gotten angry and killed her. Though Balin hadn't smelled a recent death within the walls, that didn't mean it hadn't happened.

He gripped the hilt of his sword harder and cursed.

No, she was alive—she had to be.

Pyro would see Ambrose's punishment and pain through, and if his father had sensed something was wrong with Balin, he'd made sure his son would feel that agony as well.

That meant that Jamie had to be at the games now.

Alone.

Not dead, no, she couldn't be.

He'd know, right?

It didn't matter. Either way, he had to make it to the games. Either to know for sure that both of their fates had been decided for them or to save her.

Then maybe they could get out of hell and have a life filled with something more than just the fires of hell. He'd never even spoken to this woman, but he knew she was the source of his hope. If Ambrose was also her true half, that also meant there was a chance he was part of Balin's future as well—a triad.

He'd take anything he could get.

They could be his hope.

They *were* his hope.

Balin took a deep breath and began the long trip to the coliseum where the games were held. He could only hope that in the few short hours he'd seen Jamie, that she'd been healed and prepared for the games…not *in* the games.

As a human, she'd be a huge draw due to the fact that her death would be brutal, and the demons would want to see that.

He shook his head, pissed at himself for even thinking that. He'd find her first, damn it.

Ambrose was an angel and couldn't come to hell to save her. That meant it was up to him to save her—something that made him feel stronger than he was.

Balin looked at the sturdy stone coliseum and cursed. This would be harder than just taking her from Pyro's home. There were guards, dungeons, fighters with such scarred minds that their brutality was a thing of legends.

He made his way to the back entrance of the games, knowing he'd have to sneak in. Damn, he really didn't want to do fight and kill, but it would be worth it to live and to find Jamie.

He'd have to make sure when he found her that she knew he wasn't there only for himself, that he wanted her for him as a true half, not just to save his life.

Balin was pretty sure women liked hearing things like that.

Okay, now he was getting ahead of himself.

The back door was actually a large chain and iron gate that would be hell—literally—to break into. Meaning he'd have to take a key from one of the guards.

Balin took out his dagger and leapt at the first one he found, slicing the demon's throat before he could take a breath or scream, alerting the others to Balin's presence. Balin searched him and cursed.

This particular guard didn't have a key, but he did carry a large sword, meaning he was the muscle of the operation.

Balin crept behind the other guard and made quick work of him, though each movement sucked out more energy from within. He felt his skin sweating, his body drawing on too much energy. He knew he must have looked pale and drawn, not the best condition for fighting, but it was all he could do until he found a way to save Jamie or die.

He just hoped it wasn't the latter.

The key to the door lay on the second demon's chest, attached to a chain around his neck. Balin took it from him, hid the bodies, and went in, locking the door behind him. He hoped if anyone came by they'd think the dead demons were passed out drunk, not dead, thus letting the world know there was an intruder amongst them.

There were hundreds of cells in the basement below the fighting floor of the coliseum, and it would be pointless for Balin to search them for hours, but he knew there was a list of prisoners and cell numbers in the back room where the game leaders would make bets of their own.

Instead of hiding, he strode through the place like he owned it. After all, he was a demon, scarred from war and his father; he'd fit in. Better to hide in plain sight than look like he was out of place.

He made his way to the back room, ignoring the other demons as they walked past, though they ignored him as well.

Thankfully.

The board was a mishmash of names, cell numbers, species, and fight times. There was no real order for anything, but Balin looked anyway. He scanned the names, cursing when he couldn't find her...

There.

Human. Cell 475. Midnight Death.

As far as Balin could tell, there wasn't another human on the board. Relief then fury spread through him at what she would have to face if he didn't get her out of there.

Midnight Death was the highlight of the games. A bloodbath of torture and rape before they killed their victim.

Well, fuck that, Jamie wouldn't be part of it. He'd get her out of there before then.

He made his way through the tunnels, aware he had to be careful not to draw attention to himself, though, in reality, no one knew him past a quick glimpse here and there in his life due to his father's torture, so he was in the clear.

Finally, after what seemed like hours, he found her cell.

Each door unlocked from the outside without a key so he made his way in once the guards left for another section of patrol. He clicked the door open and slid in, anticipation on his tongue.

This was it.

"Who are you?" a deep voice said from the shadowed corner.

Hell, did he have the wrong cell?

"I doesn't matter. I'm here for someone else," he answered, cursing himself for not finding Jamie right away. He didn't know who was in the cell with him, but because of the way the door was, he couldn't have seen in right away anyway.

"Who?" the voice asked.

"No one you'd know." Balin squinted, trying to see in the dark corners. When something shifted behind the large shadow, Balin's body shook, his heart connecting to something he hadn't thought possible.

"Jamie?" he asked, his voice raspy.

"What? How did you know my name?" Jamie slid from behind the dark shadow, fear and tears on her face.

The last time he'd seen her, she'd been bloody, her cheek broken, and her body chained to a wall. It looked as if Pyro had healed her before sending her to the games—most likely for more money.

Wait…what was he supposed to say now?

He'd had everything planned yet hadn't. He felt like a fish out of water. He was an alpha demon—even if he hadn't been acting like one since his world had turned on end when he'd found her. Yet the sight of this little woman who could be his—who *was* his true half, left him speechless.

The shadow moved, and Balin found himself against the stone wall, the rivets digging into his back.

"Who are you?"

Balin struggled, but he knew he was too weak at this point to fight much harder. "I'm Balin. I'm here to get Jamie out of here."

"Hunter, put him down," Jamie said, her voice soft and strong, though Balin could still hear the fear beneath it.

He didn't want to be jealous of the way she put her hand

on Hunter's arm to settle him, but hell, he couldn't help it. She was his—and maybe Ambrose's—no one else's.

"Tell me how you know her," Hunter said but lessened his grip a bit.

"I'm Pyro's son." He winced when Jamie blanched, but he continued on. "I'm not going to hurt you; I promise. I hate my father far more than any of you could hope to know, and I don't want you to fear me."

"Why are you here for me?" Jamie asked.

"Because you're my true half."

There. It was out, and he couldn't take it back, but it seemed like the best thing he could say at this point.

"No, you can't be. Ambrose is," she whispered.

Fuck, that hurt, but he let it go. If what he thought was true, then he and Ambrose would have to find a way to work together. Though he could live without this Hunter prisoner hurting him.

"It's true, Jamie. I promise. Can't you feel that connection?" He prayed she could. He knew humans couldn't, but for some reason, he didn't think she was fully human. No, there was something else about her.

"I don't know. Hunter, let him go."

Hunter grunted but relented.

Balin rubbed his neck and gave the man—no werewolf— another look. "You're Hunter, the games' lead fighter."

Hunter nodded. "And that means you know I can kill you quickly if you hurt Jamie. I've heard of you Balin, and I know you don't take souls like other demons do. Meaning you're weak."

"You don't take souls? I thought I'd read that all demons need that to live."

So she knew about the supernatural and had read about them before coming here? He'd have to make sure he found out all he could about her. Everything.

"We do need it to live. There's another way to get around that, but once we hit three hundred, it's over for us."

"How old are you?" she asked.

He gave a self-deprecating smile. "Two hundred and ninety-nine."

"Oh, Balin," she whispered.

Hades, he loved the sound of his name on her lips. This wasn't the time for that. Well, at some point, he'd have to explain to her exactly how they'd get out of hell—sex and all —but right now, he needed to make sure she was safe for the moment.

"I'll explain everything."

"The place is on lockdown at night, Balin," Hunter explained, and Balin nodded. "We won't be able to get out until they open it back up."

"I know, but I can get you out when they open. I'm a demon, and they won't look twice at me bringing Jamie out." They'd just think he was taking her for some personal play, but he wasn't about to tell Jamie that.

"Me *and* Hunter," she corrected.

Balin cast a look toward the prized fighter who was rumored to be a good man, hence why he'd become a prisoner in hell.

"Fine, Hunter as well."

"Before we do any of this, you're going to explain to me exactly who you are and why I feel the need to wrap myself around you and never let you go," Jamie said, her chin raised high.

Balin smiled and bit back a groan at the thought of her doing just that. "We're true halves, Jamie."

"And, what about Ambrose?" Her voice cracked when she said his name, and Balin wanted to curse himself.

"Why can't you have us both?" he asked, and Hunter rolled his eyes.

"Both?" she squeaked.

"Jamie," Hunter began, "you need to rest tonight. There's nothing we can do at this moment. I was going to find a way to get you out of here as it was, but now with Balin here, we should be able to find a plan."

Jamie rubbed her eyes. "I really, *really*, want to scream and cry right now like those heroines in those books who don't do a thing for themselves, but I don't have time for that. I'm going to trust you, Balin, because for some reason my heart tells me to, but that doesn't mean I get this whole true-half business."

Balin nodded, relived that she was even thinking about it, and he caught himself before he pulled her into his body so he could hold her and never let go. But, he let himself weaken just a bit and ran a finger down her cheek.

He'd been right. Her skin was as soft as silk.

He watched as a shudder ran down her body and her pretty brown eyes dilated.

"We'll talk about it all. I'll protect you," he vowed.

She nodded then pulled back, walking to her cot in the corner.

Hunter came to his side and whispered in his ear, "You're going to have to explain to her exactly how you get your strength back, you know."

Balin let out a breath. "Oh, I know."

Hades, he didn't want to scare her, but now that he'd seen her, spoken to her…touched her…he never wanted to let her go.

He just had to fight hell to get her.

Easy for a demon…right?

CHAPTER 7

The demon's scream was cut short as Ambrose sliced off his head. Its decapitated head stared back at Ambrose, his eyes wide and full of the fear he should have had from the beginning. Though the others in hell couldn't tell Ambrose was a warrior angel, and thereby thought he must have been just a normal demon, he thought at least the stupid soldier wouldn't have tried to kill him by himself.

The other man had had a weak technique and even weaker body.

It was no wonder the lowly demon had died so suddenly.

He wiped his blade on the clothes of the dead demon and sheathed it. He'd have to clean it fully when he got back to the other realm. At least, he hoped he could get back. He hadn't devised a plan in which to do so, but he hoped that Dante's friend Balin could aid him in that respect.

Ambrose looked out onto the barren wasteland of the

hell realm and shook his head. Throughout his years, he'd yet to spend any significant amount of time here. In fact, he'd only been here once before, during the last angel and demon war, a millennia or two ago.

There were no children running in the streets, no laughter or promise filling the empty space.

No, this was a place of death, the place humans fought so hard and with such vehemence not to make it to.

It was just too bad that sometimes the demons brought them, not the humans themselves. That was why, if he could find this Balin, he'd save him along with Jamie. The demon hadn't taken a soul and was dying for it. Ambrose would find a way to protect the man.

Though deep down, Ambrose knew it was for another reason. A connection, something that he didn't want to think about.

So he wouldn't think about it.

He had to save Jamie, and she was far more important than an odd feeling at the mention of a name.

Ambrose had seen too much in his long life to bury the images of what could be happening to her—what she could endure. Jamie was stronger than people thought, but that didn't mean she could survive hell.

He shook his head and tried to clear it. There was no use thinking about things that couldn't be changed.

The heat beat on him as he walked toward Pyro's territory. He'd have made it there in a fraction of the time if he could have flown, but demons didn't fly. The medallion he wore only shielded his essence if he acted the part. There would be no hiding if he suddenly sprouted wings.

Ambrose crept along the edge of a cavern and stopped when he heard the telltale sound of footsteps. He risked a peek and saw a younger demon training with a sword, his horns sticking out from his head, as only a son of Lucifer's could do.

The boy didn't look old enough to take souls, a teenager at best, and Ambrose wasn't in the mindset to kill the innocent—he never was.

He snuck behind the demon and tackled him to the ground, surprised when the boy fought back with a skill that surpassed his age.

"What the hell?" the boy asked as he struggled beneath Ambrose's grip.

"Where is the demon they call Balin?" he asked, his forearm against the kid's throat.

"Why do you want him? Let him be. He doesn't need trouble from the likes of you. He has enough on his plate."

So the boy defended Balin, meaning he had to be a friend. Or at least an enemy with a conscience.

"What's your name, boy?"

"Fawkes, what's yours?"

"I am Ambrose."

Fawkes eyes widened. "I know that name. You're the warrior angel who defeated Balin's dad, aren't you?"

Ambrose took a risk and leaned back. "They tell you of that story still?"

They both stood and Fawkes grinned and rubbed this

throat. "Of course they do. Pyro's an ass and deserved what came to him. Why do you want to see Balin?"

"Because he might be of aid to me."

Fawkes rolled his eyes. "Yeah, I figured that. Now why don't you tell me the real reason because I'm not just going to let you hurt him."

The kid had balls. That was for sure. "What makes you think I can't get it out of you?"

"Because despite this badass, old-as-dirt persona you have, you're not a bad guy."

"Old as dirt?" he asked wryly.

"Hey, I said you were a badass too."

Ambrose let out a breath. Dante hadn't mentioned Fawkes, but the kid might have been too young for the old dragon to have even met.

"Pyro stole my true half, a human woman who shouldn't have to endure the pits of hell. A friend from the human realm said Balin would be able to help."

Sadness spread over Fawkes' face, and he shook his head. "I don't know how much help Balin will be to you."

"I know his age and his choices, Fawkes."

The boy swallowed hard but clenched his jaw like a boy becoming a man. "I don't want him to spend his last days in any more pain. I will say, I've heard they brought a human woman down here for the games."

Fury spread through him. "The games? They'll kill her."

Fawkes frowned then shrugged. "That's the point with Pyro. I can't help you, even though I would if I could. I haven't hit maturity yet, and I can't get into the games without sneaking in. Plus, I don't have the strength I need. But I'll tell you how to get in."

"You're a good man, Fawkes."

Shadows filled the boy's eyes, something far darker than a demon his age should have. "No, I'm not sure that I am. I haven't made that choice yet."

Ambrose gripped Fawkes' shoulder. "When you reach maturity and you're allowed to go to the human realm, if you choose not to take souls, I will help you in whatever way I can. You didn't have to tell me where you thought Jamie was, and you didn't have to protect your friend. You're already stronger than you think."

Fawkes gave him a long, pleading look then shook it off. "I might take you up on that. I don't know my decision yet. I do know that we better hurry if I'm going to show you how to sneak in. Just keep that medallion around your neck. The last thing we need is another war. Oh, and please don't tell me how you got that, okay?"

"You know what this is?" Ambrose fingered the medallion around his neck.

"Uh huh, and that's why I'm not going to talk about it."

Curious, but more worried about Jamie, he let it slide. He followed the younger demon to the coliseum, each step growing heavier as he thought about what would happen if he was too late. Jamie couldn't survive what they would do to her in the games.

She would have stood a chance though if she'd had her powers. No, Ambrose had been an idiot and denied the both of them their mating because of his own insecurities. He swallowed hard but bit back the emotion that threatened to drown him.

The large stone structure looked reminiscent of the one in the human realm—at least how it had looked when the human one had been new. Ambrose remembered the gladiator games and had been glad the barbaric custom had died out…at least in most places of the world. Looking now at the demonic one, Ambrose suppressed a shudder.

The stone rose up to the sky like giant claws ready to break through the red clouds and watch them bleed. There were no entrances or exits easily navigable. Except for the owners and patrons, whatever went in did not come out alive.

He'd be dammed if he let Jamie become one of theirs to play with.

"I can get you in through the sewer on the other side," Fawkes explained as they crouched behind a boulder. "It isn't pretty, but it should do. I can't go in with you because my dad would shit a brick, but I can at least make it so you can get in."

"Thank you, Fawkes."

The young demon shrugged. "Don't thank me. For all we know, I'm sending you to your death. I don't like knowing humans are dying down here because of who they know, not for what they did."

Ambrose nodded and followed in silence as they made their way to a sewer drain filled with mud, rain, and other things he was determined not to think about. Considering they were at the edge of a place where demons and other creatures died frequently, he really didn't want to know.

"This is where I leave you. Head north and you'll end up right at the prisoner cells."

"You're kidding me," Ambrose said. "If they have a way out right there, why don't people escape?"

"Because it's easy as hell to get in this way, but to get out, they have to get through their doors, the guards, and magic. You can get in, but you'll need luck to get out."

"Well, hell."

Fawkes cracked a smile. "Considering you're in hell, that makes sense. The doors will be easy for you because you're not behind them. You're a warrior angel, so you should be able to take care of the guards. As for the magic?" Fawkes shook his head. "All I can say is that if you're quick enough, you should make it."

"Should."

"I don't know, Ambrose. The risk is worth it if you consider what's going to happen if you don't try."

Ambrose opened the grate, the heavy weight of it surprising him. As he stepped in the gunk that shall not be named, he looked over his shoulder at Fawkes. "Remember what I said. You make that choice, you can come up with me. We'll find a way."

Fawkes just nodded, uncertainty in his gaze. "I remember. Good luck."

Ambrose nodded back and crouched down in the sewer. He headed north for a few hundred feet amongst the rotting corpses, blood, and grime, and then he found himself at another grate with a small sliver of light shining through.

Oh, thank God.

He wasn't sure even his tough stomach could handle the gore much longer. He didn't want to think about what Jamie would have to endure when he took her back through it.

He looked through the small opening and couldn't see guards, nor could he hear them. Careful not to attract attention, he slowly slid the grate off its hinges, almost buckling from the weight. He was a strong angel, and he wasn't sure others would be able to lift the damn thing. No wonder it was a deterrent.

Ambrose crept down the darkened hallway, looking back and forth and keeping his senses on high alert. Demons occupied each cell, most dying or dead. Only a few looked like they could fight worth a damn, but they didn't pay him any attention. With the medallion around his neck, he looked like a demon with a right to be down there.

Because of the bond he held with Jamie, at least the initial makings of a bond, he had the ability to find her if she was close enough. He couldn't close his eyes and concentrate on it because he had to make sure he wasn't spotted by a guard, he could still settle into that bond and reach out to her.

He almost fell to his knees and wept when he found that thread. He followed the path in the tunnels while following the fragile thread leading to Jamie.

That meant that she was alive.

That she still had a chance.

Thank God.

After another turn, the bond felt stronger, and he stopped at a gate.

She was in there.

This had to be it.

"Who's there?" a deep voice growled, and Ambrose stiffened.

"No one you need to concern yourself with," he answered.

"Am…Ambrose?" Jamie whispered as she hesitantly made her way up to the door.

Oh, God. His knees felt weak, and he pressed his palm against the bars. She did the same, and at the touch of her soft, soft skin, he melted.

She was real.

Alive.

Bruised, but otherwise she looked okay. Her wide eyes made her skin look paler than normal.

"Jamie," he rasped out.

"You're Ambrose?" another deep voice asked, this one different from the first one.

Ambrose looked behind Jamie at the demon who'd said his name and froze.

Hell, that connection. He could feel it clear as day, just the same as it had been with Jamie, that warmth spreading through his chest, wrapping and locking itself around his heart.

This was that third, the other man he had felt for Jamie.

He wasn't just for Jamie…no, the man was for him as well.

A triad.

"Well, hell," the demon whispered as he rubbed his chest.

"What?" Jamie asked as she looked between them both. "What is it?"

"You better get in here if you don't want to get caught," the first voice said. "They won't look in the cages as long as you don't make a scene."

Ambrose nodded, took another look around him to make sure no one was there, and slid into the cell. He didn't close the door all the way so he wouldn't be locked in. Without words, he pulled Jamie into his arms, and she sank into him.

"Gods, Jamie," he whispered, his voice near cracking. He ran a hand through her long chestnut hair and down her body.

"I knew you'd come."

There. Right there. That's what he'd been missing. Faith, hope, and everything he didn't think he deserved—*still* didn't think he deserved.

"Of course I would come, Jaime. I'm not letting you go again." They had more to say, more to promise and decide, but now wasn't the time. Not with a strange wolf shifter with yellow eyes in the corner and a demon who meant change for Ambrose.

He held her a bit longer then pulled back so he could meet the other two men in the cell with Jamie. Jealousy rippled up his spine at the thought, but he pulled back and gave them his normal stony expression. It had gotten him through countless wars in the past, and he wasn't about to show his true emotions to strangers.

"To answer your question, yes, I'm Ambrose. And I'm here to get Jamie out of here."

The demon raised his chin and frowned. "You're the reason she's in here to begin with then."

Fury and guilt spread through him. "No, it was the bastard Pyro who holds that responsibility. Now who the hell are you?"

"Stop it, both of you," Jamie admonished as she stood between the two of them, small and fragile. The steel glint in her eyes was anything but fragile.

"I'm sorry, Jamie," the demon said as he brushed a lock of hair from her face.

Ambrose bit his tongue at the gesture but didn't feel the jealousy he was ready for. No, this felt right.

Well, hell, he hadn't been prepared for a true half, let alone a triad.

"I'm Balin," the demon said, and Ambrose started.

"Balin? Pyro's son?"

The flecks of red in his black eyes brightened, and he nodded. "He might be my father, but he is not my keeper."

Ambrose couldn't hold back any longer and wrapped his arm around Jamie's waist. She stiffened for only a moment then leaned into him. Her floral and spice scent tingled along his senses, and he calmed. Yes, he could scent the days she'd been down on her, but he could always find that floral and spice.

"I don't blame the son for the father. You're also Dante's and Fawkes' friend. As for that tug you feel, you know I feel it too."

"What are you talking about?" Jamie asked.

"I'll explain soon," he said as he kissed her brow, unable to stop himself. He knew he was acting out of character, but he'd been so afraid of what could have happened to her while down here that he didn't want to hide anymore.

A far cry from his usual self.

"You know Dante and Fawkes?" Balin asked, surprise in his gaze. He ran a hand through his dark hair and over his even darker horns.

"Wait, you know Dante too?" Jamie asked. "He's been a friend of mine forever. I've known him longer than even Ambrose has."

Balin lifted his lips in a smile. "Dante knows everyone, I'm sure. As for Fawkes, I didn't think he'd made it to the human realm yet. He's not of age."

Ambrose shook his head. "I met him here." He lowered his voice. "He helped me get in, but we're going to have to help each other to get out."

"And do you have a plan?" the other man, the wolf shifter, asked, derision in his tone.

"Oh, this is Hunter," Jamie said then gave a weak laugh. "I'm in a dungeon in hell where I might have to fight for my life, and I'm worried about manners. I'm sorry."

Hunter shrugged. "I was sure you'd get to me eventually. With the vibes off the two men, I say you three have more to talk about than just getting out of hell. I'd give you privacy, but as you can see, it's a little cramped in here." Tension radiated off him, and he rolled his shoulders. "I've been alone in here for years. It's a little odd to have so many people in here at once."

"Years?" Jamie asked.

Ambrose rubbed Jamie's side. She knew at least a little of what that meant. In order to live for years in the games, he'd have to have fought countless demons and other species and won.

By killing.

Hunter blinked but didn't show any other form of emotion. "I'll help you get out if we can, but I'm going with you." He let out a breath that seemed to tell the ageless tone of death and fighting. "I'm ready."

Balin looked over at Ambrose. "Do you have a plan?"

"I know of a way out of the cells if we're quick when the time comes. However, I can't get out of hell as easily. That's where you come in."

Balin shook his head. "I can't. At least not yet." Balin gave him a look full of meaning, and Ambrose held back a curse.

Of course Balin couldn't. Dante had said the demon was reaching his three hundredth year, meaning he wouldn't have the power or energy to get out of hell. The only way would be if he mated with his true half—or in his case, his triad.

Meaning they'd have to convince Jamie to form the bond in truth in the middle of hell.

Meaning he'd have to convince her to make love with two men in the middle of hell.

Yes, that seemed like an easy feat.

Much like building Rome.

"What aren't you telling me?" Jamie asked.

Ambrose let out a breath. "You know I'm your true half, don't you?"

She glared. "Yes, and I know you left me in pain for a freaking year when you went off to go do whatever the hell angels do."

"We're going to have to talk about that, man," Balin warned, and Ambrose closed his eyes.

In a matter of minutes he'd hurt and annoyed both of his mates.

Apparently, he was just that good.

"Jamie, I'm sorry. I know that's not enough, not right now, but we can talk about it more when we're out of here. The thing is, that pull I feel with you and that you feel with me, you feel it for Balin too, right?"

She gulped and gave a slight nod. "What does that mean? I thought I was yours." She blushed. "I mean, as much yours as I could be without having you. After the lightning hit us, and yes, I explained it to Hunter and Balin, I thought I'd find my true half and become whatever I was meant to be. Why do I feel the same pull toward both of you?"

At least she felt it. Ambrose let that little bit release from the tension in his shoulders. "Because not all true halves come in pairs. There are such things as triads."

Her eyes widened, and she took a step back—away from him and Balin and toward Hunter. Both he and Balin let out a slight growl.

They were both too close and too far away from a bond to watch their mate stand so close to another.

Even if he couldn't hear Balin's thoughts, he knew from the stance the demon took they were along the same lines as his.

"Triad," she breathed. "I thought that was only in the romance books I read." She blushed again, and Ambrose put that thought away for later. He'd have to see what exactly it was she was reading.

"They're in every realm, human, demon, angel alike. They're rare, but they exist."

"You're saying the three of us are like…together?" She shook her head and wrapped her arms around her waist.

Ambrose stole a look at Balin and gave him a nod. "Yes. That's what I'm saying. It's still up to you, Jamie. It will always be up to you."

"Does that mean you and Balin are together too?"

Ambrose swore he saw a blush rise in Balin's neck and face.

"A triad can be like that, or it can just center around one person," Balin said.

A little bit of hope Ambrose ripped from him. Did that mean Balin didn't feel that same tug? Had he been wrong and Ambrose wasn't to mate with Balin? He'd been with a man or two in his time, but he'd always preferred women. That didn't mean he didn't want Balin.

In fact, as he let his gaze fall over the built man in leather, he was dammed disappointed.

"I'm pretty sure Ambrose and I feel that connection.

Right?" The other man shifted from foot to foot, as if he was just as unsure as Ambrose.

Relieved, Ambrose nodded. "Yes, but since we just met, let's talk about Jamie first then get to know each other."

Balin gave a small laugh at that. "It's weird, right? I've been waiting almost three hundred years for a true half and mate, and now, I'm in a dungeon and have found them both."

Ambrose smiled at that and caught the look of surprise on Jamie's face as he did so. He'd have to smile more often in front of her, though it wouldn't be a hardship.

"I've been waiting a bit longer for mine," he said dryly. "Jamie, we can talk about all of this and what it means when we get you out." He risked a glance at Balin, who gave a small nod. "Balin doesn't have enough power to get out of hell, Jamie. That means he's going to need to gain power elsewhere."

"I thought he didn't want to take souls," Jamie said. "Isn't that how demons gain energy? I remember reading about it, and then Balin explained more." She gave a small smile. "I hate not knowing."

Balin smiled back and ran a hand through her hair. "I hate not knowing as well. And, I don't take souls, Jamie. I can also get power from my bond with my mates."

Her eyes widened. "And to do that..." She blushed. "You're saying we're going to have to have sex in order to get out of hell? You're kidding, right? That's got to be some kind of line. There's no way I'm going to have sex with anyone in hell. Plus, you know, we just met and... just no.

I'm still pissed as hell at you, Ambrose, and I don't even know Balin's last name. There's no way I'm just going to stop what I'm doing and lie down for either of you."

Hunter gave a chuckle, and Ambrose cursed. Damn wolf shifter. He'd forgotten the man was there.

"My last name is Drake," Balin explained.

Jamie shot him a look that would have felled more than one demon, but Balin merely stared back. It wasn't as if Balin had anything to lose at this point.

That thought left Ambrose a little cold. He didn't want to think about the future Balin faced without help from him and Jamie. There was nothing pleasant about wasting away from a person's own self.

"Jamie, we're going to get you out of the cells first. Then we can figure out what to do. Forming the bond seems to be the only way right now. Unless we find another demon to open a portal for us that is strong enough for three—" He looked at Hunter. "—four of us."

"Is that possible?" Jamie asked.

Balin let out a breath. "Yes and no. Yes, there are some demons out there strong enough to do that. The portals are heavily guarded, and frankly, none of them will want to help me. I'm an outcast, remember?"

Ambrose reached out and gripped the man's shoulder, surprising them both. He wasn't a man given to impulses of touch, but Balin had looked like he needed it.

They were going to make this work.

They had to.

Jamie stepped up and looked between them. "I don't

know what to do. I hate not having a plan. But first, let's get out of this cell, okay? I really, really, don't want to fight."

Fear slid through him, and he pulled her close. She let him and rested her head on his chest. He smelled her floral and spice scent as it wrapped itself around his body, centering him.

"I'm going to do all in my power not to let that happen," he promised.

Balin stood up behind her while Hunter stayed off to the side, envy in his gaze. "I'm not going to let them have you, Jamie. I just met you both, but I know there's something there. I'm not going to lose it. And even if there weren't, I'm not going to let my father win."

Ambrose kissed Jamie's brow and looked at the demon who could be his future along with the woman in his arms.

Things changed with one drop of rain, yet he could do this. He'd had five thousand years to live without them; he didn't want to lose his chance.

He just needed to get them out of hell.

CHAPTER 8

Jamie inhaled Balin's and Ambrose's combined warmth and musk, the scent seeping into her pores, calming and heating her up all at once. It made no sense she was in this situation. No, at any moment, she would wake up and find herself in her normal home, her normal bed, and her normal life, *alone*.

She wouldn't be in the depths of hell, put on a time limit before she had to fight for her life—and lose—then find herself held by two men who claimed to be hers.

Or, at least, could be hers.

No, that wasn't something that happened to Jamie Bennett.

Plus, the idea of two men?

No, that was wrong. Taboo. Something people only read about in secret because of the judgment of others...and maybe even the judgment of herself.

She'd given up, well, almost given up, the idea that Ambrose could be hers. After all, he'd left her alone for a year—a freaking year—so he could go up to the angelic realm and deal with the politics there. Though Shade and Lily had both explained that he was needed and *forced* to stay there to deal with his own people and council, it hadn't been any easier to bear.

She'd thought he hadn't wanted her.

He'd left her alone, in a state of flux with no end in sight.

And, now she was just supposed to roll over and let him back in her life?

That annoying part of her wanted to scream in joy and wrap her arms around him and never let go.

After all, she loved the bastard.

Or, at least, felt that tingling that could signal the beginning of love.

Why had he come for her? Because he felt he had to as she was one of his charges? Or because he felt something for her?

From the way he held her, she had a small hope it was the latter.

She couldn't deny that the past year had hurt.

Horribly.

And there was Balin.

She'd only known the man—or was it demon?—for a few hours, and yet she'd felt that inarguable pull toward him. At first, she'd thought she was betraying Ambrose just feeling it. It made no sense since Ambrose had only just shown a few signs of interest.

Balin clearly wanted her—and Ambrose—a fact that scared and thrilled her at the same time. If she were in the human realm and not in danger, she might have had a moment to breathe and make her own decisions, and even be giddy about it. After all, two very sexy men looking at her as though she was theirs—and they could be each other's—didn't happen every day, or any day for that matter.

Jamie should have had her whole life and choices ahead of her.

Instead, she was in the basements of hell with two men she didn't know well enough to…to do what they needed to do in order to get out of hell.

Oh, and Hunter, of course.

For some reason, she felt as though the wolf shifter just enjoyed watching the byplay. His feral attitude seemed to come and go with the blink of an eye, but she knew he was beyond ready to escape.

He'd been here way too long.

They would get out of there.

They had to.

Then they'd have to find a way out of hell…

She blushed at the thought. No, she wasn't quite ready for that. If they didn't, Balin would die. Jamie didn't know if she could have that on her conscience. It would have been nice to have the option of finding her own supernatural existence and saving a life without the pressure of losing it all.

She just wanted the choice.

Really, there wasn't one.

A dull pain slid through her at the thought of what she'd lost.

She'd lost her choices and that little bit of hope that the man she'd fallen in love with would sweep her in his arms and profess both his love and how he needed her more than his next breath.

Jamie knew she never should have read those books where the hero did just that. They'd just set her up for disappointment.

A sense of something far greater than herself settled over her. She'd find a way to get out of hell with the men who wanted to call her their own—or at least claimed to— and the man who'd been through far too much in the games, and then she'd find a way to live with her choices.

Yes, Jamie would mate—she blushed—with Balin and Ambrose, save Balin's life, and thereby save them all.

Then she'd find a way to let her mind and heart catch up.

She bit her lip as unwanted tears threatened to spill. She hadn't wanted it to be like this. No, she wanted to be back at home and go back to a year ago when Ambrose had healed her. Rather than watch him walk away, she would have wanted him to never let go.

Then she would never have met Balin, this man she didn't know but wanted to know more.

It was all too much. Too much emotion, too many decisions made for her…just too much.

"Jamie? What's going on in that head of yours?" Ambrose asked as he ran a hand down her back.

What was this? He'd never really touched her before, but now he couldn't seem to stop it. God, why had he had to wait?

"I'm just thinking about choices," she said honestly.

Something flashed in Ambrose's eyes, and he nodded. "And you feel like you don't have any."

Jamie licked her lips and watched both men's eyes darken. Well then…that was something to think about later.

"I do feel like everything's out of my hands, and I don't know exactly how I feel about that. What I do know is that we don't have time for me to wallow in it. We need to get out of here."

Balin smiled, and Jamie wanted to sit back and just watch him do it. With his dark horns blending with his even darker hair, he didn't look like the demons from her nightmares. No, he looked like some sexy, leather-clad warrior who could swagger with the best of them. Jamie wasn't too sure she was that far off on her estimation of who he truly was.

"That sounds like a good idea to me." Balin moved away from her, and she immediately felt the loss. Odd, since she'd just met the man. Maybe all true halves—or triads in their case—were like this. She'd have to ask Lily when she got back.

If she got back.

No, *when*. Not if. She'd make it. She had to. Jamie didn't want to die in hell or, frankly, anywhere or any time soon.

"So, what's the plan?" she asked, ready to get on with it. Once they got out of the cell area, she could think about the next step. Thinking about it all at once made her want to hide in a corner with her arms around herself. She'd be dammed if she became *that* type of woman. She was already one of the quieter ones of her group of friends; she didn't want to be the weak one as well.

Ambrose ran a hand along his chin, his long white-blond hair falling out of its band to frame his face. She always wondered if it was as soft as it looked…

No, not the time to think about that.

Though, if they did what Balin had suggested, the time might be closer than she thought.

"What is making you blush like that?" Balin asked, a teasing smile on his face.

She blinked and blushed even harder. "I'm not blushing. I'm just hot. It is hell after all."

Balin gave her a long look, and she knew he didn't believe her. Whatever. They had to get out of the cell first, and then she could think of a more appropriate comeback.

Ambrose cleared his throat then moved back to pace the small cell. Each step seemed to annoy Hunter if judged by the tension in his shoulders, but Ambrose didn't seem to care.

"We can get out of the cell if we move fast and get through the sewer grate," he whispered.

Sewer? Oh, that didn't sound appealing. Really, it sounded better than what she could face in the morning. Yes, much better.

"And you can just get us out? Just like that?" Hunter questioned, pure disbelief on his face.

"That's what Fawkes explained," Ambrose said, holding his hand when Hunter opened his mouth. "And from what I've seen, it looks to be the best bet. We can't go through any other door due to the guards. Balin and I can get through the wards because he is a demon and I'm wearing a medallion to shield my angelic nature. If we move fast, we should be able to bring you and Jamie through it."

"Should?" she asked, fear snaking through her.

Ambrose traced her jaw, sending shivers down her back. Damn angel. "Yes, should. I don't have another alternative, Jamie. Nothing is easy, but I vow I won't let them have you while I'm still breathing."

"I don't want you to die because of me." That fear hit her harder, almost sending her to her knees. She didn't want anyone to die for her—especially not Ambrose...and now Balin.

God, it was all too much.

Ambrose framed her face, his intensity rolling off him in waves. "I will not let you die. Do you understand me? You're more important than anyone in this room. You're everything. I won't lose you."

She couldn't doubt he meant what he said. Had he been hiding his true feelings from her all this time?

Then it hit her.

He'd lost his wife and children. Lily had told her the heart-wrenching story, and she'd broken for his loss. Now he was afraid he'd lose his chance again...and maybe that's why he'd stayed back before.

That was something to think about later, but for now, she'd stand by his side and get the hell out of...well, hell.

She'd have to think of another curse at some point.

"Then let's do it," she said, her voice only quavering a little. "Let's get out of here. I want to go home."

Ambrose nodded then looked back at the others in the cell. "We'll have to be quick, and I don't know what we're facing. I have the sword on my back, and I see Balin has his own." He pulled another sword from his cache—or at least that's what she thought she'd read it was called—this one slightly shorter but heavier looking, and gave it to Hunter. "I know you've fought with your hands for too long. Can you use this?"

Hunter nodded, taking the sword in his hand and feeling the weight. His eyes glowed gold, and he gave a feral smile. "It feels good to have a weapon again."

Jamie held back a shudder at the look on his face. Though he'd scared her when she'd first met him in the cell, she'd grown comfortable around him. She had to remember he was a shifter who could kill her with one flick of his wrist.

Once she found out what she became...maybe she could fight back.

She swallowed hard. If she did indeed mate with Balin and Ambrose, she'd find out what ran through her blood, what made her weak now that would strengthen her.

She was ready.

Long past ready.

Balin slid his dagger from his pants and nodded as well.

"Let's get out of here." She looked into those dark eyes with their red specks and didn't fear the demon in him. No, she wanted to know more about him.

Who he was. What he loved. What he'd lost.

She just needed the time.

And damn, she'd get it.

"Follow me," Ambrose said. "Jamie, I don't want you to be without me or Balin around you at all times."

"I will help as well," Hunter said, and both the men who claimed to want her growled. "I'm not saying I'm her mate, for God's sake. I'm only saying that I will protect her because she's human. I don't think the innocent should die because the ones who have fallen to evil decree it."

Jamie smiled at the wolf who'd calmed her down in the cell and now vowed to protect her. It grated on her that she couldn't do it herself, but she was human and not a fighter. She knew she was weaker than the rest, but when they got of there, she'd change that.

Maybe Balin or Ambrose would teach her to fight.

Maybe whatever she turned into would be stronger than what she was.

It was all going to change, and she relished it. As long as she got out of hell, she'd be okay.

Ambrose gripped her hand then seemed to struggle with himself before leaning and pressing his lips to hers. Shocked, she stood there, letting his smooth mouth cover hers. Though he was firm and hard everywhere, his lips were so soft she could melt into him. She closed her eyes, letting every moment and dream of what could be and what it was fill her. He parted her lips with his tongue, and she moaned. He tasted of musk and male—something she didn't know she'd craved until it was too late.

He pulled back much too soon, his gray eyes bright, his pupils large. "Stay behind me," he whispered, and she nodded.

"Wait," Balin ordered and turned so he could capture her lips. Surprised, she froze before melting into him. While Ambrose was a slow and steady heat that wound through her like a promise of more, Balin was a furnace, licking and burning with every touch, but she didn't want to let go. He tasted of heat and cinnamon, an intoxicating combination.

He pulled back and grinned. "Now we're ready to go."

Jamie swayed on her feet, the taste of both men settling on her tongue and into her pores.

Hunter growled behind them. "Now that the two of you are done marking your territory, can we go?"

Jamie swallowed hard and shook her head to clear it. "That was…well…I don't know what that was. We can talk about it when we get out."

"That's a promise," Balin said, his face turning from the beautiful smile to a stony determination.

Ambrose merely stared then, after looking out the gate, pulled it open.

"Wait? How did you do that? I thought it locked from the outside." she said. If it had been that easy, Hunter would have left long ago.

Ambrose turned over his shoulder and pressed a finger

to his lips before leaning down to whisper, "I didn't close it all the way before."

Feeling dumb, she followed Ambrose, trying to be as quiet as possible. Seeing how she was with three very large male warriors, she was the loudest of the bunch. With each footstep, she swore the sound echoed down the hall right to the guards. In contrast, the men, who seemed way too large to move like they did, made no noise.

She'd have to add that to her list of things to learn.

That list seemed to be getting longer with each breath.

They moved at a brisk pace toward a grate she could just barely make out. Tension rode in her shoulders, and her heart beat so fast and so hard in her ears she was afraid she'd have a heart attack.

They had just made it to the grate when she heard the sound of footsteps coming at them. Balin cursed then turned. Ambrose lifted the metal grate off its hooks, but it was too late. At least twenty armed guards surrounded them, and the men around her picked up their swords, steadied their stances, and looked ready to fight.

And, she had nothing.

No sword, no strength…nothing.

Damn it.

Balin reached back from his position blocking her from the guards and slid a dagger into her palm. Now, she was more likely to stab herself, but at least she had something.

"You can't escape," one of the guards said. He didn't look like Balin with his black horns curling over his head like a ram's.

Balin chuckled. "You really think we care what you say? We're not letting you have any of us."

The guards grumbled then struck. Swords clashed as Balin went against two opponents, Ambrose against three, and Hunter against four. They cursed, grunted, and killed their way through the demons, all the while not moving far from her so nothing could touch her.

Damn it. She hated being weak. She *wasn't* weak normally. There was nothing she could do but stay out of the way.

Something cold and sharp slid across her throat, and she froze.

"Stop fighting. I'll kill her where she stands if you don't lay down your weapons."

Ambrose set his sword down first, the blood of the guards covering his torso and blade, anger on his face. Balin and Hunter followed soon after, neither of them looking happy about it.

Hell, this was her fault. Her weakness.

Jamie tried hard not to swallow too hard as the blade slid across her throat as close as it could without breaking the skin.

"Follow us," the demon with the blade ordered. "The council wants to see you, Jamie. And, now they get to see all of you. I think they'll enjoy this even more."

They wanted to see her? God, her time was up. She'd be dammed if she went down as weak as she was. She'd find a way…she had to find a way.

"You can lower the blade," Ambrose said, his voice deep

and soothing, but she could hear the underlying tension. "We won't put up a fight, but I'd rather you not slip and kill her."

The demon who held her laughed, the blade digging in just that much deeper. She felt the warm trickle of her own blood trail down her neck, and she held back tears.

No, she couldn't die like this.

The demon pulled back and let his knife fall to her side. "I'd rather not let her die at the moment either. I want to see what the council has planned for her, so let's get going. Now."

Fear clawed at her belly at his words, but she kept moving, Balin, Ambrose, and Hunter behind her, held at sword point by the guards who had lived.

They would have won the battle and escaped if she hadn't been caught off guard…if she hadn't been weak. She was sure of it.

Refusing to allow self-pity to take over and drown her, she held her chin high, wincing as her neck burned from what must have been only a small cut or she'd be dead.

They made their way through the dungeon halls, the demons and other species in cages, cat calling and worse from their cells. Most would be dead soon if what Hunter said was true about the survival rate of those in the games.

The games weren't played to see who lived, but rather to see how they could die.

She didn't want that to be her.

Finally, they entered a large hall where five demons, each with various colored and shaped horns sprouting from their heads, sat on large thrones. Two were dressed in long robes, while the other three wore leather pants and chains that adorned their thick chests.

"I see you've brought us the human...and her friends," one of the ones in leather said, his voice deep and slick with something that made her want to run away.

"I'm Fury, the leader of this council," he continued. "Bring me the wolf."

The guards kicked the back of Hunter's knees, and she held back a gasp as they dragged him toward the center of the room.

"You have been our prized fighter for long enough to know an escape attempt means death," Fury said, his voice calm.

No, they couldn't kill Hunter because of her.

"I think I'd rather see you die at the hands of a demon weaker than yourself. First, though, we need to make sure that happens." With a nod, the guards beat Hunter with their fists and feet. The sound of each punch and kick echoed off the tall walls and brought bile to her mouth.

Hunter fell to his knees, and his eyes narrowed in pain as they beat him. One of them kicked him in the head, and Hunter let out a small grunt—the first sound he'd made. He let them beat him, but his eyes remained the same determined, animalistic yellow they always were.

Oh, God, they had to stop this.

Finally, after the blood flowed from a gash on his side and face, the largest of the guards moved forward and stepped on Hunter's face. Jamie gasped at the crunch of her new friend's nose breaking.

Her body shook as fear and revulsion warred within her. She wanted to go to his side and help, but she knew it was no use. She'd already caused this and didn't want to cause anyone any more pain.

She had a feeling it was only the beginning though.

They dragged Hunter's unconscious body away, and she feared it might be the last time she'd see him.

She risked a look at Ambrose, who stood tall, his face expressionless. He was an angel in a demon world. His presence alone might start a war. He'd risked it all for her.

She wasn't worthy.

Damn it, she'd make herself worth it.

Somehow.

She'd repay them all.

Another demon came from the shadows, a smile on his face, and she held back a curse.

Pyro.

"Ah, I see my son has found a way to disgrace the Drake name once again," Pyro stated as he took his seat on the empty sixth throne.

"I see you're as much of a bastard as usual, father," Balin drawled, his arms behind his back, but not tied—yet.

"I'm going to enjoy seeing you wither away and die," Pyro spat. "Not before you watch the one who was to be yours die after they rape and beat her."

Balin growled, and her body shook at Pyro's words. The picture the evil man painted made her want to either kick his ass or hide in a hole. Either way, she had to do something. She had to live.

"Pyro, enough," Fury said, his voice cool. "Jamie Bennett. You were sold to the games and do not have a choice. We, the council, own you as well, and you will do as you're told. You will fight at the midnight games as planned and will die. You will bring in more money in a fight than just by our blades now. They'll want you for more than death."

She swallowed hard at his words but didn't say anything. She'd already known what they'd planned, but hearing it didn't make her feel any better.

"Your life is forfeit."

"You cannot own a human who has done nothing," Ambrose said, his voice low, controlled.

"Ah, but we can. She's a token of war," Fury explained.

"There is no war," Balin called out.

"As soon as this angel stepped foot on our land, he caused one. Now, we can overlook it and use Jamie as our draw. Or we can fight and kill other angels. The choice is yours." Fury smirked, and Jamie felt the cold seep into her bones.

She risked the demons' wrath and turned to Ambrose. "He's lying. He's just saying that to hurt you. He would have found a way to do what he's doing whether you came to hell or not."

The weight of countless years and decisions seemed to pass over Ambrose's face, but he didn't say anything to her. He merely turned and nodded toward the council.

"And if I fight in her stead?"

"No! You can't do that," she yelled, and his look cut her off.

Fury laughed. "Oh, that would be nice. We might just use you for a fight. After all, an angel in the demon games is almost unheard of. Alas, we want the human to die painfully before that. Then Balin will waste away because he isn't demon enough to lick the shit off my boots. Then, because I know these two deaths will pain you... then I might let you die."

Pyro laughed along with Fury, and Jamie wanted to scream.

They were just bullies who didn't deserve to live.

She held no power—something she would have to fix.

Soon.

Both Ambrose and Balin stepped forward, the anger they'd been holding back slipping through their masks. Fearful they'd do something stupid and die before they found a way out, she moved quickly to place her hands on both their backs.

These two men—these two large, angry men—stopped moving forward for her, their chests heaving, their fists clenched.

Fury and the other demons threw their heads back and laughed.

"Oh, that's rich. A little female human holding back the fiercest angels of them all and a demon who used to be fierce." Fury wiped a tear from his eye as he spoke. He nodded toward the other guards "Send them to the melee cell. Let's see how well they do with that little strumpet and the other demons who could watch them. They aren't going to want to stand by and watch the other demons fawn over her and try to take her down for their pleasure."

She didn't know what he was talking about, but it couldn't be good. Before she could do anything, one of the guards gripped her arm in a bruising hold and pulled her toward the door.

Balin glared, the heat and fury in his gaze threatening to erupt and take over. Ambrose merely gave his stony expression, but she could see the calculating look in his gaze.

Maybe he had a plan.

Oh, God, they needed one.

She'd only just found out she could have a future…she didn't want to lose it.

Not like this.

PYRO SLAMMED THE DOOR TO HIS HOUSE SHUT AND LAUGHED. He bent over at the waist, his ribs hurting from his own laughter, but he couldn't help it.

Oh, this was working out much better than he'd thought it would.

That little bitch would die. Hopefully, in such pain she'd beg for death long before they gave it to her. The demons she would face rumbled that they wanted her pussy more than her death since it had been so long, and he smiled.

Yes, that would be good.

His son would finally be off his list of shit to deal with.

Yes, he should have felt something for the fruit of his very virile loins, but he couldn't give a fuck. Balin had betrayed him and his own race. Now the little bastard would watch his true half or—if Pyro was correct—part of his triad die.

Then Balin would die.

Slowly.

And, then the cream on his cake. Ambrose. He'd never thought he'd be so lucky as to have the fucking angel actually show up in hell, let alone within the walls of the games.

Fury had said there would be no war if Jamie died, but that was most likely a ruse. The council hadn't voted yet, and most here were ready for a fight. It had been too long since they'd spilled angel blood.

Much too long.

Ambrose would watch his Jamie and Balin die, and Pyro would rejoice.

After all, Jamie was just a human and held no power.

That is, no power yet. Unless Ambrose and Balin had figured out how to unlock it. Then he hadn't heard any rumblings on precisely how that would happen. After all, only one of the seven women who had been lightning struck had turned.

Pyro shrugged it off. The three had lost the window of opportunity and would die soon.

This would be a great day. He deserved to celebrate. With a flick of his wrist, he opened the door to one of his special cells and smiled at the small male he'd taken from the panther clan years ago.

"Hello, my sweet. It looks like your time's up."

He took his time, smiling as he sliced him up, and when the last bit of blood spilled from the male's neck, and, with it, his life, Pyro smiled.

Yes, he would win.

He was a demon after all. It was his turn.

CHAPTER 9

Balin cursed as the fucker behind him pushed him into the small cell. The stench of dead bodies, rot, sweat, and who knew what else filled his nostrils, and he tried to breathe through his mouth. However, the stink coated his tongue and pores, seeping into his lungs. He didn't think even a thousand showers would get rid of the smell.

He cursed as he watched Jamie shake as she had in the council chambers, her skin turning pale. She'd stood strong as the council had determined her fate. Or rather decreed it. Balin was pretty sure Fury had already known what they were going to do with Jamie long before they sent for her. It made him sick to think that he was also a demon.

If—no, when—they got out of the coliseum, Balin wasn't sure Jamie would even want to look at another demon, let alone the son of the one who'd done this to her.

Everything seemed to be slipping through his fingers faster than he could find a way to stop it.

Balin quickly searched among the other large, bloody, and dangerous occupants of the cell but couldn't see Hunter. Fuck. He hadn't wanted the other man to die, not like that. There was still a chance they'd taken Hunter somewhere else and he still lived, but Balin wasn't too sure.

He wasn't sure about anything anymore. Not when he knew his father and the rest of the council wanted not only him but those he was growing to care about dead.

They not only wanted death. They wanted pain and suffering before that happened.

Lots and lots of suffering.

He shouldn't have been too surprised. They were the demons who took their true nature to the core of what made them evil after all.

The other demons and species in the room slowly moved toward them, and Balin growled, his eyes glowing red as he let the anger that he'd tried to hold back in front of his father course through him. He hadn't wanted to do anything stupid like try to kill Pyro in front of the council, not that he could have because Lucifer's curse didn't allow that.

It had been only the touch of Jamie's small, fragile hand on his back that stopped him and had stopped Ambrose. It should have surprised him that someone as small as her could do that, but it didn't. She was to be his mate, something he'd desired more than anything his whole life.

He just had to find a way to make it out of hell alive, with her and Ambrose, and hopefully Hunter.

Easier said than done.

The other demons crowded around, their eyes various reds, blacks, and darks. Each had a different set of horns showing what caste they came from, but he didn't care. They were all in the games for a reason. Either they were truly criminal and deserved it, or they had lost in some form of battle and their vanquishers had sold them.

They were not his friends.

No, considering the way they looked at Jamie as if she were a delectable treat they wanted to taste then eat, he knew he'd have to kill all the bastards.

A wave of exhaustion slapped at him, and he ignored it. He knew he was dying. It wasn't as if it was a surprise. It still pissed him off to no end that he wasn't strong enough to protect Jamie.

Out of the corner of his eye, he saw Ambrose shift closer, so Jamie stood behind the angel and himself. The guards had taken all of Balin's weapons, but they'd been stupid to not realize Ambrose would have more. The angel —who looked damn good, by the way—had his own cache of weapons. Ambrose had even more weapons than most due to his love for his vast collection.

This could work out.

It had to.

"Looks like fresh meat," one of the other demons growled.

Balin rolled his eyes. "Really? That's the best you can do?

The entire lot of you are supposed to be the first out there, or you wouldn't be in here ready to tear us limb from limb. You can only come up with 'looks like fresh meat'? I'm disappointed."

He thought he heard a snort come from Ambrose, but he wasn't sure. The angel didn't seem to smile or laugh, except for that one time that had surprised even Jamie.

Balin would have to change that.

Hades, now he was actually thinking about his future with Ambrose and Jamie as a happy triad. Could that actually become a reality? He hadn't planned on one mate, let alone two.

Now, knowing the connection he felt between them watching the way Jamie weakened as the consequences of the lightning attacked her body with more vigor, he knew it was true.

He'd met his mates.

Plural.

He wasn't about to let them out of his sight. He couldn't lose them, not now, not when he'd just met them. Great, now he sounded like a whiny ass, but there was no way he was going down without a fight.

Fuck that.

"I would stand back," Ambrose stated, his voice low, but calm. "You forget that I'm the one with access to weapons, and no amount of brute strength can take that away from me. We mean you no harm, but don't come near us, or I'll kill you. Slowly." The angel did grin at that, but it wasn't a happy one. No, this one sent icy shivers down Balin's back, and he for one was happy the warrior was on his side.

Jamie touched Balin's back, and he wanted to melt at the feel of her hand through his shirt. She was his salvation, but she was also so much more. At least, she had the potential to be so much more.

The other captives gave Ambrose long looks filled with both fear and arrogance, but they backed away. Balin looked around and found a small corner with a bench. Without taking his eyes off the others, he led Jamie and Ambrose to a place where they would at least have a semblance of privacy.

He knew the others wouldn't kill Jamie. At least, the other captives had probably been told not to do that. Her death was to be a celebration in public, and killing her in a dank cell wouldn't accomplish anything. The bastards could hurt her…in so many ways.

No, there was no fucking way he'd allow that to happen. He looked at Ambrose and saw the same determination on the man's face.

Good. He wasn't alone in his fight.

He didn't have to be alone again.

That little bit of hope he'd found when he saw Jamie in his father's dungeon bloomed just that much more.

He could live.

Maybe…just maybe…be happy.

They just had to get the hell out of hell.

Jamie's paleness worried him, so he made her sit down

on the bench, careful not to think about what could be on it. He really, really didn't want to know.

They were as private as they were going to get, even if he could feel the other demon's gazes on them. Meaning they had to actually talk about something.

Hades, it was like high school all over again. At least high school in the human realm, since that didn't consist of torture, war, and battles—well, not as much anyway.

He'd spent his whole life trying to find a way to find a mate, and now that he found himself in the presence of *two*, he had no fucking clue what to do.

Jamie looked up at him with wide eyes and tried to smile. "Are you always so sarcastic when people are trying to kill you?"

Well then. He hadn't thought that was going to be the first topic of their decision, but he'd go with it. Then they'd talk about the whole sex-to-live thing.

Hades, they needed more choices.

Like sex-for-fun, for-love, or for-anything-but-duty.

Balin gave a small laugh then sat right beside her on the bench, unable to resist the feel of her against him.

"If I didn't shoot my mouth off, I wouldn't be me. I like inserting a bit of humor because it throws the other guys off."

Ambrose raised a brow. "I don't have that problem."

Jamie shook her head, holding back a wobbly smile. Hades, she couldn't start crying now. She'd been doing so well.

"Ambrose, dear, one look at that stoic expression on your face and they run away," she teased.

"Did you just call me ugly?" Ambrose asked, his mouth twitching.

Balin threw his head back and laughed then turned to glare at the other demons to make sure they left them alone. Tedious business, dealing with people who wanted to kill and maim.

Jamie looked like she'd swallowed something nasty and shook her head. "Oh, God, I didn't mean it that way. You know you're hot beyond reason." She blushed beneath the pale pallor, and Balin took her hand.

Ambrose knelt in front of her but kept his hand on his sword. Balin could have really used a dagger right then, but it didn't seem like the best time to mention it.

Ambrose didn't even look at him. He just handed him the butt of a dagger.

Well then, apparently, he hadn't hidden his interest in weaponry—or in the way the man moved—very well.

"Jamie, breathe," Ambrose whispered, his voice rough.

Balin had to swallow hard at the man's words. He'd been attracted to men in the past but had never gone beyond a few touches here and there. Now it seemed fate had decided he needed both a man and a woman to make him whole.

He didn't know entirely how he felt about that. Ambrose was attractive—okay, that was a mild word for the strength and masculinity the man radiated. With his strong cheekbones, his firm jaw, and even firmer body, he knew the man possessed more power in his left pinkie than some demons did in their whole bodies once they'd gorged themselves on souls.

"I am breathing," she complained. "I think that's the problem."

Balin grimaced. "I swear not all demons smell like them." He gestured to the angry demons behind him and tried to smile.

"I know that. I mean you smell really good." She blushed again, and Balin let his smile come out in full.

"See? I like that you noticed. I think we're on the right track here. Also for telling Ambrose he's handsome, which, by the way, you are." He said the latter to Ambrose, who merely lifted a brow. For some reason, that stoic attitude was hot on the angel. They'd have to do something about that, sooner rather than later, considering they were running out of time before Jamie had to fight. Another reason they needed to actually talk and get to know one another.

"I can't fight," she whispered. "I don't have any training….or powers."

She glanced at Ambrose, and he brushed a lock of hair behind her ear. Again, she seemed surprised at this action. Balin knew that Ambrose had left for a fucking year to deal with angel crap so he couldn't be with his true half. A whole year without seeing one another and no touching? The other man better have a better excuse than that.

"Plus," she continued, "I'm getting weaker by the moment." She looked between them both. "I think it's because of the whole needing-to-bond thing." She blushed again but didn't look either man in the eye. "I know Lily had attacks when her true nature was trying to get out. With me, though, it's always been like I've been getting over the flu or something."

Ambrose closed his eyes, and Balin watched as the older man framed her face then leaned in, letting his lips slightly rest on hers. He didn't feel jealous at the contact. No, rather, he felt as though it was right, like these two were meant to be together as much as they were meant to be with him.

He'd never met another triad, but Hades, he wanted this to work out.

Fate couldn't be as cruel now as it had been his whole life.

He needed this. Needed them.

"You have no idea how sorry I am that I left you alone for so long, Jamie," Ambrose whispered, his voice hoarse. "I left because I was a coward but stayed because the council forced me. You know I didn't even make it to Lily and Shade's wedding."

Tears slid down Jamie's cheeks, and Balin wanted to punch him for making her cry, but he knew they needed to get this out. Then they could find a way to keep themselves alive. With only so few moments together, they needed to use them as well as they could.

"I know," she said as she wiped her tears away. "I know you didn't want to be with me. I guess it took me being taken away for you to notice me."

Ambrose shook his head, and Balin gripped her hand. "No, that wasn't it. I've always noticed you, Jamie. I lost everything before, and I was afraid to take that chance again. I thought if I stayed away, it wouldn't hurt you."

"You know it did," she countered.

Ambrose closed his eyes, and Balin held back the urge to comfort the man. He couldn't show weakness in front of the other demons. They were far enough away that they couldn't hear the conversation, but they could still see them.

"I didn't think I could stand to lose what I had again, so I ran away," Ambrose said.

"What are you talking about?" Balin asked. Curiosity about the man who could be his mate overrode the decency to step back and let Ambrose talk only to Jamie. After all, if they were going to be a triad, they better learn how to work as three, not just two.

Ambrose took a deep breath then met Balin's gaze. "I'm over five thousand years old, Balin. I've spent countless years fighting for my people—for their safety, for their freedom. In those years, I also found a woman I thought I could spend my life with."

He met Jamie's gaze, and Balin watched as he again framed her face. "She wasn't my true half, my mate, my everything," he continued. "She was someone I loved and cared about, deeply. We always knew there could be others out there for us. That didn't stop us from getting married, from watching my best friend and her brother fall in love. That didn't stop us from having our two children, Nathan and Laura. Ilianya was pregnant with our third when the wars came to our front door."

Ambrose closed his eyes, and Balin watched as a shudder

ripped over him. Balin's mouth dried, and there was nothing he could do but listen. Hades, this man, this warrior, had had a life; he'd known that. He also saw the pain in the other man's eyes. There was no coming back from that whole.

"When they died…" Ambrose's voice broke, but he continued. "I thought I'd lost everything. I didn't want to go through that again. I'll be dammed if I lose you the way I lost them. I can't go through that again, and I won't have you suffer for my past. Pyro took you to punish me, and I won't let him have you."

Balin blinked at the promise in his tone but nodded. "And I'll be dammed if either of you suffer because my father can't give up on me. I may be of his blood, but I'm through being his pawn."

"Won't we all just be pawns if we fight like they want us to?" Jamie asked. "Or at least try to fight." The tears came again, and she shook her head. "Damn it, I don't want to cry. I *hate* crying, but it's all too much. I wanted my happy ending with flowers and a man to sweep me off my feet. Is that too much to ask?"

Balin had no idea what she was talking about. Hadn't they just been talking about dying? What was this about flowers and sweeping?

This could be why he didn't stay with women…ever.

He must have looked as confused as he felt because Jamie glared. "I know I can't fight like this. I know I'm going to have to use whatever power I can get because, like the two of you, I'll be dammed in I die here. That means I'm going to have to change into whatever supernatural creature I happen to be. Meaning I'm going to have to bond with the both of you."

Something in her tone put him off. It was almost as if she wanted another way out.

Wait, she didn't want them?

Something heavy fell in his stomach, and he rubbed his chest. He didn't know it could hurt like this.

Her eyes widened at the gesture, and she shook her head. "I'm not saying I don't want to. I'd have liked the choice. I'd have liked you two to have had the choice and to *want* to make love with me and bond—not because it could save my life. Don't you see? Pyro's winning. He's taking something that should have been just for us and twisting it for another purpose."

Now Balin understood, and he wanted to kick his father's ass—again. "Jamie…"

"No, don't try to placate me please. I don't even know you that well, and now, because of this feeling I get in my heart and because I don't want to die, I'm going to bond with you. We don't get that choice. I'd like to have thought that we'd choose each other anyway, but what do I know anymore?"

"Jamie, I chose you," Ambrose began.

"No, you chose to leave me before."

Ambrose closed his eyes but opened them and took a deep breath. "I chose you. I know you don't believe me, but I will do all in my power for the rest of my days to show you what you mean to me. And I know Balin will do the same, even if he just met us."

Balin smiled at the man, but Ambrose continued on. "I know this isn't how we wanted it to start. I had imagined something much more romantic—much more you. Right now, we're going to do everything in our power to get out of hell and go back to a life where we three—yes, all three of us—can find a life together. I know it's crazy as hell, but I'm not going to let my past take anything away from us. We're going to bond because we want to, not because we have to."

"I just said that we had to in order to live," Jamie said, her tears finally stopping.

"No, we're going to bond because it's our choice. We're going to go into this knowing we could have walked away and found another way. It might be harder and seemingly impossible, but I'd find another way if you didn't want to bond with me and Balin. Do you understand me? I'd find another way."

Balin believed the angel. Even if he couldn't think of another way, he knew just from the promise in Ambrose's tone that the other man would refuse to bond until Jamie was ready.

"The setting might not be ideal, but the outcome will be well worth it," Balin promised.

Jamie looked at them both then, after what seemed like an eternity, finally nodded. "When we get through this nightmare, we're going back to square one. I expect flowers." She tried to smile, and Balin leaned in to kiss her.

Her sweet taste danced on his tongue, and, Hades, he

wanted more, but first, they had to find a way out of the cells.

Balin pulled back and looked at Ambrose. He would have kissed the other man to show what he wanted for their future, but he couldn't risk it in front of the other demons—at least not yet. Everyone already thought Jamie was a weakness for the both of them, but for now, it only seemed the council knew of the exact weakness the men held for each other.

"You know, if we wanted space alone, we'd have to make sure it was too dangerous for us in here," Balin began and noticed Ambrose seemed to understand.

"Yes, they don't want us to die in here, only feel the fear," Ambrose continued. "If it was a real possibility, then they'd have to separate us."

"You're going to start a fight, aren't you?" Jamie asked. "I'm all for getting privacy, but I'm not keen on either of you dying. Nor am I keen on standing back and watching it happen."

Balin cupped her face and shook his head. "Even with the weakness in my bones, I can take these men. Ambrose could with his pinky I think. Right now though, it's our best option, and I want you to sit in this corner with a dagger in your hand. We won't let them come at you. And this time, we won't let them come at you from behind."

He cursed himself at what had happened during their botched escape, but he wouldn't let it happen again.

Jamie nodded, and Ambrose gave her a dagger.

"Just hold it and try not to cut yourself," Ambrose said,

and she rolled her eyes. Good, they'd get her to laugh and think happy thoughts. That had to be one way of getting out of this.

"Ready?" Balin asked as he rolled his neck.

Ambrose took out another sword and stretched. "I am a warrior. I'm always ready."

For some reason, that sounded hot as hell—something they'd have to discuss later.

The others in the cell noticed their newly armed counterparts and growled. Balin smiled and watched as a few of the demons came at them, trying to prove they were tougher than the rest. Even though he knew these demons had no-kill orders, when the opportunity to best them came, Balin knew the demons would take it.

Balin clutched the dagger in his palm and jabbed, catching a demon in the neck. Blood spurted from the wound, and the demon clutched it. Balin was faster. He struck again, sinking it into the other demon's heart, sending the man to his knees, dead before he fell on his back.

Balin hit two more demons, each time staying where he was so Jamie was safe. Out of the corner of his eye, he saw Ambrose holding his own but knew they'd have to at least make it look like they could die so Balin feigned slowing. Claws dug into his shoulder, and he cursed, falling to his knees in dramatic fashion.

It hurt like a bitch, but he still struck out at the other demon's knees, sending the bastard to the floor.

The cell doors opened with a flourish, and armed guards

stalked in. Fury was right behind them, the expression on his face resembling his name.

"Cease this at once, you fools!" Fury bellowed.

The other demons froze, clenching their fists, and Balin couldn't resist one last punch.

"I said fucking stop it." Fury stomped toward them and screamed. "What the fuck? Do you want to die? Well, I'm going to make sure my property does what it's told. And rather than split you up so you can to find a way to save the human bitch, I'm going to lock the three of you in a cell together."

Well hell, Fury was a fucking idiot. Balin would go with it.

"Lock them up!" Fury ordered and stormed out of the cell. The guards came at them, and Balin quickly gave Ambrose's dagger back to him to store in his cache. He risked a glance at the angel, who muttered something under his breath about blood on metal, but he couldn't quite tell what it was.

He pulled Jamie to his side, and she sank into him. That floral and spice scent invaded his senses, causing his dick to rub against the leather of his pants.

Considering what they were about to do, that was a good thing.

As they were led to the cell where they'd first found Jamie, he found it empty of Hunter, and Balin cursed that they couldn't find the wolf who had comforted Jamie when she had no one. He'd find a way to make that right.

The guards slid the cell door closed, and Balin let out a breath.

"So, um, yeah, how do we start?" Jamie asked as she gave a nervous laugh.

Ambrose sat on the edge of the small cot in the room and gave the small smile that Balin had begun to cherish.

They'd be okay. They could do this. He could be with the two people he knew he could love, and they would survive.

He just hoped to Hades he didn't embarrass himself.

CHAPTER 10

"First, are you both okay?" Ambrose asked, more nervous now than he had been in the other cell. "Balin, what about your side?"

Jamie's eyes widened, and she ran to his side. Her fingers lightly brushed the other man's side, and Balin sucked in a breath.

Ambrose had a feeling it wasn't from the pain of those wicked-looking gashes in his side but rather from the delicate touch of the woman they would both be having soon. He looked around the small cell and held back a sigh at the meager offerings.

He'd wanted their bonding to be something memorable, something indicative of what they were to each other. Not in a cell with a small cot, tiny blanket, and four walls.

If he were honest with himself, he'd also confess that he

was nervous due to lack of practice. Dear God, it had been over a hundred years since he'd lain with a woman.

Jamie's grandparents hadn't even been alive when he'd last had sex.

Sex couldn't have changed too much in that time, right?

It seemed to have tamed for a few centuries there, but now, if the media were any indication, it had become even more fierce.

He just had to make this about Jamie, and he'd be okay.

Ambrose risked a glance at Balin. Okay, it would also have to be a little about Balin. Right now, they needed to focus on Jamie. Ambrose was pretty sure if they both made love to her tonight, then she'd find her new power.

She wouldn't be anywhere close to having the ability to control them, but she'd get the strength that came with being more than human.

That's what they needed. That and the ability to escape.

The plan had been to avoid getting her in the arena, but that might not be an option.

When she won her match, and if they found a way to help her do it, they could get out of hell, and he and Balin would find their own path.

It would be too much too soon to scare Jamie with what the two of them could do.

Or would do.

"Jamie, dear, I'm fine; I promise. It's but a scratch." Balin tried to remove her hands, but she shook her head, her body shaking.

"You're hurt." Jamie bit her lip, and Ambrose wanted to soothe the sting…then soothe her everywhere else.

His cock throbbed, and he took a steadying breath. They'd have to be quick in cementing their bond before the guards came, but he wasn't about to throw her on the floor and ravish her.

At least not this first time.

"I know, but I had to make sure the guards and Fury believed we could have lost. Don't worry. I'll heal."

Ambrose spotted the lie on Balin's face and held back a curse. As the hours ticked by, Balin was close to his end. Only with the bond would he be able to live. And, that wasn't even a true fact. Balin had let his body fade to the point that it might take more than a mating bond to heal him fully.

They would get to that.

Soon.

As for the gashes on Balin's side, there was something Ambrose could do now. "I can heal you, Balin."

Jamie's eyes widened. "That's right. You healed me from Striker. That's because we're true halves, right?"

Ambrose nodded. Anger coursed through him with the memory of her body, broken by the hands of a now dead angel.

"Wait," Balin interrupted. "Who the hell is Striker? And how did he hurt you?"

Jamie shook her head. "It's a long story. One we will tell you when we get home. I promise. Ambrose can heal you."

She turned to him. "Can you heal what's making him weak as well?"

He shook his head, letting a little bit of that defeat slide through him. "No, I can't heal something of that magnitude. We'll see what happens after the bond, okay?"

Jamie blushed again, and he could have cursed himself for saying that so casually.

Ignoring the heat and nerves in the room, he stood and walked over to Balin. Without looking directly into the other man's eyes, he pressed his palms against the wounds, sending a little bit of power through the fragile connection between them. It wasn't a large one. No, it could have broken with the slightest wisp of air, but it would be cemented soon.

Maybe not today, but after they bonded with Jamie.

The claw marks stitched themselves together, the skin tightening. Balin winced, and Jamie held the demon's face soothingly in her hands.

She was always doing that, trying to care for others even when she was scared beyond reason.

That was why they were doing this. Not because Pyro was going to kill them but because he wanted that light in his life. He wanted Jamie, and now that he'd met him, he wanted Balin as well.

Call him selfish, but after five thousand years of war and pain, he deserved happiness. He couldn't let it slip through his fingers the moment he caught a glimpse of it.

Ambrose pulled back once he sensed the healing was complete, and Balin let out a breath.

"Thanks," he said. "I didn't know you could do that."

"I didn't know I could before I healed Jamie. It was just something that came to me when...when I found her like she was."

"You saved me that day, Ambrose," Jamie said as she wrapped her arms around his waist.

He ran a hand through her hair and kissed her softly, relishing in her touch, her taste. "I was almost too late."

"You weren't."

"And you two promise you'll tell me this story?" Balin asked, his shredded shirt on the floor, his hands on his leather-encased hips.

He felt Jamie's heart speed up at the sight of Balin's chest and ripped abs. And, if he were honest with himself, his own heartbeat increased as well. Even though Balin was weaker from not eating souls, that hadn't changed his physique. No, the man had the body of a warrior—a toned one.

And Ambrose was a lucky man—as long as he let himself be.

As lucky as he could be in hell, but they would make the most of it.

"I'm not sure what to do." Jamie whimpered as he ran a hand down her back, cupping her ass.

She let out a little gasp, and he smiled. Her eyes brightened when he touched her, and he knew his plan of smiling more was working.

He'd wanted her from the first time he met her, though he'd denied himself. And, though they were forced into making their decisions quicker than they'd have liked, he'd make sure she enjoyed it—enjoyed him.

"We're going to love you, Jamie," Ambrose vowed as he leaned in to run kisses up her neck. She shivered in his hold, making his cock just that much harder. "Slowly, one at a time at first, and then we'll take you in every way possible. For right now, we're going to take it as it comes."

Balin came up to her other side, running a hand down her back. "This is just the three of us. And, for now, we'll make sure we don't scare you with too much, too soon. Later? I'm going to fill every inch of you, and then I'm going to do the same to Ambrose. How does that sound?"

Ambrose let out a groan at the images Balin presented.

"So you're saying you're both going to make love to me individually before we get to the more complicated things?"

Balin let out a chuckle. "Yes, I won't push you today. Maybe tomorrow, because I want to see how far you'll go, but not too far now."

Ambrose could practically taste Jamie's arousal, and he knew Balin was on the right track with being open and honest. He wasn't as good with words as Balin, so he let him take the lead. One day soon, he'd show the demon that he wasn't as submissive as he acted now.

From the glint in the other man's eyes, they were both on the same page.

This wasn't about life and death, choices and fate. No, this was about Jamie, Balin, and him.

Nothing more, nothing less.

He leaned down and captured her lips, parting them

with his tongue. She opened for him, soft, innocent, letting him take the lead. Because his eyes were closed so he could drown in her intoxicating taste, he couldn't see Balin move, but he felt the other man rub his hands up and down Jamie, cupping her breasts, his hands brushing along Ambrose's chest.

Shivers of need cascaded down his spine, and he deepened his kiss, running his hands down her sides, causing them to tangle with Balin's.

He pulled back, raising a brow as Jamie chuckled.

"Does something amuse you?" he asked, cupping her breast, watching as her eyes darkened and hearing her breath quicken. Her nipple pebbled beneath his palm, and he held back a shudder. It had been so long since he'd had a woman, and he'd never had the one woman who could fill his heart like no other. He didn't want to embarrass himself and explode from just the feel of her in his hands.

From the look on Balin's face, the demon wasn't far behind him in arousal.

"I'm just feeling you and Balin trying to figure out how to touch me without choreographing your moves," she teased as she arched into his palm. Balin slid his hand up her shirt, cupping her other breast, and she closed her eyes.

"I'm sure Ambrose and I will find a way to move as one with you between us, under us, and even watching us," Balin said as he bit her earlobe. "Yes, we're going to bump heads." He grinned. "And other things."

They all laughed at that, even though they were all moving, touching, feeling.

"But," Balin continued, "even if we mess up and find ourselves in an awkward position—literally—that's what learning with those who are with you in a lifetime of grace is for. We're mates, Jamie. You, me, and Ambrose. We're a triad—a rare and beautiful thing. Even if we totally suck at making love—which we won't—we'll still be together, learning."

"I just don't want to do something wrong," she whispered, and Ambrose finally did what he'd wanted to do and kissed her.

When he pulled back, he cupped her cheek with one hand then moved to cup Balin's with the other. "You won't do something wrong when we're making love." He met Balin's gaze. "Either of you."

Balin smiled, the red flecks in his eyes glowing. "Now, where were we?"

Ambrose watched the man who was to be his mate and leaned in, ready to cement his promise. Balin looked startled for only a moment before leaning over Jamie to brush his lips against Ambrose's. Ambrose deepened the kiss, and Balin growled. This was not a gentle mating of mouths but rather the ferocity of two warriors who would test and battle themselves before they crashed into the abyss of bliss. Their teeth clashed and their tongues fought for dominance, but Balin's heady taste settled on Ambrose's tongue, mixing with Jamie's gentle one, causing him to groan.

He pulled back, enjoying the way Balin's chest rose in sync with his own.

"Dear Lord, that was hot," Jamie said then giggled. "Who knew I'd like seeing that?"

Ambrose smiled full out, rubbing his thumb along her chin. "You like the sight of two men kissing?"

She nodded. "You should see some of the books I have in my store." She winked. "Seeing it in person? I think most kissing is pretty hot, no matter who the participants are, but the two of you are…well, you're better." She ducked her head, and he smothered a laugh.

"We're better because we're a part of you," Balin explained. "Or at least, we will be part of you. Now, enough talking. I want to taste you, and I don't like waiting."

Jamie turned and faced their future mate. "Then make love to me and stop talking about it."

Ambrose growled but wasn't as fast as Balin, who lifted her in his hold. Jamie wrapped her arms around his waist, and Balin walked her to the wall. Ambrose followed them, shucking his clothes as he did so.

Jamie's eyes widened at the sight of his naked body, her gaze fixating on his cock, which stood at attention, throbbing and ready for release. He knew if he didn't get it under control, he'd explode as soon as he touched her.

Balin gulped as he looked over his shoulder at Ambrose then pressed Jamie against the wall, rocking his groin to her core. "I see. I have this soft, beautiful woman in my arms, and you get naked first so she can look at only you."

Ambrose shook his head. "Lower her feet to the floor so we can strip her, and then you take off those leathers. I know they must be tight on that erection of yours."

"Glad you noticed."

Jamie squirmed in Balin's hold. "Please."

Balin set her feet down, and Ambrose walked up to her, his cock bobbing against his stomach. He slowly stripped off her shirt, her breasts full in her bra. He lowered one cup and licked her nipple, loving the way she shuddered and tangled her hand in his hair. Balin reached behind Ambrose and undid the leather band holding his hair back.

"I want to see your hair down when you enter her," the demon said.

Ambrose nodded then went to his knees, unbuttoning then sliding off Jamie's pants and panties in one swoop. She raised each foot so he could remove her pants totally, and then he leaned back so he could stare at the magnificent sight before him.

God, her caramel skin looked like sugar and spice, ready for his tongue. Her hips flared out, ready for his grip. She'd shaved or had a wax done before she was captured, so he could see her pussy, wet and ready for his cock.

Or Balin's. Ambrose would be fine watching, touching then, in the future, playing as his other lover filled her.

"Hades, you're amazing," Balin whispered as he undid her bra. Ambrose looked up as her breasts fell, heavy, ready for their hands. Balin leaned over and kissed her then ran his tongue down her chest, flicking her nipple, alternating between his hand and tongue.

The other man had stripped down as well, his cock practically resting on Ambrose's shoulder, but he didn't mind.

Balin's wasn't as long as his own but thicker and tilted to the left, so he knew Jamie would always know who filled her.

That thought almost sent him over the edge, so he licked his lips, then leaned in to taste her. He ran his hands up her legs then gripped her hips, steadying her to the wall so she wouldn't fall. He breathed cool air on her pussy, loving the way she shuddered.

Ambrose spread her legs a bit so he could see her fully then licked her clit.

"Oh, God," she groaned. Ambrose looked up, still licking, sucking, tasting as she squirmed in their hold.

Balin suckled her breasts while Ambrose sucked her clit. They worked in tandem as Jamie's sweet honey coated his tongue. He moved one hand so he could insert one finger then two in her tight channel, teasing, preparing, and she came.

Hard.

She buckled against his face, and he greedily licked up every drop of her.

He pulled back and watched the blush on her skin darken then he stood, his cock in his hand. He wanted to watch Balin take her first. He'd already had her come on his tongue. Balin needed to feel her on his cock.

"Fill her, Balin," he ordered. "Fill her while I lick those pretty breasts."

Balin groaned and moved to stand in front of her. Jamie stroked his horn, and the other man almost fell to his knees.

Jamie's eyes widened. "Does that feel good?"

Ambrose laughed. "Jamie, baby, that's the equivalent of stroking his cock."

Jamie's mouth dropped. "Really?"

"Really," Ambrose said as he stroked the other horn.

"Fuck," Balin said, panting. "You two can horn-stroke me anytime you want but, for the love of Hades, stop. I need to come in her, not against the fucking wall."

Jamie giggled then stopped. "Wait, we don't have any condoms."

Ambrose shook his head. "No, but we don't have diseases."

"What about a baby? Wait, never mind. I don't know why I thought of it. We have more to think about," she whispered and bit her lip.

The thought of her round with their child—his, hers, and Balin's—made him want to fill her right then to make it happen, but he stopped himself, barely.

"Then we make a baby," he said. For a moment, he thought of the children he lost but pushed them out of his mind. He would never forget them, but it was past time to at least move forward.

"Jamie, you're ours. We're not leaving you," Balin promised as his cock teased her entrance.

"Okay," she whispered. "Ambrose, come here, please. I need to touch you while he's in me. I want you both. I know that makes me a slut, but I don't care."

Ambrose growled, "Never say that again. Do you hear me? You're not a slut. You're ours. You're not in the structured human world anymore. You're in a world with triads and love that crosses those boundaries you've been told exist. No matter what you've learned, you should know that we won't treat you like a toy, like nothing. You're ours. You're our mate."

Her eyes widened. "I've never heard you say so much at once."

Ambrose growled. "Then don't anger me by calling yourself names. Now, Balin, sink into her while I get this pretty little hand wrapped around me. Then, Jamie, I'm going to lay you on the floor and make love to you while Balin touches you. Do you understand?"

She nodded and wrapped her hand around his cock. He sucked in a breath, seeing stars. Well, hell, this might not have been his best idea considering he was about to come. She squeezed and gasped as Balin entered her slowly.

She stroked him as he leaned down to kiss them both while Balin thrust in and out of her, increasing his speed with each movement. Her breasts bounced, and her strokes stopped as she blushed then came. The cords on Balin's neck stood out as he followed her, her name on his lips.

Balin pulled out, his cock still hard, wet from their love-making, and Ambrose moved to catch Jamie as her knees buckled.

"I've got you," he whispered. Balin staggered to the cot and pulled the small blanket to the floor. Ambrose gave a nod then laid their mate down on it.

Jamie spread out before him, her hair tangled, her body sweat-slick and rosy.

"I can't believe I get to do this," she said as she gave a wobbly smile.

Ambrose checked her for any signs of weakness or her change because he knew that even though they were making love because they wanted to they were also doing so to change her and save Balin.

She looked the same, only more relaxed. Maybe it would take the three of them together.

He leaned over her, his cock at her core. "Are you ready?"

"Please, Ambrose."

Balin lay down on the floor, his hands roaming over Jamie.

Ambrose entered her slowly, inch by inch, and waited as he slid in to the hilt. Hell, she was wet, hot, and still as tight as a glove. Her eyes widened, and she smiled.

"You feel different from him."

Balin kissed her hard. "Good, then you'll always know."

Exactly what Ambrose had thought, but he couldn't form the words, his mind only on the fact that his cock was in the woman he wanted and finally had.

Then he moved, slowly then faster. Balin kept his hands on her, dividing her attention, but Ambrose didn't care. He pounded into her until his balls tightened and he came.

He felt the walls that surrounded him shudder as she came with him, and he smiled. Her soul reached out to him, and he felt the bond between them click into place as her bond with Balin had cemented theirs.

This was bliss.

This was a triad.

He closed his eyes as her walls continued to shudder around him. Three times wasn't that bad considering they were in a cell in hell.

That sobering thought brought him back to the present.

He pulled out, watching as her eyes widened.

"Oh, God," she whispered. Then she convulsed, her body shaking, her eyes rolling in the back of her head.

"What the hell, Ambrose?" Balin cursed, his voice laced with concern.

Though Shade had told him what had happened to Lily, the knowledge didn't make a bit of difference. Ambrose gathered Jamie in his arms as she thrashed and yelled in pain. Light shot from her skin, radiating from pin pricks, then almost to a blinding hue, and Balin scooted to wrap his arms around the both of them.

"She's changing, Balin. Shade said it would be like this, but…but I didn't know it would hurt this much." His voice broke as she moaned in pain. He covered her lips with his own in case the guards came at the sounds, but tears burned in the back of his eyes.

Please, Jamie, please be all right.

He pulled back as she stopped thrashing, her eyes closed, her chest heaving. Delicate spiral tattoos wrapped their way up her arms, legs, and sides. Her body glowed with a soft white light and a slight aura of wispy smoke surrounded her.

She opened her eyes, fear and anxiety filling the now translucent violet irises.

"Djinn," Ambrose whispered.

She was a djinn.

That had not been on his radar of potential choices, but now that he looked at her, he knew she was the most beautiful creature he'd ever laid eyes on—just as she had been before in her human form.

She was djinn.

More powerful than he.

More powerful than most.

CHAPTER 11

Balin sat back as he gazed over Jamie's new body. Well, that wasn't quite right. She still had the same basic structure, the same curves, the same soft feel.

She was a djinn.

The small and intricate designs on her arms, legs, sides, and spine were a dark coal that faded to a light lavender when she breathed. He knew from meeting another djinn in the past that djinn would regulate to show their moods while they were in this form. Like all supernaturals, she would be able to turn herself back to her human state, so she would be able to blend in. He could have done that before to hide his horns and eyes but had wanted to show Jamie just who he was normally, not who he'd be when he hid.

"What...what am I?" Jamie asked as she looked down at

her skin. The glow brightened as her voice broke, and he held her closer, kissing the top of her head.

Ambrose leaned down to kiss her, running his hands down her newly tattooed arms.

"You're a djinn," he whispered, his voice holding the same amount of awe Balin felt.

Djinn weren't only rare; they were practically extinct.

Balin wasn't even sure there were many, if *any*, females in existence. If the djinn council found out that Jamie was now one of them…

He closed his eyes and tried to gather some semblance of control. They would deal with that when it came. They had enough problems on their hands without adding more to it with speculation. He met Ambrose's eyes and knew the other man would keep this from her as well.

Just until they got out of hell.

Then they would tell her what her future might look like because knowledge of what would come was the best weapon.

Nothing in his life had been easy. It made sense that his mating wouldn't be either.

"A djinn?" Her brows scrunched as she said the word. Her newly violet eyes were mesmerizing. He knew that if others looked into them they would be lost in their power. He was pretty sure he and Ambrose would be immune, but they'd have to be careful.

Hades, things changed at the drop of a dime.

"Like a genie, with the silk pants and lamp?" she asked,

her tattoos changing from light lavender and back again as she struggled with her emotions.

Ambrose shook his head. "No, that is the television version. Djinn are a race of people who are very secretive, so I don't know their history as well as I should, but I will find out more. I promise."

Balin agreed. "Yes, we'll find out more together."

Her body shook as she sat naked between them. Balin cursed and went to get their clothes so she could at least be dressed and somewhat comfortable when they discussed what she was and what powers she might have.

Damn, once she reined in her powers and learned to control them, she could probably win the games. That would take time, and that was something they didn't have.

They pulled on their clothes, Jamie's hands shaking as she did so. "What do you know though?" she asked.

Ambrose took her hand, sat on the cot, and forced her onto his lap. Balin sat beside him, taking her feet in his hands so he could rub them down. He knew she must be freaking out, and he had no idea how to help her.

"Jamie," Ambrose began, "you're a djinn. That means you've got power in your blood greater than most supernaturals. In order to tap it, you're going to need to learn control. I can help you do that."

Her chest rose and fell as she took a deep breath then traced his jaw. "I know you know control, Ambrose. It's all I've seen of you before now."

Regret passed over the other man's face as he leaned down to kiss her brow. "We'll learn together. You already see your physical attributes, and you'll be able to hide those when needed."

"Like Lily with her gold skin and you with your wings?" she asked, and Ambrose nodded. "Balin, can you hide your horns and eyes?" She bit her lip. "Not that I don't like them. I mean…oh, I'm sorry."

He shook his head and rubbed her calf. "Don't apologize. I knew what you meant. And, yes, I can hide them when we get to the human realm."

The very idea that the possibility was at their fingertips surprised him. Then he froze.

He didn't feel any better.

No, in fact, he felt a bit weaker.

He'd felt his bond with Jamie and one with Ambrose that he knew would strengthen once they made love, but he didn't feel that cycle of energy between the three of them.

He was still dying.

Balin swallowed hard then forced his expression to lighten as Jamie and Ambrose discussed her physical attributes and calmed her so she could turn back to looking human.

"Well, at least that works," she said. "I can feel the power running in my veins. It's sweet, like honey. When Lily changed, and we found out that the rest of us might follow down her path, I never thought it would actually happen. Oh, I'd hoped because that meant I'd be with you." She ducked her head and blushed while Ambrose kissed her brow.

Balin didn't take any offense that she didn't mention him. After all, before today, she hadn't known him.

Had it really only been a day? He had no idea how much time had passed in the human realm considering hell ran on its own timeline, but he'd felt like he'd always known her and Ambrose.

And always would.

No, that wasn't right.

He was still dying.

It was as if someone had stabbed him in the heart with a cool blade, the ice settling over him as his fate called.

He'd lose them.

Without his strength, he couldn't get them out of hell.

They'd lost.

"Balin?" Jamie asked, her voice laced with worry. "What's wrong?"

Ambrose cursed and rubbed Balin's back. The feel of the other's man's touch settled him.

"It didn't work, did it?" he asked. Balin shook his head, not surprised that Ambrose would know what he was thinking about.

"What didn't work?" She looked between them, her voice high. "I can feel you in my heart, so I know the bond is working. What's wrong?"

Balin gave a self-deprecating smile. "I'd thought our bond would work like a cycle, giving me the energy I need. I would think I'd have to bond with Ambrose the same way, but I know other triads form their bond from sex like we had, not necessarily with the three of us in every which way."

Her face fell as tears rose in her eyes. "No. No, it has to work." She scrambled off Ambrose's lap and fell onto his. "I can't lose you. I just found you. There's got to be something you can do."

Balin crushed her to him, burying his face in her hair, inhaling that spicy floral scent that he didn't want to lose.

Her body shook as she sobbed in his hold, and he let the few tears fall from him that he'd held in for almost three hundred years.

"There might be a way," Ambrose said as he stood to pace the small cell.

Jamie looked up and faced him while Balin grabbed onto that small lifeline that Ambrose had thrown out. He didn't know what the other man would say, but it had to be better than the loss that cascaded deep within him.

"The djinns have the ability to bestow three wishes on those they love," Ambrose began, and Balin's heart beat in his ears.

He bit his tongue so he wouldn't interrupt.

Jamie slid off his lap and put her hands on her hips. "Then tell me what do to. I'm not going to let him die."

Ambrose gave a small smile, and Balin stood so he could wrap his arms around her.

"From what I know, which isn't much, you will have to use that aura, the smoke you saw before surrounding you." At her nod, Ambrose continued. "You'll use that to surround the person you love and make your wish."

Jamie nodded and pulled from his hold. "Okay then. Let's get started."

Ambrose shook his head. "It's not that simple."

"Of course it isn't," she complained and wrapped her arms around her middle.

"You only get three, Jamie. Just three. Then you can't use your magic to make drastic changes. I know you don't understand what it is you can do exactly, but we'll find out. Djinn can use their powers to protect and harm, much like a witch's power. You'll be stronger, faster, and more in tune with the world around you. You'll also be able to use your magic like a weapon once you're trained. You'll be able to use it for other things that don't require your aura, but other than that, you'll be powerless."

"Fine, then we use this one. I'm not letting Balin die."

Balin took a deep breath and closed his eyes. He knew Jamie would do anything for those she cared about. He'd already seen during their short time together. He couldn't take her wish and leave her with only two for the future.

He opened his eyes to find Jamie standing in front of him with her own narrowed. "Don't you dare think you're not important enough for my wish, Balin Drake."

"How did you know what I was thinking?"

"Because I know you in my soul." She pressed her palm between her breasts, over her heart. "You don't get to sacrifice yourself for something that *could* happen later. I'm not losing you. I want to get out of hell so the three of us can figure out what we're doing with our futures. Plus, I miss my friends, my job, my *life*. So, you don't get to be selfish and decide whether or not I get to use *my* wish on you. Got it?"

He nodded, proud, scared, and a little turned on at her tone. He looked up at Ambrose, who stood there smiling.

"Since she explained to you what we're doing, we can begin," Ambrose said, and Balin wanted to flip him off, but it didn't seem like the right time.

"What do I need to do?" she asked.

"You'll need to change back and try to extend your aura to him."

Jamie closed her eyes and Balin watched as she focused, her body changing into her djinn form, her aura brightening.

"Should she be holding me or something?" Balin asked. "To make it easier?"

Ambrose tilted his head in thought then nodded. "I think the others can do it from afar as long as the person they want to bestow their wish on is in their sight, but since you've only been a djinn for about five minutes, I don't think it could hurt."

Jamie nodded then wrapped her arms around Balin's middle. Balin kissed the top of her head and hugged her close.

"Now think about your djinn state, Jamie," Ambrose whispered. "You can do this."

The hair on the back of Balin's neck tickled, and power washed over him like a warm blanket as Jamie changed to her djinn state.

"Now imagine that aura surrounding you and think about it wrapping around Balin."

"Are you making this up as you go along?" Jamie asked as her face scrunched. Her aura flickered but didn't move toward Balin.

Ambrose let out a sigh. "I'm a five-thousand-year-old angel. I think I can wing this."

Jamie and Balin laughed.

"Wing it?" Jamie said. "Get it?"

Ambrose cracked a smile then nodded as Balin felt Jamie's aura slowly creep over him like a warm blanket.

Jamie's eyes widened. "You did that on purpose."

"You're relaxing," Ambrose explained. "Now, when it's completely over him, make your wish."

"Will it hurt?" Balin asked. "No, not me. I don't care if it hurts me. Will it hurt Jamie?"

"I don't care if it hurts me either," Jamie said.

"I'm not sure on either account, but Jamie, you're there. You're aura is where it needs to be. Now make that wish."

Jamie looked into Balin's eyes, and he warmed. Her aura was hot, spicy, caring, and...*her*. She was pure, peaceful, and everything he'd dreamed he could find in a mate.

And, she was his.

No, he looked at Ambrose quickly. *Theirs.*

He looked back at Jamie after Ambrose's slight nod and met her gaze.

"I wish for Balin to fully be healed," she stated. "Healed in all ways, spiritually and physically. I wish him to be whole."

His body buckled, not in pain, but from the amount of energy that coursed through him like a heated furnace. The bonds between the three of them pulsed, the cycle he'd been begging for rushing like a river after a harsh winter snow's melting.

He was whole.

Jamie's aura pulled back as she exhaled, and he kissed her hard.

"It worked," he whispered as he pulled back and Ambrose snuck in to kiss them both.

Tears made stains down Jamie's cheeks as her body faded to its human form.

"We're okay. You're okay," she said over and over again.

"Are either of you weak? How is your energy?" Ambrose asked the both of them.

"I'm fine. No, better than fine," Balin answered. "I haven't felt this good since before I was twenty and I wasn't yet in maturity. No, that's not even right. I feel better than that."

Ambrose cupped his cheek. "Good. You have a future ahead of you, and with that, we all do."

Balin nodded, emotion clogging his throat.

"Jamie, what about you? Did it hurt? Tell me." Ambrose took her in his arms, and Balin didn't protest. They'd all need to learn to share, but at the moment all he could think about was Ambrose's words.

They did have a future.

For all his hopes and dreams, he'd never thought it'd be possible.

They were his everything, and he owed them even more.

Thankfully, he had an eternity to make that happen.

"I'm fine," Jamie said. "I promise. It didn't hurt at all, and it didn't even drain me. It was invigorating."

"Thank God," Ambrose said as he kissed her temple. "Don't show off your new powers, Jamie. We can't get out of the cell using Balin's replenished power because of the coliseum's wards, but we *will* get out of here. I'd rather them be surprised by your new strength."

"Won't they be able to tell right away?"

Ambrose shook his head. "With it so new on you, I think they would be able to tell only by getting very close. And, even if they did, you're stronger now, Jamie."

She closed her eyes, and Balin saw the relief spread over her face.

"Thank God."

"Thank God for what?" a voice called out behind them.

They all turned. Balin pushed Jamie behind himself and Ambrose. A guard stood in the hall.

"I've been told to bring you to the games. The human gets to die tonight."

It seemed their time alone was over, but they wouldn't be going down without a fight.

No, they wouldn't be going down at all.

Jamie wrung her hands together as she stood in the empty cell underneath the coliseum floor. They'd taken her from her men—her men, that was a nice thing to say—and thrown her in this cell. They'd also given her an outfit to fight in.

She rolled her eyes as she looked at what she wore. The leather corset forced her boobs almost to her chin, quite an alarming feat considering she didn't have the biggest breasts in the world. The tight-fitting torture device stopped right at her belly button and the short leather skirt she wore showed about five inches of stomach and way too much leg. They'd also given her leather boots that laced up to her knees and thankfully didn't have a heel so she could at least walk—or run, which was likely to be the case.

She looked like a whore.

Caring more about what she wore and how she would move in it made more sense than freaking out about the fact that she was about to die.

Or, at least, fight to live. She just had to figure out a way to get out of the games alive so Balin could take them home.

The thought of home with both Ambrose and Balin made her body stir in an altogether pleasant and heated way, but she pushed that back.

She'd deal later with the whole ideas of a triad and mating, living with two men—if that's what they did—the reality of her life being nothing like it used to be, and the fact that she was pretty sure she was falling in love with both of them.

Jamie couldn't deal with that right now. Now, she'd ignore it and bury the feelings until she was back in the human realm, alive and whole. Then everything could come crashing down on her because they hadn't exactly discussed the future.

Yeah, they'd said some vague things about it, but nothing concrete. And she needed concrete.

Her greatest fear—beyond being eaten alive within the next hour—was that Balin would decide that he was done with them once they escaped hell and had just been using her. Then Ambrose would leave because he was still too in love with his late wife and didn't want to deal with another loss, so he'd leave before she left him.

As if she'd ever do that.

She knew they'd said the words they needed to say to get her to change in a time of dire need, but that didn't mean that when the chips fell where they may and life returned to peace that they would stay.

No, she wouldn't think about those fears yet.

Or, she would at least pretend they weren't in the back of her mind, festering and building on top of one another.

Jamie took a deep breath, the corset digging into her sides as she did so. A man had to have designed the damn thing because surely no woman would purposely stick herself into one of these.

She had no idea where Ambrose and Balin were, and her fear for them lodged in her throat. She told herself that Fury and Pyro didn't want them dead right away. No, they'd rather have Jamie dead first.

After whoever was out there raped her.

Hence the whore outfit.

Well, screw that. She wasn't going to just lie down and

prepare to die. She'd fight. Though she had no idea how to use these new powers of her, she could still feel the strength running through her veins. She could at least fight back.

Jamie swallowed hard, closing her eyes.

She wouldn't die weak.

That didn't mean she wanted to die at all.

Suddenly, the ground beneath her feet trembled, and the roof opened up above her. She shielded her eyes from the red glare of the sky as the noise from the crowed nearly deafened her.

The floor below her rose, and she almost fell to her knees but caught herself. She would not look weak when they brought her in. With her hands fisted, ready to fight if she had to, she rose into the coliseum, dead center, surrounded by thousands of demons in the stands who screamed, roared, and called for her death.

Her heart beat loudly in her ears and her newfound powers threatened to push through, but she held them back. Ambrose had told her to remain human for as long as possible to shield herself and take the others by surprise.

It was her only plan.

"Quiet!" Fury yelled into the speakers, his voice rising over the roar of the crowd.

They hushed in an instant, the raw power of Fury's voice sending shivers along her sides.

"We all know why we're here today. This human," he spat the word like a curse, "is here to die painfully at the hands of our proudest warriors. Now, to make matters even better, we have the two men she cares about with us to watch!"

The crowd roared, and Jamie turned to where Fury stood. Ambrose and Balin kneeled on either side of him, blood dripping down their faces and the cuts along their skin.

Her stomach lurched, but she stood strong.

She had to.

"Now, who will she fight? Or at least try to fight?" He laughed as he asked, and the crowd laughed with him. "Why, our strongest competitor for sure!"

The crowd started chanting, and it took a second for the name to register.

"Hunter! Hunter! Hunter!"

No, not him. Not the man she'd just met who could be her friend.

She watched as he rose up from the cell below, chains around his arms, legs, and neck. He looked like a caged animal, but Jamie had seen the goodness in him.

Maybe they could work together to find a way out.

Jamie looked into Hunter's gold eyes, and he clenched his jaw, defeat washing over his face.

"And to make the pot more tempting, whoever wins this fight gains their freedom!"

The crowd roared, and Jamie blanched.

Fury had his perfect fight—two competitors who didn't want to kill each other but wanted freedom.

Hunter growled, attacking his chains, and Jamie shuddered.

No, this couldn't be happening.

There had to be a way out.

"Begin!" Fury yelled, and Hunter snapped his chains.

He came at her like a freight train and, before she could take a breath, tackled her to the ground. She twisted, scratching at him with her nails, trying to free herself.

"Keep fighting me," Hunter said, so low she wasn't even sure she'd heard him at first.

"Why?" she whispered back.

"I can feel your new powers. You're strong, Jamie. When Fury tires of seeing me not kill you, he'll send in more demons because he can't help himself. Then we'll fight them together. I promised you I'd get you out of here. As soon as we find a way to escape, we'll get your men and go."

Relief hit her hard, but she still fought him off. He nudged his knee between her legs, and she shuddered.

"I swear to you I won't hurt you. I just have to make it look good."

She nodded, still twisting as tears threatened.

"Don't change yet," he whispered again.

"Enough! This wasn't worth the price of admission, not yet," Pyro yelled.

"Bring in more demons!" Fury yelled, and the crowd cheered.

"Get up and change as soon as the first demon comes at you. You're stronger than you think, Jamie. The rules state they can only have one competitor per competitor, so they can't bring in more than one per person."

She nodded as the floor shook beneath her. Hunter

jumped off her with a grace that surprised her and waited for her to stand.

Her legs shook as two thick-muscled, long-horned demons rose from the ground, scars and cuts marring their bodies from long battles.

Hunter squeezed her hand, and she took a deep breath. She could do this. At least she could try. If they won, they'd be free; or at least she hoped.

"I can kill them both, Jamie," Hunter said. "You just run and stay alive. Fight if you have to."

Jamie nodded, not liking that Hunter would be doing the work. There had to be something she could do. She couldn't just stand back and not help.

The crowd chanted, each curse more vile than the next. The two demons before her threw their heads back in unison and roared, and Jamie clenched her jaw.

With one last roar, they charged, their bodies moving with a grace that she hadn't expected as they came at her and Hunter.

"Now! Change!" Hunter yelled as he planted his feet, his eyes glowing.

Jamie closed her eyes, trying to concentrate on the power within her. She felt the djinn power wash over her, her body growing in strength.

"No! What the fuck is this!" Pyro yelled as she opened her eyes and saw that she had changed fully.

Like before when she'd changed in the cell, she felt empowered, stronger, like she could do anything. Her senses where heightened and she could feel other people around her like she hadn't before. Ambrose had called it her aura. That would be something to get used to.

Pyro screamed again and she blocked him out. She didn't have time to worry about him. When one of the demons charged at her, she feigned left then ran right as fast as she could go, far faster than she could have as a human.

She felt the demon behind her, giving chase. Out of the corner of her eye, she saw Hunter fighting the other one and winning. Blood spurted from a wound at the demon's neck, and he went down to his knees. Hunter gripped its head and twisted, decapitating it with one movement.

Dear Lord, Hunter was strong.

She changed directions, sweat pouring down her back. She knew she must look like an idiot, running around with a demon chasing her. Hunter ran to her side and stopped her with one arm, wrapping it around her waist and bringing them both to their knees. The other demon lashed out, slicing Hunter down the arm.

With his scream, Jamie wiggled free and used her new strength to push the other demon back. The demon seemed surprised she fought back, but screw him.

She wasn't just going to lie back and let him kill her.

As the demon roared and charged at her, she took off again, this time to the corpse of the other demon. Her heart beat in her ears, blocking all other sounds as she threw her body down behind the corpse and picked up the horn of the dead demon. She reached up and pierced this demon's stomach. The now bleeding demon flipped over them, and Jamie pulled the horn out then stabbed him in the head.

Dear Lord.

How the hell had she done that?

Her new power coursed through her veins, strengthening her.

She'd killed a demon on her own.

Go her.

Bile rose in her throat, but she pushed it down. The last thing she needed was to throw up like a loser in front of the crowd.

"No!" Pyro yelled and shook his fists.

Fury yelled something in a language she didn't understand, and the floor shook again. This time at least twenty demons rose from the floor.

"I thought they couldn't do that," she said, her voice breaking.

"They can't," Hunter spat then cursed.

"Cheat!" Balin yelled, and Jamie turned to her mate. He and Ambrose broke through their chains as Ambrose's crystalline white wings burst from his back, spreading out, and he grabbed Balin around his torso and flew to the center of the fighting area. They dropped to her side, pulling her into their hold. She pulled back to stand on her own two feet, though she loved that they were close.

Their scents surrounded her, grounding her.

"You can't be in there!" Fury yelled over the din as the other demons quieted. "You're an angel; you've started a war."

Ambrose shook his head as he brought Jamie to his side. "No, you have. If there will be a war, you have caused it.

You've broken your own laws by bringing those demons in here. This game is forfeit."

"Jamie and Hunter are ours," Balin yelled. "We claim them in consequence of your deceit. Now, give us our freedom, and we'll leave. You have no say here, Fury. You've lost by your own impatience and lies."

Jamie wanted to cry in relief but held back everything she could. She didn't trust Pyro or Fury, not in the least.

One of the other council members held Fury back before speaking.

"It is the law, my son," he said, his voice old but strong. "Let them go, and they can *try* to leave hell."

She wasn't too sure she liked the emphasis the demon made on *try*.

Fury smiled, his teeth looking sharper by the minute, even if it was only a feeling. "Yes, you can go. If… no, when we find you, we'll kill you."

"You have no say and no jurisdiction outside of this realm," Ambrose stated as his grip tightened on her hand.

"So be it," Fury spat, and Pyro shook beside him.

Balin pushed her toward a side gate as the three men flanked her. "Let's get out of here."

Jamie wanted to sink to her knees and weep, but she didn't think this was the right time. By the look on Hunter's face, she wasn't the only one warring with their emotions. The wolf looked as if he couldn't believe his fate, as if he'd resigned himself to dying and now had a chance at life.

She didn't know what came next, but whatever it was, she'd survive. She had to.

Anything was better than what she'd just seen.

She knew the demons might come after them at any moment, but she'd take a breath because she could.

Because she had to.

At least she hoped.

The fear slowly slipped from him as Ambrose led the way to a group of rocks outside the coliseum doors. He knew they weren't safe until they were behind wards in the human realm—or really any other realm other than hell —but the jagged fear he'd had watching helplessly as Jamie ran for her life ebbed away.

As soon as he could, he'd take her in his arms and never let go, just to confirm she was really there.

He'd never been so helpless and so proud at the same time, watching her in the games. She'd never shown a hint of fear, though he'd been able to feel it through the bond. He and Balin had been forced to watch on their knees, chained to the ground.

Though he could have—and did—break free easily, he didn't at first. If he had done that before Fury had cheated, it would have cost Jamie her life, and there was nothing in the world more precious than her. He'd had to stand back and watch, holding his own emotions in check while everything he'd ever wanted could have been lost. He'd had to wait for his moment—one he hadn't been sure would come.

Now they had even more things to worry about. Namely, how to get out of hell. He could hear the crowd behind him and knew it would not be easy to make a portal and leave with them ready to give chase.

"Balin!"

Ambrose turned to find Fawkes running toward them, a huge smile on his face.

"Fawkes!" Balin said as they hugged each other, relief in the younger man's stance evident from his sagging shoulders.

"I couldn't watch, but I heard what happened. Congrats by the way on finding your true halves." He turned to Jaime and bowed. "I'm Fawkes, a friend of Balin's."

Jamie hugged him tight, surprising him. "I know what you've done for both of my men. Thank you."

Fawkes blushed and shook his head. "It was nothing. I do know that an angry mob is on its way, so I'm going to go make a distraction so you guys can divine a portal."

Ambrose smiled. This young demon was a far greater man than he gave himself credit for.

"Can't you come with us?" Jamie asked as Balin pulled her into his arms.

Hunter stood back, watching it all with that same fierce expression on his face. Ambrose was glad the wolf could escape, even though he looked more feral than sane.

"I can't go," Fawkes said, a frown on his face. "I still have a bit of time until I'm in my maturity...then..."

Balin nodded, and Ambrose took the kid by the shoulder. "When you make your choice, come to us. We'll find a way to help."

Fawkes gave a wobbly smile then coughed. "I might take you up on that."

Balin moved forward to give the kid one last hug. "You better."

"Now I'm going to go blow up a couple things, but don't worry, I'm faster than they think. Make that portal quick though."

Balin nodded. "I'm strong enough now to be able to take my mates easily, plus another, so it won't be a problem."

The roar of the crowd grew louder, and with one last nod, Fawkes ran off.

Ambrose hoped to God that the boy would make a choice that could lead him back to their lives.

That wasn't for him to decide.

"I don't want him to get hurt," Jamie whispered as Balin started to draw his rune to open the portal. Absolute glee at the new power he held shone on their lover's face.

His lover.

He liked the sound of that.

Ambrose tucked a stray hair behind her ear. She still wore her leather costume, that he had to be honest looked sexy on her, and he knew she was uncomfortable.

"He'll be okay. He's stronger than most. And I have a feeling we're not done with him."

"Good."

"Ready?" Balin asked as he stood in front of the portal, a swirly vortex of light and darkness that would lead them to, presumably, the human realm.

"God yes," Jamie said as she turned back to human. Ambrose had long since tucked his wings back, and Balin changed to his human form, which was still the same strong, good-looking man, just without horns and red specks in his eyes.

Balin took one of her hands while Ambrose took the other. Hunter grabbed Ambrose's free hand, the desperation evident in his stance, and they made their way through the portal. Sharp pinpricks of pain danced along his body, but unlike last time, it wasn't the flames of hell that greeted him, but the twilight of a setting sun in Jamie's hometown.

They were home.

Well, not exactly home. At the moment, they were in an alley near Jamie's home. He was pretty sure he'd heard Jamie give Balin the directions to where she lived before, but he'd been too caught up in making sure there were no demons following them, he'd missed it.

"Oh thank God," Jamie whispered. He caught her around the waist as her legs gave out.

"Are you okay?" Balin asked, worry etched on his face.

"Was it the portal?" Ambrose asked, not knowing how she'd fare.

"I'm just glad to be home."

Hunter came to her side and knelt before her. "Thank you, Jamie, and all of you for saving my life."

Jamie shook her head as tears slid down her cheeks. "You saved mine."

Hunter let out a breath. "I'm going to my Pack now since they're close to here. I don't know how long it's been…" He closed his eyes, clearly struggling for control. "I will come back to all of you. I will never forget what you've done."

"Nor will any of us," Ambrose promised.

"You've found an ally in me, all of you," Hunter explained as he stood. "I don't know the state of my Pack, or even if I have a title anymore, but when I come back, I will find a way to repay you."

"You owe us nothing," Jamie said.

"You gave me the option of a future. That is something I will never forget." With that, the wolf walked away, wearing only leather pants and his boots.

Considering how they all were dressed, they should probably get out of sight soon.

Balin looked around as if he'd never seen the human realm before, and Ambrose brought him in for a hug.

"You're home now," Ambrose whispered, and Balin shuddered.

"I've been here once or twice, but it's been too long."

"Let's get to my home, and then we can get clean and never move again," Jamie said as Ambrose took her hand and led the way.

He used his powers to shield them from prying eyes in case anyone saw two leather-clad people walking with another man who didn't wear leather, but looked just as dangerous.

Once they made it to Jamie's house, she almost collapsed in the doorway.

"Home," she whispered.

Balin leaned into her side as Ambrose walked to the living room, noting the window that had been broken before had been replaced. He quickly went to the phone to check the date and cursed.

"What is it?" Jamie asked.

"It's been two months."

"What?"

"It's been two months since they took you."

"No, that's not right."

Balin shook his head. "Hell is the only plane that works on a different timetable. And, since it flows like a wave, you never know if you're losing time or gaining it. Also, because it averages out, over time, it doesn't really matter and people end up aging the same."

Jamie's eyes widened, and she sank into the couch. "Two months."

Ambrose knelt before her. "I'm going to call Shade and tell him we're back and to let the others know. I'm also going to tack on that they should give us time alone to process."

Jamie nodded, her gaze far away. "We can meet at Dante's tomorrow."

"Dante? We can see him?" Balin asked, awe in his tone.

Ambrose nodded. "We'll see everyone tomorrow and learn what we've missed. Though it's going to be tough for Faith to stay away," he teased.

Jamie cracked a smile. "Tell her I need to shower and sleep and that I will see her tomorrow."

"Of course."

He quickly made the call, and the relief in Shade's voice was unmistakable. He and Lily promised to keep everyone away from the house, knowing the new triad needed time.

Everything had changed. He'd lost what mattered most to him before and almost lost it again. He wouldn't be letting go easily.

He wanted Jamie in his life, his bed, and in every single aspect of his life. And as he looked at Balin, who stood shell shocked in the living room, he knew he wanted Balin by his side throughout it all.

He loved Jamie.

Loved her.

He knew he was falling for Balin.

It might have started with a bond and genetics, but it was more than that, more than fate. He saw the way they both took care of those they loved and fought for more than just themselves. They were true warriors, and he wasn't about to let them go.

"We should get cleaned up," Ambrose said as walked toward his mates.

Jamie absently nodded then shuddered. "I'd really like to get out of these clothes."

"I can help with that," Balin said, a smile on his face.

Jamie rolled her eyes. "Really? You're thinking about sex right now?"

"Jamie, darling, I'm always thinking about sex." Balin lifted her into his arms, and she let out a squeal. "I will say I like this leather number on you."

Ambrose let out chuckle at the look of mutiny on Jamie's face.

"You would, you deviant. I look like a whore." She puffed up her cheeks and let out a breath. "At least they didn't give me heels. I could actually run."

"As much as I like that leather on you, we need to get you out of it so we can all be clean," Ambrose said as he led Balin toward Jamie's bathroom. "Though I might have to get you something with leather in the future."

Balin groaned behind him, and Ambrose's cock pressed against his pants.

"Done. We're doing that as soon as possible," Balin teased.

"Fine, but then I get to dress you both in leather."

"Deal," both men said at the same time.

Ambrose looked behind him at the younger man who had a more carefree air about him. He knew Balin had been through wars, near death, and in almost constant pain his whole life, but the demon still joked and tried to make light of things—completely the opposite of how Ambrose dealt with life.

He had a feeling Balin would be good for him.

He looked at Jamie's tired face, yet he knew she was full of life and hope. Good for the both of them.

Jamie let out a small sigh as they entered her bathroom. Her house wasn't the largest of houses. In fact, it could have fit in just one of his living rooms, but her bathroom was breathtaking. She'd bought the place because of it, and he knew from Shade that she was planning on building onto her home but would keep the bathroom the way as it was. She had a large claw-footed bath that could fit two people—something they'd have to work on since there were now three of them.

It was her shower that made Ambrose want to weep.

It was a large, glass-enclosed shower. One showerhead came from the ceiling then three more showerheads jutted from the walls to make sure every inch of skin could be heated, wet, and clean.

Not to mention the fact that it was large enough for six people and had a bench in it.

Perfect for what he had in mind.

"Well, Hades, I'm in love with your bathroom," Balin said as he set Jamie on the bathroom counter.

Jamie smiled and wiggled, clearly uncomfortable in her skirt—something that could quickly be remedied.

"I love my shower, though now, I guess it's yours too, right?" She blushed and Ambrose froze, not wanting to break the moment.

Balin stood by her. "Jamie, darling, I'm never leaving your side. Nor am I leaving Ambrose. I'd love to stay here with you and make a future. I love you, Jamie Bennett." He cupped her face and kissed her softly.

Tears stained both of their cheeks, and Ambrose moved so he was closer to them. "And I'm not leaving you—either of you. Though we don't have to stay here, we can go wherever you want, whenever you want. You both are my future, and I'm not going to be stupid and walk away from it—again. I'm going to do all in my power to show you that I'm worthy of you, Jamie. And you too, Balin."

He kissed her then, her lips soft, needy beneath his. "I love you," he whispered.

She pulled back and hiccupped a laugh. "Oh, I love you both. I can't believe I got this lucky." Then she laughed again. "I don't know why that's funny because, really, we just went through hell—literally—but I feel like the luckiest girl in the world that I get the both of you. I have no idea how we're going to make everything work, but hearing you both say that makes me believe that it can work. That it will work."

Balin wrapped an arm around Ambrose's waist and leaned on his shoulder. Ambrose shuddered a breath and turned to let his lips rest gently on Balin's. "I love you too, Balin," he whispered. "I don't know how it happened, and I wasn't expecting you, but I'm not sorry."

Balin grinned. "Good to know because you're stuck with me, old man." He leaned in to kiss him harder. "And, of course, I love you too. Right now, all the emotions in this room are a bit thick. Why don't we shower and show Jamie what it means to be with two men? And let me show you what it means to be with me. We have a whole future to plan and figure out, but I'd rather take the next few hours just being us."

Happiness spread through him as he slowly undid Jamie's corset. Not a single mark marred her skin from her ordeal, and he was grateful that her newfound abilities seemed to have sped up her healing process.

Though he could have healed her, it was good to know she could do it on her own. He'd just have to make sure he pampered her in other ways.

She exhaled loudly as he undid the last of the strings and removed the binding. Her breasts fell, heavy, her nipples hard.

Smiling, he leaned down to press a kiss to the tip of one while Balin did the same to the other. When Balin turned slightly, Ambrose captured the other man's lips above her chest and bit down hard.

Balin pulled back and laughed. "Feisty, are you?"

Ambrose merely raised a brow. "I am a warrior after all."

"Oh, God, I really am the luckiest girl ever." She leaned back and smiled, her eyes dark with arousal.

Balin undid her boots while Ambrose turned on the shower. The water flowed, and steam started to fill the room.

"How is it you two can get me so hot with just a little touch?" she asked as she squirmed on the counter.

Balin slowly slid off her skirt, and Ambrose cursed.

"You weren't wearing panties this whole time?" he asked.

She blushed from head to toe, her nipples darkening.

"No, and let me tell you, it's hard to fall to the ground with your legs crossed so you don't flash a whole mob of demons."

"Was it really a mob?" Balin asked. "Or was it more of a gathering? Or a grouping?"

She smacked his shoulder as they both laughed, the tension easing.

Ambrose stripped off his clothes, glad to be rid of them. He had more clothes in his cache for himself and Balin later.

Balin stripped down as well, and Ambrose picked up Jamie and headed toward the shower.

"You two do realize I can walk, right?" Jamie asked as she buried her nose in his throat.

"Why should you?" he asked as he stepped in the stall, setting her down on the bench.

She wrinkled her nose as she looked down at herself. "I smell like a sewer."

Balin laughed as he walked in naked behind them, shutting the stall door. "No, you smell like mine."

"If you think the smell of dirt, trash, and God knows what else is yours, then we have a problem," she teased.

Ambrose shook his head as the two of them teased each other then turned on the ceiling showerhead.

Balin moved out of the way quickly, shaking his head like a wet dog. "I can't believe you just did that."

Ambrose shrugged but hid his smile as the water heated, and then he turned on the other three showerheads so steam filled the stall and the hot water poured over them.

Jamie leaned back against the wall, the water running down her body, between her breasts, down to her core.

Hell, he hadn't meant to get as turned on as he was in the shower. He'd wanted to make sure they were all clean and taken care of, and then he'd make love with the both of them.

Balin smiled at him as if he knew exactly where Ambrose's thoughts had run off to. By the look of the other man's cock, Balin's ran on the same path.

Soon, he told himself, *soon*.

With the soap in his hand, he moved toward Jamie, brushing by Balin, who sucked in a breath. He might have been older than dirt, as Faith liked to joke, but that didn't mean he was dead and cold.

No, far from it.

"The water feels wonderful," Jamie whispered as tears ran down her face, mixing with the water.

"What's wrong?" Ambrose asked as he knelt between her legs, leaning his forehead on hers.

"Just coming down off my high I think," she whispered.

Ambrose kissed her softly, letting the sobs rack her body. Balin took the soap from his hands and slid it over her body, comforting her.

"I was so afraid."

Ambrose put a small amount of shampoo in his hands then began to massage her scalp. She moaned at his touch, and his cock filled even more, but this was not the time.

"I was too," he said, his voice stronger than he expected. "When I saw the window in your house—" He took a deep breath and washed the soap from her hair, continuing his massage. "I never want to go through that again."

Jamie managed a smile as the tears ebbed. "I don't either."

"And now you're stronger than you were before," Balin added as he washed his own body. Ambrose's gaze followed the man's hands as he slid them over his washboard abs then stroked his cock.

He blinked then turned back to Jamie, knowing they had to get this out before they could enjoy each other to the fullest.

"You're stronger now, Jamie, but we still need to train you."

Jamie nodded, her eyes filling with worry, and he cursed himself for bringing it up.

"We can talk about that later. Just know that since we're out of hell, we have the advantage. We'll protect you."

Jamie shook her head. "I want to protect myself and you both."

Balin nudged Ambrose over so they were both kneeling before their mate. "The three of us are in this together."

She nodded then smiled. "Good."

Ambrose took the soap from Balin and quickly washed himself. Before he could turn off the water, Jamie stood, taking the soap from him.

"I just want to make sure you didn't miss a spot." She quirked her mouth in a smile, and Ambrose held back a smile.

Little minx.

He felt Balin's hands in his hair, and he groaned, closing his eyes as both his mates washed him.

"I love his hair, don't you?" Jamie asked as Balin worked his hands along Ambrose's scalp.

No one had ever washed his hair before, and he wanted to sink to his knees and let them have him. They took care of him, loved him.

Why had he wanted to run from this?

No, he wouldn't think of that anymore. He'd moved on from his insecurities—or at least he was on the right path. He'd do all in his power to prove worthy of his mates.

Balin walked him beneath the celling spray, running his hands through Ambrose's hair to get all the soap out.

"All clean, I believe," Balin whispered and smacked his ass.

Ambrose turned, loving the delight and mischief on the man's face. "Did you just smack me?"

"I have no idea what you're talking about."

Jamie laughed behind him, and Ambrose pulled her around so she stood in his arms. "Is something funny?"

She widened her eyes, biting her lip to hold back laughter. "Oh no, wise one, nothing like that."

Ambrose closed his eyes, biting back a laugh of his own. "You two make me feel old."

He felt the small grip of Jamie's hand around his cock as she squeezed. "You sure don't feel old to me," she purred.

Balin reached around them both to massage Ambrose's ass, and Ambrose groaned. "We'll just have to prove it to you."

Ambrose narrowed his eyes. "Oh, no, boy, I'll have to prove it myself. Meaning we should get his one," he squeezed Jamie's hip, "under you so sink her over that cock of yours, and then I can fill you."

Jamie blinked at his words, and he gave a dangerous smile. "I might be old, but I know how to take what I want. What I need."

Balin smirked. "I can let you take me this time, old man. I will have you."

Ambrose nodded, knowing they needed to set their own boundaries and needs. "Then let's get this one ready."

Jamie laughed. "Dear Lord, I'm past ready." She wiggled from their hold and left the shower, grabbing a towel on her way to the bedroom.

Balin ran a hand down Ambrose's side, tender yet strong. "I like the way she moves."

Ambrose sighed. "I can't believe I almost lost her because of my own ignorance and then my past."

Balin leaned in to bite his shoulder—hard. "Get that thought out of your head. We're moving forward, remember? I'm not going to let Pyro and what happened between you and Jamie before me ruin this. Yes, we have a lot talk about. And, we will—later. Got it?"

Ambrose nodded, leaning in to brush his lips across his lover's.

"Now, we have a willing woman waiting for us in the bedroom. What in Hades' name are we doing in a cooling shower?"

Ambrose laughed as he turned off the water then walked naked to the bedroom, still wet but too eager to wait.

Jamie sat at the edge of the bed, her teeth digging into her lip.

"What's wrong?" he asked as he walked toward her, Balin on his heels.

"I'm just tired I think."

Ambrose didn't need to hear anything else and picked her up. Balin seemed to understand as he pulled back the covers. He set her down in the middle of the bed and climbed in to spoon her while Balin got in on the other side to hold them close.

"I thought you wanted…" She closed her eyes and snuggled closer to the both of them, her ass nestled against his cock.

He brushed her hair back so he could suck on her neck, marking her gently with his teeth. "We have a lifetime for that. You've been through so much in the past few days, and now you're back, and two months have passed. I think you're allowed to want to sleep."

Balin kissed her softly then did the same to Ambrose. "We'll be here when you wake up. Just sleep."

She sighed and wiggled once more. "I like the both of you in my bed."

Ambrose kissed her neck. "Good, because we're not leaving it."

"Though we may need to get a bigger bed." Balin groaned as he scooted closer.

"Later," Ambrose whispered as his lovers fell asleep.

Soon after, Ambrose woke to hands roaming over his body as both his lovers pet and held him.

"I thought you wanted to sleep," he rumbled.

"Oh we will, but I want you first," she said, her voice strong and steady with her new powers. She'd turned back into her djinn form, her aura washing over them, warming them.

"What do you have planned for me, little one?" he asked even as she moved from him to roll under Balin.

"We both have plans," Balin teased, he too in his non-human form. "I'm going to take Jamie while you take me. It's about time that we have each other."

Ambrose nodded, his cock hardening at the thought of sinking into Balin.

He quickly got out of bed and got the lube out of the nightstand drawer. His eyes narrowed at the tiny bottle. Oh, they'd need more in the future.

His cock throbbed as he watched Balin suck and nibble Jamie's breasts, her aura shuddering along with her body at each stroke. Then Balin ever so slowly sank into her wet heat and Ambrose had to swallow hard.

These two were his.

His alone.

Thank God.

Shaking his head to clear his thoughts, he knelt on the bed behind his demon and ran a hand down his back.

"She feels fucking amazing, Ambrose," Balin panted. "Then again, you already know that."

Ambrose chuckled. "Oh, I know. But now I want to feel how amazing you are."

As Balin fucked their mate, Ambrose readied Balin, touching, teasing, licking. Balin leaned down and bit into Jamie's shoulder, marking her as his, something Ambrose would do soon. Soon, Balin was ready and Ambrose positioned his cock, ready to take him with all his power.

"Ready?" Ambrose asked, his body shaking as he fought for control.

Balin stopped moving and Jamie whimpered. "Yes, please, I need you. *We* need you."

Ambrose nodded, then rocked his hips, slowly breaching that tight ring of muscles. He stilled for a moment while Balin groaned and relaxed, then pushed in with one quick stroke.

He knew that with Jamie, they'd have to go slower, but Balin was different.

He'd like the slight sting more.

When we was fully seated, he moved back and began to thrust. Balin matched his rhythm so Ambrose felt like he was not only fucking Balin, but Jamie as well.

Sweat slid down his back as his balls tightened, sending him over the edge, his seed filling his lover as Balin and Jamie followed soon behind.

Exhausted and sated, he pulled out, knowing they'd have to clean themselves in the morning, but not caring.

"We'll do that again, yes?" Jamie asked, her voice fading as she fought to stay awake.

Ambrose leaned over to kiss her, then Balin.

"Every day," he answered. "Always."

He tugged them closer, letting their scents wash over him.

The dangers were still out there, but this... this was contentment. He'd do anything to protect it.

KOBAL LOOKED AT THE NOTE IN HIS HAND AND PACED. HIS longtime ally—not a friend, as it would be his downfall if he'd made friends with a demon—Pyro had sent him the missive, and Kobal wouldn't believe his eyes.

The rumors were true.

The gods or *something* had deemed seven human women worthy of supernatural powers. He sneered at the word human. They weren't fit to lie under his shoe. He knew the other djinn didn't think the same way he did, but they didn't matter.

He was the leader of the djinn council, and he refused to allow this abomination the courtesy of living.

No, he didn't care about the brownie or whatever the other five women turned into. He only cared about this djinn.

Or, rather, this tainted bitch who didn't deserve the title.

He was a pureblood djinn, one of the last alive. There were others like him, some male, only two female, but *they* were the future of their race. Not this diluted, lightning-struck whore.

Pyro had noted that the bitch had bonded with not one

but two non-djinns, tainting her blood even further. There was no coming back from that—no excuse.

So, Kobal would do what was needed and aid Pyro in the extermination of this abomination.

And, he'd enjoy every moment of it.

Their species was pure—or at least would be.

There was no need for the lightning-struck…no need for this Jamie.

She would die.

Soon.

CHAPTER 13

She'd woken up to an arm wrapped around her middle and the other resting between her legs, and Jamie had never wanted to move. Ambrose and Balin had had other ideas on how to wake her up.

Needless to say, her body was delightfully sore in all the most intimate places, and she was pretty sure Balin was as sore as she. Her face heated at the memory of Ambrose taking their lover with all the passion he'd taken her.

Things had changed to the point she'd never thought possible. She was a djinn. Someone with a power she didn't understand but would be able to use. She'd never thought she'd be in a relationship with two men, let alone get to watch those two men love one another.

And they were *hers*.

Meaning she would be able to watch them again…and be loved by the two most powerful men she knew…again.

How freaking lucky could she get?

She stretched her fingers, letting her new power fill her slowly. It was like another person within her, no, that wasn't right. It was more like a warm blanket that she would always know was there, helping her kick ass if she needed.

She couldn't wait to see what else she could do with it.

"Ready?" Ambrose asked as he pulled her car into Dante's Circle's parking lot.

She nodded as he parked and turned off the engine. They were about to meet the girls, Shade, and, most likely, Dante so she could tell them about her journey. It still boggled her mind that they'd been waiting for two months for her to return.

She'd lost so much time.

Jamie couldn't even think about what she was going to do with her store and her life, not to mention she needed to call her parents back so they wouldn't worry. Though she knew they probably hadn't even noticed she'd been gone for so long since they only talked every few months as it was.

How was she supposed to tell them that she was in love with two men?

"Hey, stop thinking so hard," Balin said as he reached around the seat from the back to hold her.

She gave a shaky laugh. "I can't help it."

Ambrose opened his door and looked back at her. "We're going to figure it all out together. Now let's get inside so you can see your friends. They've been worried, and I think they'll be good for you."

She smiled at him, her heart so deeply in love it was a

little sickening. He was right. Her friends would freak out, worry, then totally make her feel better. They were another facet of her family after all.

Balin tickled her chin. "Plus, you need to introduce and then protect me from them. I'm a little worried about this Faith."

She'd given a little background on each of her friends and had explained that, even though all her friends would want to know who this new person in her life was, Faith would be the most aggressive. That's why Jamie loved Faith —bitchy attitude and all.

Ambrose led them inside the bar that was like a second home, and Balin followed. They were always blocking her from the outside world and threats. Normally, she would have been pissed that they thought she was the little woman, but now that she'd been through hell she was okay with them doing what they thought was needed…at least for now. As soon as she gained more experience with these new powers of hers, she'd have to sit down and have a talk with them. There was no way she'd let either of them get hurt because of her. She didn't think she'd be able to live with that.

"Jamie!" Eliana yelled as she ran to her, shaggy red hair falling around her face.

Jamie found herself embraced in hard hug then more arms and hands grabbed at her so Jamie wasn't even sure who was holding her. All six women gathered around, talking, laughing, crying, and hugging.

Jamie pulled back, tears running down her cheeks. "I can tell you missed me."

Faith slapped her upside the head and cursed. "What do you think? You go away for two months and you expect us not to worry?"

"Oh, I've missed you're bitchy self," Jamie teased and kissed Faith's cheek.

"Did you just call me a bitch?"

"No, you're just bitch-like. And I know it's all the hard candy shell because you're sweet as milk chocolate underneath," Jamie explained as Faith narrowed her eyes.

"Oh, God, I've missed you," Lily said as she laughed. Jamie looked down at her friend and bit her lip.

"You're showing! I missed it!"

Lily shook her head and placed her palm on her rounded belly. "I'm not that far along, dear, don't worry. I'm just glad to have you back."

Amara wrapped her arms around Jamie's waist. "Don't do that again, okay? I don't think we can take it."

Becca snorted. "Right, like she had a choice. Good to know that we can count on Ambrose to bring her back." She narrowed her eyes at the man in question, and Ambrose just tilted his head.

Nadie shuffled, her steps tentative, to Ambrose's side and gave him a hug, surprising them all. "Thank you for bringing her back. We knew you would."

Jamie watched as Ambrose swallowed hard and wrapped his arms around her. "It was my honor."

"It's about time you realized that," Faith added. "Now,

are you going to introduce us to this fine specimen?" She smiled at Balin, and Jamie let out a little growl. "Oh, it's like that is it?" Faith teased.

Jamie pulled away and stood between her men. "This is Balin. He saved me, too, and he's…he's my other half. Just like Ambrose is." She blushed and quickly looked around the bar, feeling like an idiot that she'd just blurted it out like that. Then she remembered that Dante had closed it for their celebration.

Thank God.

"That is so hot," Eliana said and then laughed, cutting through the tension as the other women joined her.

"What's hot?" Shade asked as he walked toward Ambrose from the back of the bar, giving him a strong hug. "Good to have you back, my brother." He walked toward Balin and hugged him the same. "Welcome to the family."

This was why she loved Shade like her family. He just went with the flow and brought in his family as people took care of one another.

Dante walked out behind Shade, his long black hair in a ponytail. He nodded toward Ambrose and picked Jamie up in a bone-crushing hug.

"Don't do that again, okay?" he whispered in her ear, and tears prickled the back of her eyes. Dante was like the brother she'd never had. It must have killed the dragon in him not to be able to go to hell to get her.

Dante moved to Balin and hugged him just as hard. "It's good to see you, Balin. It's been too long."

Balin snorted. "Yes, a century or two could be considered that. Too bad you couldn't come down for a visit."

Dante rolled his eyes. "You know damn well why I couldn't."

Jamie could tell that everyone wanted to ask why, but even Faith seemed to know better than to question a dragon.

Ambrose cleared his throat. "That reminds me." He took the medallion that had saved his life in hell—all their lives—out of his cache and handed it to Dante. "Thank you for your assistance. Even though you couldn't accompany me, you were the only reason I was able to go on my journey."

Dante nodded then left without a word, presumably to put his medallion away—wherever it was he hid his things. That dragon sure had secrets, but she didn't mind. He deserved them. If he didn't do something about the longing looks he shared with Nadie, Jamie would have to do something.

Apparently, being in love caused her to wish all her friends were in love.

Wasn't that just sickening?

Oh, Faith would love it.

Becca wrapped her arm around Jamie's shoulders. "Come on over to our table. We all brought in food, and we have the normal bar food too. You can tell us all about your....trip, and we can tell you what's been going on here." They all sat around the table, Balin and Ambrose on either side of her. "Plus, when we get you alone, you can dish on those two men of yours."

Balin laughed. "There really are no secrets between women."

Faith narrowed her eyes. "Nope, so that means if you do something wrong, we'll all know about it. So, no funny business."

"Behave, Faith." Jamie scowled as she took a bite of her nachos. The taste exploded on her tongue, and she moaned. She'd eaten that morning but hadn't had any food in hell so she was still trying to eat everything in sight.

Balin rubbed her back, a glint in his eyes.

"No, stop thinking about that," she whispered, and Shade laughed across the table.

Damn supernatural hearing.

"Be nice." Lily giggled.

"I have no idea what you're whispering about over there but leave it in the bedroom please," Eliana said as she picked up a chicken wing. "Now, before you tell us what you've been up to… and by the way, I love how we're talking about this ordeal like it's a freaking vacation… but whatever… anyway, you should know that, between all of us, we took care of your shop and your bills so you don't have to worry about that."

A huge weight slipped from her shoulders as she looked at her friends. "You did all of that?"

Amara shrugged. "Of course. We knew you'd be back."

"Ambrose wouldn't have had it any other way," Nadie added, a wistful note in her tone.

"Well…just…thank you. When I found out we'd been missing two months, I had no idea what I'd be able to do with my store. As it is, I'm pretty sure I'm going to have to close it."

"Why?" Balin asked.

Jamie shrugged, trying to act as if she didn't feel like a failure. "It's a small indie bookstore, and the brick and mortar stores are a dying breed. I've done all I can think of to make it worthwhile for people to come in, but ebooks are all the rage. And, frankly, I love my ereader, so I can't blame them. I don't have the room in my house for more books, so I understand people's logic."

Balin traced her jaw. "Even if you understand why it's happening doesn't mean it doesn't hurt."

She closed her eyes, grateful that he understood.

"Don't give up hope yet," Ambrose said. "We can find a way to make it work. Or at least try."

"As much as I'd like to believe you, I've been through it all before, Ambrose."

"Then let me and Balin take a look."

Jamie narrowed her eyes. "Are you saying that the big strong men should handle it while the little woman hides in the corner?"

She heard the rumblings of her friends at the table, glad they were on her side. Her men would have to get it through their heads right now that she wouldn't back down and let them control her.

"Not at all, Jamie. I've been around a long time, and it never hurts to put a new set of eyes on the problem. I know you've done everything you can think of, so let me help. If it doesn't work, then we'll find something to make you happy."

She nodded, not completely convinced. If they wanted to take a look, why not? It wasn't as if she could afford to be stubborn.

She knew Ambrose's late wife had been content to stay at home with the babies, but Jamie needed to have a job and do something more. Now she sounded like a bitch considering her own mother had been a stay-at-home mom and worked harder than anyone she knew.

She just needed a nap.

Or a drink.

While they ate, she detailed her ordeal in hell, pausing to wait for the gasps and comments when she mentioned Pyro and the others. No matter how detailed she got, she couldn't describe the fear, the smell, and the pure terror.

"So, you're a djinn?" Becca asked. "That is so cool. Now we have a brownie and a djinn. I wonder what we'll have next."

Amara shuddered. "I'm just fine how I am. Thanks."

"We'll just take it as it comes to us," Faith said as she crunched on some celery. "It's not like we're all alone, right?"

Right there, that's why she loved her friends. They were there with her no matter what happened.

She leaned into Ambrose's hold while Balin ran a hand up her leg. And, now, she had the two loves of her life. What more did she need?

❄

BECCA GROANED AS SHE THREW THE TRASH BAG IN THE dumpster. Even though it wasn't her shift, she wasn't just going to leave the trash around for Dante to clean up. She liked the man—no, dragon—more than that.

It was really too bad that she and Dante weren't true halves since they got along so well, even when they were yelling at each other. Alas, she didn't feel those special tingles or that weird weakness that came with finding a true half.

Nope, she was just plain old Becca.

Healthy and boring.

Plus, she was pretty sure Nadie and Dante needed to get together, but she had no idea why they circled each other the way they did. Nadie didn't seem as weak as Lily and Jamie had, but something was off.

Becca on the other hand, felt nothing.

She let out a breath and ran a hand through her too-long hair. At some point, she should probably cut it, but she didn't have the time to make it look nice. It was just easier to let it go crazy around her head or put it up in a ponytail.

Plus, she had the absolute worst luck with haircuts.

She blocked the image of the bang incident from her memory.

Footsteps sounded behind her, and she turned, expecting to see Dante or one of her friends. The fist to her chin knocked her off balance, and she hit the ground hard, her elbow taking the brunt of it.

"What the hell?" she asked as fear clawed at her.

"Give me your money, bitch."

Mugged. Really? She was getting mugged. Now she knew she had the worst luck of anyone she knew.

"I don't have my apron on me," she explained. "I have nothing you want."

The man, his hat shadowing his features, cursed. "Fuck, lady," he said as he ran his hand over her body, and she tried to break free. That's when she noticed the knife in his hand.

"If you don't have any money, then I'll take something else from you." He reached up to unbuckle his pants, and she opened her mouth to scream. "Make a sound and I'll fucking kill you."

Her body shook, her mind trying to find a way out of this. Her friends were right inside that building and would come out for her if she took too long. At least she hoped.

Oh, God, please come out.

"Get off her, you prick," a deep voice said from behind her attacker.

The mugger twisted her nipple hard and laughed when he looked over his shoulder. "I don't see a fucking knife or gun on you, so why don't you get lost?"

"Have it your way," the stranger said as he moved quicker than humanly possible, taking the mugger by the throat and throwing him into the wall. The man fell to the ground, unconscious. The stranger stalked toward him, and Becca was sure she was about to witness a murder—not that the mugger didn't deserve it.

"Wait, don't kill him."

The stranger turned to look at her, and her breath caught. He was beautiful. Strong cheekbones and lush lips made him look like a model. His brown hair brushed his shoulders, making him look dangerous. His eyes…they were yellow.

And totally not human.

The stranger's nostrils flared as he stalked toward her. "He hurt you and would have done worse if I hadn't been here. He doesn't deserve to live."

"And you don't deserve to have that blood on your hands."

The man froze then shook his head, as if the possibility had never occurred to him. "I can call my Pack to take care of him."

"Your…Pack?"

The stranger nodded. "I can smell Ambrose and Jamie on you, so you must be one of the friends she talked about in hell." He reached down to trace her jaw, sending shivers of something she didn't want to think too much about down her spine. "And from your milky-white skin and hair that looks caught by the sun, I would say you are Becca."

"Hunter? The…wolf that saved Jamie?" Her heart beat against the wall of her chest as she lay on the ground, staring at the man who had saved not only her best friend, but had now saved her as well.

They'd said he was almost feral, and they had been right. Becca caught the look of something stronger than that in his eyes…something that needed…her?

What was she talking about?

She didn't even know this man.

She watched as he quickly made a call to someone, then hung up. Before she could breathe, he had her in his arms and strode toward the back door of Dante's.

"I can walk you know," she complained, even as she leaned into his hold. He smelled wild, like the forest and even a bit of wolf. Though she didn't know why she knew that. For some reason the heady combination made her want to sink into him and never let him go.

Apparently, she'd hit her head when she'd fallen.

"I know you can, Becca, but you don't have to. I'm going to take care of you."

Well then, maybe should get used to that.

Maybe.

"I CAN'T BELIEVE BECCA WAS ALMOST RAPED, AND WE WERE SO close to her," Jamie said as she wrung her hands together. "What use are our powers if our friends can still get hurt?" She closed her eyes, biting her lip. "Thank God Hunter came when he did. I know he only came to see us, but it seemed like fate had something to do with it."

Balin nodded as he watched his mate and love pace around their bedroom. When Hunter had brought Becca into the bar, chaos had erupted. The other girls had thought he was a crazed killer with the way he walked in holding Becca. While the three of them knew he didn't have the ability to hurt one of Jamie's friends.

As none of the people in the bar were healers to those who weren't their mates, Becca left with the bruise on her face, as well as a few on her body that he knew hurt Jamie to see. The single girls rallied around Becca and had taken her home, leaving a longing Hunter behind.

Balin had an idea of why the wolf looked so crestfallen, but he wasn't about to bring it up—not with the dangers lurking about from common thieves as well as demons.

Walking up behind her, he brought Jamie to his chest, inhaling her sweet scent. That act alone calmed his body from the rage he felt that it could have been her—though other parts of his body had the exact opposite effect.

"She's okay," he whispered as he nuzzled her neck. "Hunter got to her in time."

She turned in his hold, wrapping her arms around his waist. "What if he hadn't chosen that exact time to visit us?"

He rubbed small circles on her back, willing her to believe. "Stop thinking in what-ifs. All it will do is make you worry more. She made it, and now that we got that scare, Ambrose, Shade, Dante, and I are going to teach you all self-defense. I won't have any of you hurt because you didn't know what to do."

Jamie took a shuddering breath, and he hugged her tighter. "I just wish the rest of the girls would find their true halves and find their inner supernatural. That way they'd be stronger and have a fighting chance."

He leaned down to kiss her, unable to hold it back any longer. "Fate will provide it when necessary."

"You put a lot of stock in fate, Balin."

"I have to. Fate brought me you."

Jamie looked up at him, a small smile on her face. From that smile alone, he knew he'd at least brought her out of the darkness of feeling helpless.

"About that…"

Balin froze, a slow terror creeping its way along his spine.

"About what?" he asked, surprised his voice was so steady.

"I hardly know you, Balin. I know everything down in hell made us feel like we had to bond in order to live…"

His heart stopped. No, she couldn't be doing this. He couldn't lose her.

"No, don't look at me like that. I want you, Balin. I *love* you. I don't want it to be just because of magic. I mean I just met you. I need to know more about you. I need to know *you*. Plus, there's this whole future thing. We're in a triad, Balin. Humans don't live in triads. Or, if they do, it's taboo, and people think it's a dirty, sinful thing."

Balin narrowed his eyes. "And you think our bond is like that?" Anger, yes, anger, was a better feeling than the hurt and loss that threatened to take over.

She shook her head, her eyes filling with tears. "No, of course not. Maybe before I started reading so much romance, I would have. After reading about those fictional characters in triads, I thought that at least emotionally, it could be done. That's fiction. I *know* emotionally we can handle being a triad. I feel it in my heart, in my every breath. That could be because of the magic, but I don't care.

Balin, how is this going to work in real life? I figured the three of us would live here or in Ambrose's realm. You're a demon, how would that work? Would they accept you?"

Balin took her by the hand and led her to the bed, needing to sit down and let his mind work. Yes, he knew it would be difficult, but to be honest, he hadn't thought past *finding* his mate. He hadn't thought about actually *living* with her.

Or, in his case, them.

"Jamie, I don't know, but I know we'll work it out."

Jamie stood up and broke his hold. "How? I need specifics. It's all well and good that we're great in bed and we love each other. We know the bond's the reason it all started. I love you and Ambrose in spite of the bond, Balin. The bond might have started it, but what I feel for you finished it. You have to believe that. I love the way you two take care of each other and me, I love the way you joke when you're upset, I love the way you try and be better than you think others think you are. I know all of this just by watching you for a short time."

His body sagged in relief. The rest was just details. Details she needed. Details they needed.

"What do you want to know, Jamie? Ask anything. I want to know all about you, and I want you to know me beyond what you see."

Jamie walked toward him, a frown on her face. "What about your mom?"

Pain slid through him at the question. Of course that was the first thing she would ask. "She's dead."

Jamie's eyes filled with tears and she moved to settle on his lap. "I'm sorry, Balin. I didn't mean to cause you pain."

He held her close, that familiar ache settling in. "She died when I was a baby. Or rather, Pyro killed her when she wanted to leave with me."

He didn't remember her, not really. He'd only seen the photos later in life. Even though he'd never known her, he missed her.

"Oh, Balin," Jamie whispered. "I'm so sorry."

Balin inhaled her scent, the sweetness settling him. "It was a long time ago. Pyro didn't make her death hurt either, according to others. He at least loved her that much."

Jamie pulled back, a frown on her face. "That's not love, Balin. Not even a little bit."

He shrugged, not arguing. "It is for Pyro."

"You're not Pyro, Balin. You're stronger than that. You're better."

He cracked a smile. "You and Ambrose might be the only two who have ever said that."

"Then the others are idiots."

He shook his head, holding back a laugh. "Only you would call a whole contingent of the most evil of demons idiots."

She rested her head on his shoulder. "How is this going to work?"

He hugged her tight, needing her more than she knew. "One step at a time."

"I know it's going to take time to get to know one another.

"Who cares what people think? Jamie, we love each other. We'll deal with what comes together."

"It's just new, and I'm freaking out. I'm sorry, Balin."

"Don't be sorry. I know it's not going to be easy, but we can find a way to make it work for the public. It's what happens in private and with our friends that truly matters. And from the way the girls treated us, I don't think they care that you're with two men."

"So it doesn't make me a slut?"

Balin growled and turned her over his knee in a quick movement. "What did we say about using that word?"

Jamie laughed. "You are *not* going to spank me, Balin Drake."

"I really don't think you're in any position to argue," he said as he slid his hand up her leggings to rest his palm under her dress.

She wiggled as her laughter died. "Balin…"

"I won't hurt you. I'd never hurt you."

"I'm not a submissive. I know what that word means and what the world entails. I don't want to have a master or a Dominant."

Balin smiled and patted her bottom. "I'm not a Dominant, Jamie. Neither is Ambrose. I can enjoy bringing you pleasure." He pulled her leggings down below her ass and pulled her dress up so her thong-clad bottom was ready for his gaze.

"And you think spanking can do that?" she asked, her voice a little breathless.

"There's only one way to find out. Plus, I told you not to call yourself a slut."

He slapped one cheek, not enough to hurt, but to sting just a little.

Jamie let out a little moan as she wiggled again. "Oh."

Balin chuckled. "I will never use anything on you but my hand, Jamie. I just want you to feel good, and then I'm going to fuck you hard against that wall over there."

He spanked the other cheek, and this time her moan was a bit louder, a bit longer.

"What is it with you and walls?" she asked.

"I have no idea. I just like fucking you against them. And, later, I'm going to fuck Ambrose against the wall as well."

He spanked her as he said the last part, her body flushing, her cheeks pink.

"Oh, I think I want to see that."

He pulled her off his lap, standing as he wrapped his arms around her waist. "You see? This isn't wrong, Jamie. It's the three of us loving each other and bringing each other pleasure. Ambrose and I have spent long enough without happiness, and we're not letting you go. You might be younger than us, but it's time you see what true happiness can be. We're going to make this work."

She nodded and he kissed her hard, their teeth clashing, their tongues tangling. He quickly stripped her of her clothes and followed suit, leaving them both bare and needy.

He ran his hands down her sides, loving the feel of her heated flesh in the cool room.

He ran his tongue ran up her neck, licking to her ear. "We haven't been using condoms, Jamie. We can start right now if you don't want to make a baby."

She shook her head. "I know it's crazy when we're still learning everything about how to make this work, but I don't want to interfere with fate."

His body shuddered under the weight of her statement. He couldn't wait to see her round with his and Ambrose's child. No matter who the father was, they'd both raise the child as their own. He'd rather have the child be half angel so they wouldn't have to deal with the idea of souls and death.

"Why are you frowning?" Jamie asked as she ran her hands up and down his stomach.

"Maybe I should wear a condom."

Hurt crossed her features as she took a step back.

"No, that's not what I mean. Hades, I want a baby with you. What about when the baby needs souls?"

Jamie shook her head. "That's something we'll deal with when it comes. The baby would be half djinn, so that might change how things work. We will raise our child so they have the values you have, Balin. Our baby will be good. Don't you understand that? We'll do all in our power to make sure they have a chance at life."

He nodded, liking the way she talked of their future. "We'll make sure they have a chance."

"Yes, now, please, don't leave me wanting."

Balin smiled and turned her to face the wall. "Place your hands on the wall and stick your ass out."

She looked over her shoulder, a coy smile on her face. "You're going to do this from behind?"

He growled and gripped her hips, letting his cock slide between her cheeks. "Hell, yeah. I'm going to fuck you hard while playing with your ass so you're ready for my cock when Ambrose and I have you between us." They'd talked of a true threesome that morning, and he knew she was on board, if not a little scared.

"Anything, just please."

He slowly slid into her heat, pausing to control himself. Hades, she fit like a glove. He pushed in until their bodies were flush against each other, his own body shaking.

Balin pulled out, loving the way she whimpered as he did so, then thrust in—hard. He pistoned into her, his cock throbbing as her pussy clenched around him. He let one hand run its way up her stomach to palm her breast. Her breaths ran ragged as he plucked and rolled her nipples.

With his other hand, he moved to flick her clit.

"Push your ass back, baby," he said on a breath so he could keep his rhythm. She did so, his cock going deeper than before.

He rubbed circles around her clit then pressed hard as he rolled her nipple. Her pussy fluttered around him, her body coming hard as she yelled his name.

Balin fought for control, trying not to come right with her as her pussy squeezed his cock.

"Hades, you feel good. I'm not done with you yet."

"Balin," she whispered as she came down from her high, but he wouldn't let her come down too far.

One hand went back to gripping her hips as the other took some of her juices so he could ready her back entrance. As he kept his pounding rhythm, he slowly entered his finger into her ass, her body tightening around him.

"Oh, God," she called out, and he stopped moving.

"Push out against me, baby. I won't let it hurt you."

She shook her head. "It doesn't hurt. You couldn't do that to me."

She pushed back, and he thrust his finger in and out, loving the way her walls tightened around his cock as he did so.

Slowly, he went back to a rhythm, removing his finger and replacing it with his thumb, loving the way her body blushed at his attention.

He moved at a steady pace, sweat rolling down his back as his balls clenched. He twisted his thumb as he pounded into her harder, and he came, his cum filling her as she came again.

Balin moved to take her hips in both hands, his cock still inside her as she rested against the wall.

"I love you, Jamie. No matter what happens, we'll make it work." He kissed her neck, nibbling where he'd bitten her that morning.

"You and Ambrose are it for me, Balin. We'll find a way."

Damn straight they would. He wouldn't let doubt take hold and ruin this. He knew the dangers weren't over. Their time of peace would only last so long.

CHAPTER 14

Jamie sliced the last of the chicken and added it to the hot oil. She might not have been as good a cook as Lily, but she could at least make a decent stir fry. Even though the amount she made now rivaled that of a small army considering how much her men ate.

Her men.

That had a nice ring to it.

She was still a little worried about people's reaction to a real life triad, but she was getting over it. She loved her men too much to let it be an issue. At least a big issue. She still had no idea how she was going to tell her family about Ambrose and Balin.

Or tell them—if she could—about the fact that she'd have to watch them grow old and die while she stayed the same.

She set the knife in the sink as her power flared, needing

to take action where none could be made. How was she supposed to watch her family die? She wasn't as close to them as she'd have liked to be, but she didn't want to see them fade away while she had a new purpose.

It wasn't fair.

Hands wrapped themselves around her middle, and she leaned back into Ambrose's hold, a tear running down her cheek.

"What's wrong?" he asked, his voice settling deep in her heart.

"Just thinking."

He turned her around to face him, his large hands framing her face. "What makes you sad, my Jamie?"

She swallowed hard, closing her eyes. "I'm going to live forever, Ambrose. How is that fair to my parents?"

He took a deep breath as his thumbs rubbed the tears from her cheeks. "I know it's not fair. We can only sit back and watch those we love age and fade from time but not from our memories. That is how they'll live in our hearts and minds. I've been talking with Dante and Shade about this, and we think you should be able to tell your parents about who we are if you choose to. Lily has chosen against it as she never sees or talks to her family. It will be easier for her to cut ties. That is not the case with you. If you want to tell your family about this so they know what to expect, you can."

Her heart warmed at his words. This would break the rules of their people, but it would keep her happy, so it would be worth it.

"I don't know, Ambrose. I'll have to think about that. Thank you for….just thank you."

He leaned down to kiss her then turned quickly to stir the chicken.

"Oh crap, I'm sorry. I got distracted."

Ambrose shrugged and wrapped his arm around her shoulders. "I was the one who turned you away from it. And it's not burned, just a little more brown on one side."

She took the wooden spoon from him, needing something in her hands as Balin walked in the room, leaning down to kiss her then doing the same to Ambrose. She loved watching the way the two men in her life found the path that worked well for them. She couldn't wait to see them make love again, showing each other how much they meant to one another.

"I heard the last part of what you were talking about and just know, Jamie, that I'll be by your side no matter what," Balin said as he leaned against the counter.

Jamie gave a small smile. "And that's all I need. I know it's not going to be easy, but we'll find a way."

As she dropped in the veggies, the hair on the back of her neck stood on end. The power deep within her flared, almost sending her to her knees.

"Ambrose?"

His grip on her hip tightened. "I felt it too."

She turned to see him grab a sword from his cache as Balin took a dagger from his side.

"What's going on?" she asked as she stood between her two warriors.

"Someone's coming," Ambrose said as he moved to stand in front of her. "Balin?"

"Demons," he growled, and fear slid through her.

Her body shook, and her djinn powers took over, her tattoos running up her arms as her body shifted.

Ambrose looked behind him and nodded. "You're stronger in that form, but if the need arises, you run. Do you understand me?"

"I don't want to leave you. I can fight."

Balin rolled his neck as he left the kitchen. "We don't want you hurt."

Damn it. She wasn't some weakling. Not anymore.

The glass window that had just been fixed shattered as three demons rolled into her home, their horns out of place in this human world. Balin roared and attacked first, leaving Ambrose to cover her as she stood in the kitchen with only a wooden spoon to fight with.

She watched as Balin slashed one demon in the neck with this dagger and Ambrose rushed to fight against another demon. These demons were stronger than the ones she'd seen them fight before.

Much stronger.

The third demon dodged a blow from Ambrose as her lover fought the second demon. With a gasp, she stepped back as the demon charged at her, a growl escaping his lips. Her power flared out, attacking him, but even as slices appeared on his skin as if she'd cut him, he moved forward intent in his gaze.

Ambrose turned, and the demon he'd been fighting

slashed at him with his claws, leaving a trail of blood in its wake.

"No!" she yelled as she ducked from the demon chasing her. The demon stormed toward her again, this time knocking her into the stove and onto the tile. The pan hit the floor, sending hot oil along her face and arms, as well as on the demon.

Her body burned as she screamed from the pain. The oils scalded her, weakening her. She scrambled up, biting down on her lip as the burns intensified.

She couldn't just stand down and let the demon win.

No, she was stronger than that.

She lashed out with her power again, this time sending the demon to his knees, blood spurting as he growled. She limped to the sink, still hearing the sounds of fighting behind her. The knife felt heavy in her hands as she gripped the handle and swung at the demon beside her. She used all the strength that came with her new powers and slid the blade into his neck, the skin parting like butter.

His claws lashed out again, this time raking down her side, but she moved through the pain, lodging the knife deeper in the demon's neck. He moved again, even though his blood poured out of him.

Jamie scrambled back, the burns on her skin searing her, and she hit a wall—no, a chest. She looked up, scared that it would be a demon, but she let out a breath at the sight of Balin's face. Ambrose came from around him, limping as he beheaded the demon right in her kitchen.

Her knees buckled as the pain hit her hard, the adrenaline quickly fading from her system.

"Fuck, Jamie, baby," Balin said as he looked over her body.

"He burned you?" Ambrose asked as he limped toward her, the slices on his side still bleeding.

"I'll be okay," she said through clenched teeth.

Balin shook his head and quickly picked her up. "I'm taking her to the bathroom to clean what I can."

Ambrose nodded. "I'll heal what I can as well."

Jamie shuddered. "What about you two?"

Balin growled as he set her on the bathroom counter. "We'll be fine. Just a few gashes and scrapes. Damn, baby, he got you good."

She trembled as she brought her palm to rest on his face. "Have Ambrose heal you as well."

"I will, Jamie," Ambrose said as he gently placed his hands on her burns, the pain excruciating. "First let me heal you."

Warmth spread through her at his touch. She felt the skin at her side stitch together—a really freaking odd sensation—and the burn start healing. The skin around where the oil had seared her skin began to itch, and she struggled not to fall into Ambrose's arms in relief.

"Who were those demons?" Jamie asked as the worst of the pain subsided.

Balin growled as he cleaned her off. "Some of my father's top men. That's why it took so long to take them down. Pyro must be fucking pissed if he sent them."

Jamie shuddered. "It's never over, is it?"

Balin framed her face, careful of the healing burns. "It will be soon. I can promise you that."

"Didn't you say you couldn't kill your father yourself because of Lucifer's curse?"

"Then I will kill him," Ambrose said as he pulled back. "Something I should have done long ago."

"You can't blame yourself for this," Balin said as he cleaned a bit of blood off Ambrose's cheek.

"Then you cannot do the same," her angel ordered.

Jamie rolled her shoulders, the pain not as great as it had been.

Balin sighed. "I can't believe we let you get hurt."

She narrowed her eyes. "Oh, no, you two don't get to act all alpha and blame yourselves. You said that those demons where higher-ups, and I saw that they were stronger than the others. You did all you could, and I didn't do too badly myself."

Ambrose ran a hand through her hair. "You fought bravely. And starting tomorrow I will teach you how to fight like a warrior."

She heard the honesty in his tone so she didn't have to kick him for placating her.

"I'm going to call Dante to help us clean this up," Balin said as he pulled back, not kissing her like she'd hoped.

Maybe he was just worried and wasn't really pulling back like he seemed. Without another word, he walked out of the bathroom, leaving her hurt and alone with Ambrose.

"What was that?" she asked as she leaned into him. She'd

already had to deal with Ambrose leaving her before. She didn't want to deal with the pain of Balin doing the same.

"He just needs space to think."

"We can't let him wallow on his own, Ambrose. That doesn't do anyone any good."

He kissed her temple then went to turn on the shower. "I know, Jamie mine. I know."

She couldn't let Balin wall himself up and take on the guilt of his father's actions.

Pyro screamed as the report of his demons' failure reached his ears. He'd sent the best of his men to deal with the problem, and they'd failed. Their deaths didn't matter to him, but the fact that they hadn't even taken *one* of the fucking triad down pissed him off.

He stomped to his desk and threw a large, metal paperweight against the wall. The resounding crash did little to soothe his anger. He needed to kill something. Or, at least, make it feel pain.

Damn Lucifer's curse. He couldn't fucking kill his own son because Lucifer had been an asshole. Now, Pyro had to sit back and watch others fail to kill the demon who didn't even deserve the title of demon.

Balin should be dead.

That fucking Ambrose deserved it just as much.

Pyro ran his hand down the scar the warrior angel had given him all those years ago and cursed. Ambrose deserved to pay for what he'd done. Instead, he was free to roam with his newfound mates, happiness leaking from the bastard's pores.

Soon it would be blood.

It wasn't as if Pyro didn't have a back-up plan.

He'd already sent the note to Kobal that would start things in motion. He knew the djinn leader wouldn't want Jamie to live. And with Pyro's help, Kobal would take out that newly-djinn whore. Of course, her men would fight to protect her, leading to their deaths.

Pyro would be able to take on Ambrose while he would let Kobal take on Balin.

The djinn whore would die as well.

It was really too bad about his demons, but Pyro was a planner and would not let his son live.

He'd waited long enough for the bastard to die.

It was time.

WITH THE FINAL STRIKE OF THE HAMMER, AMBROSE HAD THE board in place over where the window had once been. This was the second time that he'd had to watch the glass in Jamie's window cease to exist, and he didn't think he could take a third.

It wasn't so much the glass, as what it represented.

They weren't safe.

Not here, not at his home in the angelic realm. Not anywhere.

Not with Pyro still alive.

He would have taken Jamie to his home high up in the skies, but that would mean he'd have to leave Balin behind —something he would never do. He might not know his other lover as well as he did Jamie, but that would change with time. Balin was just as much his mate as Jamie was—a fact that wrapped itself around his heart like fate's caress.

Ambrose still hadn't told the council he had mated a djinn *and* a demon. He knew they would rejoice in Jamie as they had when Shade had met his Lily, but Balin would be another issue.

Ambrose wasn't sure there were any matings between an angel and a demon. At least not to his recollection. Considering he'd been alive for eons, that was saying something.

If he had to give up his sword and lose his title, he would. He'd fought for his people for thousands of years and had given and lost everything in the process. He couldn't let the council govern his life beyond that.

Not anymore.

If they didn't approve of a demon entering their world, they could block Balin from their realm. Meaning their triad would be forced to stay with the humans for eternity.

Sadness swept over him at the thought. He loved his home, his people. He wanted to fly his mates within the clouds, watch their faces as he showed them the caverns and structures that had been erected before his time.

He wanted to show them the history and beauty of the angels.

He didn't know if that was possible.

So, for now, he would stay with the humans and with his mates.

He couldn't go down to hell, not again, and risk another war. Meaning he'd have to wait for Pyro to come to him. How long would that take? How many people would be injured or die in the process?

What cause was worth his own life?

There had to be something that could be done to prevent war and loss.

What?

He let out a breath as he walked back into the house. As a warrior, he'd asked himself that question thousands of times and had yet to find an answer.

Maybe there wasn't one.

Maybe one just drifted from fight to fight, barely being able to hold onto the precious moments of peace and love in between.

"What put that frown on your face?" Jamie asked as she walked up to him, her body sweaty from her work out and training session.

This is what he'd been missing all these years—someone to come home to. Someone to love him for who he was and stay by his side. Now that he had two of them, he wasn't going to let them go, not for any price.

She set the book down and came to him, wrapping her arms around his waist, her soft body molding to his. With Balin at Dante's, meeting to talk about things they'd missed over time, he and Jamie were alone for the first time.

Something that he'd love to take advantage of.

"Why did Balin leave?" she whispered. "And don't tell me it's so he can catch up with Dante. He barely even talked to us before he left. What's going on with him?"

Ambrose's arms tightened at her words. He'd hoped she hadn't noticed the distance Balin had put between them and himself, but he knew Jamie was more observant than that.

"And don't give me that silent act you've perfected. I know he's putting up a wall, but I don't know why."

He kissed her temple, letting her scent wash over him. "I think he feels responsible for the demons coming here and trying to hurt you—for actually *hurting* you. Even though Pyro did all of this to hurt *me.* "

Jamie pulled back, her eyes wide before they narrowed in anger. "Seriously? He's going to blame himself for his dad's decisions? He's spent his whole life making sure everyone knew he wasn't his father and now he's taking on his father's guilt? It doesn't make any sense."

"He can still feel guilt over his father's transgressions—even if it's misplaced."

"Well, that's just stupid. We'll have to make sure he knows we don't blame him." She pulled back and paced the living room, anger and sadness radiating from her. "He doesn't get to pull away from me like you did."

He winced as the shot hit home.

She turned, regret on her face. "I'm sorry. I didn't mean it like that."

"Yes, you did. I deserved it."

She shrugged as she wrapped her arms around herself. "I still don't know why you left for a year. Yes, I know that you stayed for so long because of the council, but you didn't have to cut ties completely. You didn't have to make me feel like nothing."

Pain sliced at him at what an unworthy angel he was, almost sending him to his knees. He'd hurt her because he'd been a coward—nothing more, nothing less.

He didn't deserve her.

Didn't deserve Balin.

He wouldn't run. He'd prove he *could* be worthy.

Ambrose walked the small distance between them and fell to his knees, needing to be near her but not tower over her.

"I was a coward. Nothing. I wasn't worthy of you," he said as the words in his mind tumbled and thrashed. "I'm still not, but I'll prove myself. I left because I couldn't stand to lose another person in my life. I was scared."

He was an angelic warrior and would never admit to the fear coursing through his veins…but this was Jamie.

She was *his*.

She ran her hand through his hair, and he leaned into her touch.

"You've said that before, Ambrose. You're not a coward. I want to move on though. I don't want to talk about the choices we made, just the ones we're going to make. I want to know more about you, about Balin. I want to know what our futures will hold and how we'll survive together. I don't want to look back. Not anymore."

He leaned forward, kissing her belly, wrapping his arms around her waist. "Our future will be ripe with anything you desire, anything you need. All you have to do is ask."

She gave a shaky laugh, and he looked up at her torn expression. "I just want us to be happy. I want Balin to come back and not feel guilty. I want you to not feel it as well. I just want us to live our lives while I try to figure out how to live with two men." She grinned at that last part, and Ambrose shook his head.

"We can do that." He stood, keeping her in his hold. "I've noticed we're alone at the moment, and I don't think I've had you just to myself."

Her eyes narrowed. "You aren't jealous, are you? Because you don't get to be jealous of sharing me with Balin. We're a team."

He leaned down to take her lips, loving the way she moaned into him. "I'm not jealous. I'm just pointing out that I can have you alone for a moment. I want to share you with our demon, but I also want you under me, just me—and I know Balin wants the same."

She nodded, understanding in her gaze. "And the two of you will want to be alone."

He smiled. "Yes, we're not just a triad, but three couplings."

"It sounds very complicated," she teased as she ran her hands up his shirt, her skin soft, delicate.

"I'll make it easy for you," he whispered as he slowly slid up her dress, his hand gripping her ass. "I'm going to love you, fill you, and make you quiver. Then later, we'll do the same to Balin. How does that sound?"

She nodded, and he pulled the dress over her head. She stood in her panties and bra, barefoot and perfect.

He nibbled up her neck, her taste settling on his tongue as her hands roamed his back. He pulled away to let her take off his shirt.

He cupped her breasts, her nipples stiffening through her bra.

"I want you, Jamie. All of you." He crushed his mouth to hers, their bodies moving together toward the couch.

He pulled away and turned her around so she faced away from him, her perfect bottom ready for his hands.

"Put your hands against the couch," he ordered.

"What is it with you two and taking me from behind?" she said as she wiggled her ass.

He spanked her hard, and she gasped. "Balin told me you liked that, and I wanted to see. If you think we're doing too much of the same thing, I'm sure I can change that."

He quickly shucked his pants and stripped her of her bra and panties, leaving them both naked and panting.

"I'm going to let you ride me, Jamie-mine. How does that sound?"

She smiled as he sat down and she straddled him. He held her hips steady as she tried to slide over him, not wanting to take her just yet.

She looked like a goddess, *his* goddess.

"What's wrong?" she asked, her breasts heaving as she panted, wanting.

He slid one hand up between her breasts and collared her throat. Her eyes darkened, and he smiled.

"I want to make sure you're ready for me," he whispered, letting his hand fall back down to her pussy. He circled her clit, loving the way she rocked into him, her mound brushing up against his cock.

He slowly traced his fingers over her, letting them tease and pet. When he slowly slid two fingers within her and twisted to rub her in that place she loved so much, her body shook.

"Please, Ambrose, I want to come on you, not without you."

His cock throbbed at her words, wanted her more than ever.

He slowly removed his fingers and brought them to his lips, tasting her sweet juices.

"Gods, you taste amazing."

She blushed, her breasts going pink at his words.

"You don't like it when I talk dirty?" he asked, teasing.

"I love it. It's just different coming from you," she whispered. "You're usually so stoic."

He slowly lifted her up and then down his cock, one inch at a time. Her eyes widened as her pussy clenched around him.

"I'm yours, Jamie." He said, needing control. "You're mine. I want you to know the thoughts in my head as I take you. I want you to know *who* is taking you."

He let her slide down a bit more until finally—*finally*—he was fully seated within her, her heat pressing around him on all sides, ready to milk him at just one thrust.

"I know it's you, Ambrose." She tried to rock, and his

grip on her hips tightened, stopping her. "Please," she begged.

Unable to deny her, he lifted her slightly so he could thrust into her, hard, fast, with everything they both needed.

She threw her head back, pushing her breasts closer to his lips. Giving into temptation, he sucked one nipple into his mouth. She moaned and tried to move.

"Please, Ambrose. You said I could ride you," she said as she panted.

He pulled back, letting her breast go with a *pop*. "So I did."

He stilled his hips and let her move. And, God, did she move. She rolled her hips, letting her body take him in deeper, then moved up and down, resting her hands on his shoulders. He rested his hands on her hips, their gazes meeting.

His Jamie rode him hard like the goddess she was, their magic mingling, their bond flaring in a tangle of desire, lust, and promise. And, when they came together, hard, and inviting, she rested her head on his, their chests rising and falling as one.

He'd almost missed this.

He wouldn't let her go again.

She was his, and he intended to keep it that way.

No matter the obstacle.

CHAPTER 15

Balin stepped out of the shower and dried himself off. He'd purposely waited to take one until Jamie left to go help Lily with a baby thing so he wouldn't be tempted to bring his mate in with him.

He closed his eyes with a groan.

Really? This was how he was going to handle it?

Hide from his mates and refuse to touch either of them?

He knew it made no sense to them, and it really didn't to him either. He didn't have a choice.

He'd almost lost both of them because his father wanted him dead. Not only dead, but broken and beaten from everything imaginable until he begged for death. Pyro would take away his mates and force him to watch—that was the type of sadistic bastard his father was.

Well, there was no way Balin would let that happen.

He knew he was cutting himself off at the neck, but

there wasn't any other choice. Ambrose and Jamie were more important than anything in his world, anything he could ever hope to have.

He pulled on his jeans and ran a hand through his wet hair. He missed his horns, but he wasn't about to wear them on this plane. Since he wasn't used to hiding because he'd always been in the hell realm, he'd probably forget to pull them back and scare the poor unsuspecting neighbors. As it was, they probably thought Jamie was crazy with two men staying with her and the sound of broken glass reaching their ears every few months.

If he stayed, they'd have to move to a home hidden in the forest or in another realm that would accept them. That way they could be themselves.

That was a big *if* though.

Balin shook his head and walked out of the bedroom. He knew the choices he was about to make would only hurt the ones he loved, but he'd rather them be hurt than dead.

Ambrose stood in the living room, his broad back shirtless. His wings slid back into the slits where they hid in the human realm.

Balin's gaze trailed down his muscular lover's body, his legs encased in jeans that were just snug enough in the thighs that Balin had to adjust himself. As Ambrose turned to him, Balin noticed that the top button was undone, showing that blond happy trail that Balin wanted to lick with his tongue.

Hades, walking away was going to be harder than he thought. He loved the way Ambrose looked—strong and protective—compared to the way their Jamie looked. While she was soft, yet deceptively tough, Ambrose was steel-encased fragility.

His gaze followed his lover's thick chest, defined by an ageless amount of strength and battle. His hair was out of its band, falling to his shoulders as his head tilted to the side, confusion on his beautifully chiseled face.

"What's wrong?" Ambrose asked as he stood there, his hands on his hips.

Images of just what Balin wanted to do with those hips, along with just about everything else on this man, filled his mind. He might have preferred women, but he wanted Ambrose in every way possible.

No.

He had to remain strong and pull back. It wouldn't hurt as much if he didn't touch his mates.

Hades, who was he kidding? It was going to hurt like hell no matter what he did, but at least this way, they would be alive.

"Balin?"

He blinked as Ambrose took a step toward him, a frown on his face.

"I'm fine," he said, his voice low.

"No, you're not. Jamie and I have noticed it, Balin. You can't hide from us, no matter how hard you try. Why are you pulling back?"

Balin swallowed, not liking the way they saw right through him, even before he'd actually left.

"I don't know what you're talking about," he lied.

Ambrose fisted his hands and stalked toward him, danger seeping from his warrior's pores. "Really? You don't know what I'm talking about? Let's see, you've shut yourself off from me. You don't look at me, except right now it appears your cock likes me. I can see the way it's pushing at your zipper, is it because I have my shirt off?"

Balin's cock pushed harder against his jeans at Ambrose's words. He opened his mouth to speak, but Ambrose cut him off.

"Let's not forget that you've pulled away from Jamie as well. You don't look at her; you don't speak unless you're spoken to. You purposely spend your days with Dante, even though you haven't seen the dragon in over a hundred years. You're hiding from us—hiding from her. Don't you see you're hurting our mate? She's our true half. Don't you get that? With each step backwards you take, it's another slice to her heart…another slice to mine."

"Ambrose…" His throat constricted at the pain he'd caused.

"No, I don't know if I want to hear it. I get that you're scared."

"I'm not scared," he lied again.

Ambrose moved to stand right in front of him, their similar heights bringing them to eye level. "Don't fucking lie to me. I might have been able to get over the fact that you're killing me with each decision to pull back, but I won't forgive you for hurting Jamie."

"You hurt her first," he said, lashing out like a child, unable to take the anguish in his angel's eyes.

Pain crossed Ambrose's face, and Balin immediately regretted his callous words.

"You're right. I did. And, no matter what I do, I will never earn the forgiveness I don't deserve. Right now, I'm standing by her while you're pulling back. Is it because you're afraid of Pyro? You know that no matter what you do, Pyro won't stop. He doesn't want to hurt Jamie and me just because of you. You remember that I'm the one who scarred him. I'm the reason he took Jamie in the first place. This isn't just about you, so stop being so selfish and stand by our sides. We can't lose if we stick together."

Ambrose cupped Balin's cheek and leaned in to brush his lips across his, soft, tentative.

This man.

This angel.

This mate was the one to break him.

Hades, he was fucking stupid.

"I don't want to lose you or Jamie," he whispered, his breath mingling with his angel's.

"It's not going to happen. By blocking yourself from us, you're just making us all more vulnerable. Don't you understand that? We're stronger as a team, not as a fragment of what could have been."

Balin leaned forward, his forehead resting on Ambrose's cheek. "I'm an idiot."

"Yes, yes you are. We've all been one at some point in our lives. I was one when I tried to save Jamie from a life with a warrior—when I tried to save myself from a potential heartache because it was all I knew. Now it's your turn."

Balin looked up, and reached around to set his hands on his lover's hips—right where he'd wanted them before.

Ambrose quirked his lips and ran his hands down Balin's back. "You're going to have to make it up to us and promise never to leave our sides because you're scared. You will come to us if that ever happens again. Jamie and I will stand by your side and be with you no matter what."

Shivers ran down his spine as Ambrose continued to caress, touch. He'd made love with his angel once before with Jamie watching, but now it would be just the two of them—of that he was sure.

He leaned in and took Ambrose's lips, wanting, needed. He tasted of coffee, musk, and male—a heady combination.

He pulled back but kept his hands on his lover's hips. "I'm sorry."

Ambrose ran a hand up Balin's back, collaring his neck. "I know. Just don't do it again, okay?"

"We're all alone for a bit. Jamie will be home later and then we're going to meet the djinn delegation."

Ambrose froze as tension radiated from them both. "I had tried to forget that. I don't like the way they summoned her."

They'd received a missive the day before that told them they were to meet on the djinn plane so Jamie could be set before their council. Though they'd tried to prepare Jamie for it, both men had been, and still were, worried about the tone of the missive. Even though Lily had been accepted by the brownies and had found a new family with them, it didn't mean it would be the same for Jamie or any of the other women in their group.

As it was, djinn were some of the most secretive supernaturals out there and were a dying breed, much like many of the other supernaturals who only wanted to mate with other true bloods.

Considering Jamie was not truly of their blood…

The potential deadly outcome wasn't something any of them wanted to think about but one they needed to prepare for.

"It wasn't as if we could hide what she was considering she showed her true nature in the middle of the demon games."

Ambrose ran his hands down Balin's sides and pulled him closer so their jean-clad cocks rubbed together, eliciting a moan from both men's throats.

"We won't let her out of our sights, and you'll be by our side," Ambrose said as he leaned in to nibble at Balin's jaw.

Balin tipped his head back, letting the angel taste and lick. "I won't leave. Right now, all I want to do is show you just how much I want you."

He pulled the other man closer and crushed his mouth to his, letting their tongues tangle, their chests heaving as he kissed him with all his strength. He ran his hands down Ambrose's back and gripped his ass, rocking his own erection into his lover's.

Balin pulled back and leaned to whisper into Ambrose's ear, biting down hard on the angel's ear lobe before he did so. "I'm going to fill you up and fuck you against that wall behind you. You've already had me and Jamie wrapped around that cock of yours, I think it's my turn."

Ambrose chuckled. "Taking turns, are we?"

Balin grinned. "Damn straight. But, first, I want to make sure you're ready."

Ambrose lifted a brow. "Oh, really? And how are you going to do that?"

Balin got to his knees, and Ambrose laughed.

"Oh, I see. That's how you're going to do it."

"Hey, don't knock it. Of course, if you'd rather me not suck you down my throat, just let me know and I'll get up."

Ambrose tangled his fingers in Balin's hair. "I think I can stand a bit longer," his angel teased.

Balin smiled and slowly slid down Ambrose's zipper, knowing full well his lover didn't wear underwear—much like himself.

He pulled down Ambrose's jeans so they were just under his ass, his thick cock standing straight out, ready for Balin's tongue.

Greedily, he licked the small drop of precum at the tip then fisted him.

Ambrose groaned, and Balin watched as he let his head fall back, his fingers still in Balin's hair. Balin swallowed the head, squeezing Ambrose at the base of his cock, then licked his way down the length of him.

He sucked, licked, hollowed his mouth, taking as much of him as he could. The tip of his cock reached the back of his throat, and he tightened his grip.

Ambrose did the same, tightening the grip on Balin's

head, keeping Balin steady before he thrust his hips so he fucked his mouth—hard.

"I can't do this with Jamie. I don't want to hurt her because she's so tiny. You can take me, can't you?"

He pistoned his hips into Balin's mouth as Balin looked up, greedily sucking up as much as he could.

Ambrose ran a finger down Balin's check then cupped his jaw. Balin rolled Ambrose's balls in his hand and sucked with all his power until Ambrose shouted and came on his tongue, the salty taste unlike anything Balin had ever known.

Balin swallowed it all, not letting one drop get away from him, then pulled away, a smile on his face.

"Face the wall," he said as he stood.

Ambrose's eyes darkened even more and his angel kicked off his jeans before doing what he'd been told.

Fuck, that was hot.

Balin quickly shucked his pants and fisted his cock, already ready to pop at just the sight of his lover's muscled back and fucking-hot ass.

He couldn't wait to take it.

"What is it with you and walls?" Ambrose asked. "You've already taken Jamie against one a few times."

Balin gave a deep chuckle and softly cupped his lover's ass. "There's nothing like the feeling of sliding into someone as they're pressed up against a wall, helpless to our desires."

He slid his finger along the crease of Ambrose's ass and froze. "Fuck, I need to go get the lube. I don't want to hurt you."

Ambrose shook his head. "Check my pockets."

Balin laughed and pulled out a small bottle. "So, you just carry this stuff around for emergencies now?"

Ambrose laughed with him. "No, I had planned to fuck you out of your mood if words didn't work."

"Yet it looks like I'm about to fuck you."

"I don't care, just get it done please," Ambrose said, his voice breathless.

"You sound like you want it over," Balin teased as he inserted one lubed finger and rubbed that tiny bundle of nerves that made his lover's knees weak—and pretty much did the same to him.

"Dear Lord, I like that," Ambrose whispered and moved his hips to take Balin in.

"Good. You're going to love the feel of my cock."

Ambrose nodded. "I just want you, you know. I know it's crazy since neither of us have wanted men for more than just a passing glance in the past. It's different with you."

Balin let out a breath, feeling the same. He worked Ambrose's hole, with one then two fingers, loving the way his angel shuddered.

"I know," he answered as he pressed the head of his cock against Ambrose's opening. "It's just the three of us, nothing more, nothing less. I was a fucking idiot for trying to throw that away."

"Don't think about that, just think about what you're doing," Ambrose whispered.

Slowly, oh so slowly, he slid past the tight ring of

muscles and stopped. Hades, his angel gripped him tighter than a glove.

"Push out," he said as he moved his hips in shallow thrusts. Ambrose did as he was told, and Balin slid home.

"Hell," they both groaned at the same time, their bodies frozen in place, their legs flush against the other's as Balin stayed still so Ambrose could adjust.

"Move," Ambrose said, his voice low, needy.

"Anything, my love," he whispered, meaning the word more than ever before. He'd never felt so close to Ambrose, not like this. He knew the man's history, his hopes, his dreams, and so much more that made him love the angel. It was this closeness, this giving up and releasing the control that made Balin want to scream in happiness. That this man, this warrior, would relinquish all control and let Balin lead made him feel as though he were on top of the world and there was nothing that could break them.

He'd be damned if he'd let the doubts and fears that had plagued him before ruin this. Not ever. Not again.

Balin pulled almost all the way out then slammed back home, eliciting the trembling and groans of a man in love. He thrust in and out, harder and harder as Ambrose's hands fisted against the walls.

"Make yourself come," Balin ordered. "Take yourself in hand and come when I do." Balin's fingers dug into Ambrose's hips as his lover did so.

That telltale tingling wrapped up his spine and clenched in his balls as he came, shouting Ambrose's name as his angel came against the wall with a groan.

Balin rested his head on his lover's sweat-slicked back and smiled. "We're going to have to do that again."

Ambrose chuckled. "Anytime. You just have to *be* here for it to happen."

Ashamed, but still in the haze of bliss, he kissed Ambrose's back and smiled. "I'm not going anywhere."

And, with that decision firmly in place, it meant the death of Pyro.

Good.

SHE WAS PRETTY SURE SHE'D ALREADY SWEATED THROUGH HER dress and she'd just changed, but Jamie didn't have time to go back and put on another one. No, no matter what she did, she couldn't get out of this.

This being a summons from the Djinn council.

Apparently, there was no way out if it. It wasn't as if she could have prepared for it either. After all, not even Ambrose had been invited to the djinn realm, meaning they had no idea what they were up against. She had a feeling it wouldn't be all unicorns and rainbows like Lily's experience with the brownies had been.

Yes, her friend had been hurt in the process of finding Shade and having her true heritage revealed, but that was a far cry from how Jamie's transformation had been. She'd already been sent to hell, forced to complete the bond when they weren't ready, and broken open her life, transforming it into a new one where she still couldn't quite gain her footing.

Not that she didn't love her men—she did—but she would have rather gone in gradually than cannon balled into a triad relationship rife with emotions, tender feelings, and way too much politics considering there were three councils to deal with.

They hadn't even begun to deal with Ambrose's council and the fact that he'd mated a demon—though Ambrose said he didn't care.

That was a problem for another day.

No, today was all about Jamie's new powers and the fact that the djinn wanted her to face them. She would have just gone with it and hoped for the best, but her men couldn't hide their tension. Though she knew they tried, they just weren't very good at it when it came to her.

"We'll take care of you," Balin said as he reached up from the backseat to run a hand down her arm. She sat in the passenger seat as Ambrose drove to the edge of the city where they could pass through the wards into the djinn realm. She still didn't fully understand how things worked with the different realms, but she knew that, unless they were actually *part* of a certain realm, they had to find portals and entrances into the new place, rather than just open a seam and enter where they wanted like Ambrose could with the angels and Balin could with hell, once he'd regained his energy.

Maybe in the future she could do the same with the djinn—if they even let her in to begin with.

"You know, if you two keep saying you'll take care of me, it'll just make me more nervous," she said as she cracked her fingers, just trying to do *something*. "If it wasn't going to be an issue, then you two wouldn't be acting as protective as you are."

Ambrose shook his head. "We're always going to be protective. That's the price you pay when you mate with two warriors."

Jamie let out a breath, hiding back a smile. "You two are going to be a pain about everything, aren't you?"

Balin laughed, easing some of the tension out of her stiff body. "Yes, but that's why you love us."

"Sure."

Ambrose pulled over to the side of the road and shut off the engine. "We're here. I can feel the portal."

Tingles fluttered over her skin as she opened the door and neared the place where Ambrose pointed, though she wouldn't have needed him to do so. She felt the call of it in her blood, bringing her closer.

Ambrose settled his arm around her waist and pulled her close. "Your people may be in there, but we're yours as well."

She nodded and leaned into him, placing her hand into Balin's as she did so.

As if someone had lifted a curtain, she felt the pull toward the other realm deep in her bones.

"Come," a voice said from beyond the veil. "Your presence is required."

Well, not the most welcome of welcomes. That didn't seem to bode well for the rest of the "visit."

Ambrose moved to take her hand and led them in. Warmth spread over her like hot cocoa on a winter afternoon as she made her way into the djinn realm. When they passed the barrier, she gasped.

Brightness.

Such brightness.

It wasn't like earth, or the human realm, or whatever people called it, not by far. They were still in a forest, but the trees seemed brighter, and an aura resembling the one that had surrounded her before surrounded them now. In the distance, she saw a city of bright lights and tall, white structures. It was something out of a fantasy novel, with diamonds and other crystals twinkling in sunlight that seemed too bright for her eyes.

Standing before them was a group of about twenty or so djinn, their eyes sparkling violet, their auras shimmering along their glowing skin and tattoos.

She'd chosen to remain in her human form before they crossed, and now she felt as though that had been a mistake. Closing her eyes for courage, she shed her human image and became djinn, her skin tingling as she did so.

The soft caress of wings against her side told her that Ambrose had let his wings out, though she hadn't seen him take off his shirt to do so. She turned to the side, and yes, her angel was shirtless in all his glory, looking like the proud warrior he was. She looked the other way at Balin to find his black eyes speckled with red and his horns curled back, mingling with his hair.

This was the three of them in their true forms.

She surely wasn't in Kansas anymore.

The other djinn looked at her men in disgust before turning toward the closest structure, one with a tall steeple that seemed to reach toward the gods in an almost regal fashion. To her, it brought to mind a prison, and she didn't know why.

This wasn't going to end well.

Not knowing what else to do, she followed the other djinn into the building, her men flanking her, their wariness entwining with her own.

The inside of the building was even more grand and opulent than what she'd imagined. Large diamond chandeliers hung from the ceilings, and art pieces hung from the walls. Everything was glass, crystal, diamond, and white.

For some reason the vision of blood spilling across it made her want to shudder. Not a real vision, just the idea that blood would look so stark against it scared her.

She didn't know why she thought it, but the idea scared her more than the depths of hell. Where the demons could be evil and deadly, their malice wasn't secret. For some reason, she was more afraid of the cool and precise djinn.

These were her people?

No, she wanted Ambrose, Balin, and her friends at home.

She didn't want to be here.

With one look at the council leader—or whoever it was

who stood before her on the dais—she knew that wouldn't be an option.

"I see the rumors are true and you've turned…djinn," the leader said, his voice layered with disdain.

Ambrose stiffened ever so slightly next to her, and she held her breath.

"You are not really djinn though, are you?" the man asked. "No, you're an abomination. A *nothing*."

Frozen, she couldn't speak. The danger and threat underlying his words made her want to flee, not fight, and that angered her more than anything he could say.

She was not weak.

Not ever again.

"I am the leader of the djinn," the man continued. "If you were truly one of my people, you would know my name is Kobal and that I could tear you limb from limb. You don't know that. You're just a copy of what was once a beautiful people. The gods deemed you worthy of our blood? Well, I disagree. You are nothing. You. Are. Not. Djinn."

With each word, his voice rose, the crystals in the walls vibrating with his fury.

"I'm djinn because that's what the gods declared," she said, surprising herself with her words. "I might not have been born of your people, but I am not nothing. I'm more than you think."

Kobal glared at her, his lips twisted in a snarl. "You think to speak to me, girl? You're lucky I don't kill you where you stand."

"Watch how you speak to my true half," Ambrose

warned, his voice low but carrying the threat of ages of war and battle.

Her power flared, her aura wrapping itself protectively around her men. Out of the corner of her eye, she saw Balin grip the edge of his dagger, ready to fight at a moment's notice.

This wasn't how she wanted to meet the people who she'd thought could be hers.

This wasn't like Lily and the brownies.

No, this meant death.

She wouldn't go down without fighting though. She wasn't that bookstore owner anymore.

No, she was stronger than that.

"You are the mightiest of angelic warriors, Ambrose the White," Kobal drawled. "You are not one of us. *She* is not one of us," he said as he pointed to her. "We are the djinn of pure blood. As the leader of my people, I sentence this abomination to death. All who stand in our way will perish by her side."

Jamie gasped. What the hell? She'd been there all of two minutes and they'd already called out her death? She'd lasted longer in hell.

If this was the way the paranormals wanted her, she wasn't sure she wanted them.

Balin growled by her side as Ambrose took out his sword.

"You cannot hurt my true half," her angel said. "You have an accord with the angels. Do you really want to start a war over something you cannot win? Your people are dying, and my men can wipe you out with just their swift blades. Let us leave your realm and we won't return. Be warned, once you step foot in the human realm with the intention to harm my true half, it will be war."

Pride filled her at Ambrose's words, and she prayed the djinn would listen. She looked around at the others in the room and couldn't find a friendly face among them, but neither did she see the hatred that she saw on Kobal's.

"Let them go, Kobal," a woman said from the crowd. "You know your views are as archaic as you are."

"Temperance," Kobal warned, "watch your tongue."

"No, I will not. You are only on that throne because we allow you to be there. Let this girl go with her men and she won't be a problem. We can deal with your attitude later, but we cannot let you start a war because of your prejudice."

Kobal growled, and Jamie wanted to weep at the woman's feet. At least not everyone wanted her dead. That seemed to be a step in the right direction.

Kobal sneered and threw up his hands. "I do not want war nor do I want this abomination in my sight."

This man made no sense considering he'd been the one to summon *her*, but whatever. She just wanted to leave—now.

"We'll leave," Ambrose said as he walked backward to the doors, pulling Jamie with him. Balin turned to face the others, keeping her between her two men, protected.

"I will find a way," Kobal threatened as they left the sterile building.

Balin practically carried her to the edge of the forest and

through the portal, and Ambrose followed them, Kobal's threat lingering in the air.

"I don't trust that man," Balin said as he slid her into the car, looking over his shoulder.

Ambrose cursed under his breath and got in as well, starting the car and kicking up gravel as he sped out of the spot. "I don't either. We didn't have a choice in making an appearance. At least we know their true colors."

Jamie gulped, her anger rising. Screw tears. It looked as if she wouldn't have that new family she wanted. No, they hated her. As she looked at her two men, she felt at least a little at ease.

There was no way to know what the djinn and Kobal or the demons and Pyro would do, but they'd make it.

They had to.

CHAPTER 16

"I need another drink," Jamie said as she closed her eyes, letting the music in Dante's Circle and the lull of her friends' conversation wash over her. The weight on her shoulders lifted ever so slightly with each sip of her drink. It wasn't the healthiest way to deal with her problems, but after the time she'd had recently, it didn't seem like it would hurt.

It was better than hiding in a corner and weeping because that sounded like a grand idea to her. Everything was just too much. Had it really only been a little over a year since she and her friends had been struck by lightning and set on a new course, a new destiny?

Lily had already found her path in life and was relishing it. The others were all in various stages of shock and acceptance—or apathy. And, here Jamie was, with two men and a new life.

She'd already been to hell, run for her life in the demon games, and bonded to two men who cared for her more than she'd ever thought possible. Yes, Pyro and Fury most likely still wanted to kill her—okay, *really* wanted to kill her—but they'd had a plan to get through that. At least the makings of one. She would have been just fine eventually.

Then she'd met her people—or at least the people who *could* have been hers.

Jamie hadn't had any grand ideas of open arms and a place in their society, not like what had happened with Lily, but she hadn't dreamed of the open hostility and death threats. Why couldn't there be a happy medium? Somewhere between roasting marshmallows on an open fire and roasting on a spit over said fire.

Jamie held back a snort and drained the last of her drink.

"I think you've had enough," Faith said as she stared off into the distance. All her friends had been especially subdued after Jamie had told them about her story with the djinn. It also didn't help that this was their first time meeting at the bar after Becca's attack.

Jamie glanced at her redheaded friend and gave a small smile. Of all of them, Becca seemed the most together and acted as though she wasn't worried about going outside alone again. It had to be a façade though considering Jamie knew her friend better than that.

By the way Hunter and Becca kept avoiding each other's eyes, Jamie thought her friend had another secret to tell.

As in finding her true half...

That wasn't Jamie's business.

She'd already resigned herself to staying out of Nadie's and Dante's way and now she'd do the same with Becca and Hunter—if there was anything there.

Jamie looked between her two men seated on either side of her and let out a breath. Yes, she could wish the best for her friends, but for right now, she wanted to sink into her men's embraces and never leave.

Call her selfish, but she'd had a bad week, month, and year. It was her turn to try and be happy.

"Wait, why can't I have another drink?" she asked Faith as her friend's words finally registered.

Faith shrugged as Amara, seated next to her, rolled her eyes.

"We've all decided to have just one drink so we don't wallow in our sorrows and all the changes around here," Amara explained as she played with her water.

Jamie let out a laugh. "Okay, if that's what you think is best. It *has* been a shitty week."

"Tell me about it," Eliana said as she nibbled on a pretzel.

"Well, aren't we just the happiest group of girls ever?" Lily said, her voice as dry as the pretzels on the table.

The hair on Jamie's arms rose as her stomach clenched.

Something was wrong.

She looked around at her friends, but only Hunter, Lily, Shade, Ambrose, and Balin—the ones with magic—seemed to be aware something had changed.

"What is that?" Lily asked as she placed her palm over her gently rounded belly.

"I don't know," Jamie whispered as she slowly stood up, the men at the table doing the same.

"What's going on?" Faith asked, tension in her tone. "What are you guys feeling that we can't?"

"I don't know," Jamie repeated, her voice low. "Something's just off."

Lightning flashed outside the bar's windows, and Jamie gasped while a few of her friends screamed.

"It's just a storm," Nadie whispered, her underlying terror not masked even in the slightest.

"That's not a normal storm," Dante whispered as he walked from the back, his fists clenched at his sides. He turned to the customers who weren't part of their group and gestured. "It looks like it's going to be a bad one soon. You guys better head home."

People nodded, fear rising so thick in the air Jamie could practically taste it, and left Dante's after throwing cash on the table. From the way the dragon looked, she was pretty sure he didn't care about money at the moment.

"Shouldn't we be going with them?" Faith asked as she put on her jacket, some of the others doing the same.

"No," Ambrose said as he pulled out a sword from his cache.

"Really?" Eliana asked, her face pale. "A sword? What the hell is going on?"

Balin pulled Jamie to his side and kissed her temple. "I don't know what the last storm was like, but this one doesn't feel right. I don't think it's nature's choice."

Jamie wrapped her arms around Balin's middle,

breathing in his scent. "I didn't have the same senses before, so I don't know if it's different from then, but it doesn't feel right at all."

Dante walked up to the window, Nadie on his tail, and he reached out to keep her behind him. That casual and caring gesture broke Jamie's heart, but she pushed it down. There were more important things to deal with at the moment.

"It's different from the last time," Dante said as he pulled Nadie closer.

She watched as Hunter sniffed the air and shuddered. "You said it was the gods or something along those lines that started the storm before?"

Becca walked up to him and shrugged. "Maybe. We're not sure. We just know the lightning hit us, and now things are changing."

"This isn't the same," Dante repeated. "If we're correct, then the last storm was from the gods, bringing in a new light and direction for the paranormals. This isn't god- or manmade. No, this is magical, of its own accord."

He turned to Jamie, and fear clawed at her belly.

"Djinn," she whispered.

"How do you know?" Amara asked as she gripped Eliana's hand.

"I don't know," Jamie said. "It just feels like magic I should know...magic that's part of something I am or could be. I can't really explain it."

"I think you explained it perfectly," Ambrose said as he nodded toward Shade. "If it's a djinn storm, then they've declared war. They can't show their powers in the human realm in a fashion that can destroy all our secrets. It's the first rule in any realm."

Shade nodded and hugged Lily close. "We'll stop them."

"How?" Jamie asked. "What's the point of starting a storm here? Is this Kobal?" She turned to Ambrose as Balin's arm tightened around her.

The windows shook as the wind hit the bar hard. She heard the wind howl and the rain slapping against the window. Off in the distance a siren wailed, and Jamie shuddered.

This couldn't be because of her.

It couldn't.

As the magic within her swelled to the taste of the storm, she knew it was true.

Pyro wasn't their only enemy. No, now Kobal wanted her dead, and it looked as if he was doing all in his power to make it happen. She hoped it was Kobal because, if it wasn't, that meant they had yet another enemy.

"What are we going to do?" Jamie asked, ready to take a stand. She was tired of hiding and running.

Ambrose looked out at her group of friends, and she followed his gaze. All were pale, wide-eyed, but not backing down. This was her family—not a group of djinn who didn't want her. Why had she felt as though she were nothing when the djinn rejected her? They didn't matter. Her friends mattered.

Jamie would be damned if they were hurt or worse because of a pure-blood prejudice.

"We're going to stop whoever is doing this," Ambrose said simply.

Balin growled. "I don't like that the storm tastes only of djinn. This would be a perfect time for Pyro to attack."

The wind hit the door hard, emphasizing his words.

"Hell," Hunter mumbled as he rubbed his chest. "I want to kill that fucking demon."

"Stand in line," Jamie said then flinched as the rain pattered against the window harder.

"Okay, I want those without powers to go to my room in the back and stay there," Dante said over the howling wind, getting louder with each passing moment.

Dear Lord, it sounded like a freaking tornado out there.

Jamie thought about all the innocent people out there and shuddered. Damn Kobal. They couldn't let this stand.

"You just want us to hide while you guys go out and fight?" Faith asked, her hands fisted on her hips.

"Yes, that's exactly what we want you to do," Balin spat, his body morphing into his demon form, his horns curling against his hair. "We need you to be safe while we take care of it. Yes, it sucks, but what can you do against magic? Until you find your true halves and change, you're still human. Deal with it."

Faith narrowed her eyes and opened her mouth to say something that probably wouldn't help matters, but Eliana help up her hand.

"Balin is right," Eliana said.

"What? We're just going to listen to the big bad men now that they're here? What are we, little women who need help?" Faith glared, but Jamie saw the fear in her eyes.

"No, you are people we care about who can't fight against this. Not yet, anyway," Jamie explained in the calmest voice possible.

Faith raised her chin, but Amara tugged on her hand. "No, don't fight. We'll let them deal with this because we have to." She turned toward Balin and Ambrose. "But if Jamie or any of our friends get hurt, then we'll have to have some words."

"Deal," Ambrose said.

"Lily's going with you," Shade ordered then kissed his mate hard. "I'm not letting you or our baby get hurt."

"Okay, but only for our baby."

"I'd force you back with the others, but since we're pretty sure this is Djinn magic, we might need you," Ambrose said as he traced Jamie's jaw. "Stay with Balin and me."

She nodded, the love for both her mates flaring.

They could do this.

They had to do it.

As Dante led the girls to the back room, a gust of wind hit the door, tearing it off its hinges and shattering the windows.

Jamie screamed as Balin threw his body over hers, her shoulder hitting the ground and sending pain down her side. She heard the other girls yell out, and one scream in a gut-wrenching sound of pain.

The wind wrapped around them, whipping in dangerous

funnels, sending tables, chairs and everything else not nailed down flying around the room.

"We need to find cover," Balin yelled over the raging storm.

"Where? We're inside!" Jamie hollered back as the rain slapped at them—icy shards digging into her skin as her clothes clung to her body.

She could barely see though the sheets of rain and debris but could make out forms on the floor, moving as carefully as they could to somewhere safe.

There wasn't anywhere safe.

They weren't safe.

"There has to be something we can do," she said as Balin tugged her beneath the bar, which offered a bit of shelter, at least for now.

"Where's Ambrose?" she asked, her heart in her throat. She still felt their bond but couldn't see him. He had to be okay.

"I don't know, baby, but we'll find him."

She leaned into his heat, grateful that she at least had him, but it wasn't enough. Her friends couldn't get hurt or die because of someone who wanted her dead.

That wasn't the way things worked.

She was a djinn—at least by blood, if not title. If it was a djinn fighting them, then she should be able to fight back.

There had to be a way.

She closed her eyes, letting her aura wash over her, her body strengthening in its djinn form.

She could taste the magic of the storm, the vile taint that

should have been something as good and beautiful as normal djinn magic but had been transformed and mutated into something unwanted and dirty.

This was the fault of someone insane.

She closed her eyes tighter and concentrated on the magic she felt. It was almost as though strings or cords reached out to farther places in town and closer to the bar—as if it were propelled by magic. They were almost tactile as if she could reach out and touch them if she knew how.

Maybe she could counter it with her own magic, as she had when she'd wrapped her aura around Balin and given him his strength back with her first wish...

She could use a wish here and try to save her friends. Would it work?

Instead of wishing aloud and possibly wasting it, she let her own magic flow from her, cords of power flaring out from her center as they counteracted the evilness of the storm.

She let the cords of her own power reach out and grazed the cords of the other one. It was almost like a snake attacking another in the beauty of it. The other cord pulled back as if stung and retreated to a place she couldn't see. If they were right in thinking it was Kobal, that must be where he was hiding. Maybe if she followed that path she could find him...

"Stop, Jamie, you're hurting yourself," Balin called out, his voice faint, as if he were far away.

She did as he told her because she trusted him with every ounce of her being, and her eyes fluttered open.

"Did I help?" she asked, her voice almost a croak.

Balin's throat worked hard as he swallowed and nodded. "You got the storm out of the building, but it's still raging outside. Never fucking do that again. Do you hear me?"

She tried to lean on her elbows but almost fell back from her lack of energy. "I helped. Why are you yelling at me?"

"You almost died. You used too much fucking energy without training."

"Oh, I didn't realize."

"Well, you do now. Don't do it again." Balin kissed her hard, and she tasted the desperation and relief on his lips.

"Where's Ambrose?" she asked as she pulled back.

Balin's eyes widened, and he stood quickly, pulling her with him so fast that she got a head rush.

"Ambrose!" Balin yelled as he ran to the other side of the room, dragging her behind him.

"I'm fine; it's just a small cut," Ambrose said as he tried to smile away his pain.

Fury raged through her as she went to his side. How dare someone hurt her mate? It wasn't a small cut, not by far, but it wasn't a mortal wound. Angels and the like couldn't die by a small wound and could heal faster than others, but that fact didn't stop the fear from crawling over her. It looked as if a piece of metal had slashed across his torso, but the bleeding looked like it would stop soon.

"Thank God," she whispered and hugged him on his good side.

"I'm okay," her angel whispered as Balin brought both of them into his arms.

"We're okay," her demon said.

A pained roar echoed in the room, pulling them out of their thoughts. It sounded as if a thousand deaths layered in anguish had ripped from Hunter's throat.

She turned and froze, all the blood leaving her face. "Becca!"

Becca against the wall, her eyes wide as her breaths became shallow. No, Jamie was wrong. She wasn't standing.

Becca's toes barely touched the ground as she struggled to free herself from the large piece of wood that impaled her. Blood poured from the wound, a dark red that surely meant something far worse than a normal wound.

Hunter gripped her hips and kept her body from sliding down and tearing at her flesh even more.

"No, you don't get to die," he growled. "You need to live. Do you understand me?"

Becca blinked, and Jamie pushed through her other friends who stood there, their bodies cut and bruised but alive… unlike what she feared Becca would be soon.

Jamie's body shook as the sobs threatened to take over, but she pushed them back. She needed to be strong. She couldn't show the fear that made her helpless.

"Becca, we're going to take care of you," Jamie said, her voice shaky.

Becca tried to smile, and a small trail of blood seeped from her lips. She coughed, sending a spray of red along Hunter's chest, but he didn't flinch. He just kept her steady so she wouldn't hurt more.

Oh, God, no. It couldn't end like this. She couldn't let Becca die.

She turned to Ambrose, whose face was unreadable. "What can I do?"

He reached out and slowly cupped Becca's face. Jamie's heart cracked open.

No, no. This couldn't be happening.

"For God's sake, do something!" Faith yelled, her voice hoarse with tears. "Don't just stand there and let her go. You're magic for fuck's sake."

Balin pressed a hand against the small of Jamie's back. "You've lost so much energy, but I don't think you have a choice now."

Jamie nodded and moved to stand beside Hunter. The feral wolf who'd saved her life didn't spare her a glance now. No, his gaze locked with Becca's, the untold story of what they would have been—no, what they could still be—blatant in their eyes.

Blood pooled around Becca, and her best friend's body was so horribly pale Jamie was afraid she'd be too late. She had a feeling that her wishes might be able to save the living, but not the dead.

God, don't let it be too late.

She closed her eyes and let her aura wrap around Becca like a warm blanket. Much like it had been with Balin, Becca's aura was nearly non-existent, fading with each passing second.

"Hunter, I don't know how to wish that she be okay with her body still impaled. You're going to have to move her."

Her voice cracked at the end, and someone sobbed behind her.

Hunter growled, low, deadly. "Wish quickly," he said, the sound of his voice more animal than man.

She kept her eyes closed, concentrating on keeping her aura around Becca. She felt Hunter move, and Becca screamed.

A scream so full of agony Jamie wanted to weep.

"I wish for Becca to be healed fully, and to live" she whispered, hoping her words would be enough.

She opened her eyes as Hunter slowly lowered them to the floor, Becca in his arms.

"Did it work?" she asked as her own body sagged. Balin caught her and lifted her to his chest.

Hunter didn't say anything, his hand tracing along Becca's side. The blood had stained her friend's clothes so much that Jamie couldn't see past the stain to a wound.

"Did it work?" Amara repeated.

Hunter nodded. "She's healed," he whispered, and Jamie let the tears fall.

"Oh thank God," Eliana said.

Jamie pulled away from Balin to look at her friends, tears on their faces, blood on their clothes, but standing.

They were alive.

They could get through this.

"Thank you," Hunter said as he looked toward Jamie. "I owe you more than my life."

The others stood still at the words that made his intention clear.

Becca was his mate.

"You owe me nothing. She's my best friend. Take care of her," Jamie ordered as Ambrose knelt down to check on the wound.

"You're down to one wish," Ambrose said.

"I know, but it's worth it."

"It's not over yet," Balin said, indicating the storm still raging outside.

"Then let's make it over. I think I know where Kobal is. I felt his magic." She rubbed her arms, remembering the tainted taste of the djinn's magic.

"Then that's what we'll do," Balin said.

"Hunter, stay with Becca and those who can't fight," Dante ordered. "At least not yet," he added as Nadie glared at him.

"We're going to stop this," Jamie said, her voice stronger than before. "He can't take everything from us."

"Then let's do it," Balin said as he ran a hand down her side.

She gave one last look to her human friends and followed Ambrose to the door, where beyond the storm raged like a dying king, ready to take all down in its path.

She was djinn, and she wouldn't let others fall for her leader's lack of grace.

She was stronger than Kobal thought. Jamie glanced at her mates.

They all were.

❄

Hunter looked down at the woman in his arms and fought back another howl. The other women in the room had tried to take Becca from him, but he'd merely growled and they'd stepped back. He'd ordered them to the back as he carried Becca behind them, his touch as gentle as it could be.

Though the blood on his hands would never wash away.

Twice he'd almost lost her before he had her.

He knew the woman in his arms was his mate, and he'd do all in his power to keep her alive and by his side.

Not yet.

First, he had to make it safe for her to be with him, and considering his Pack had fallen while he'd been gone, he knew it wasn't the time.

But soon.

Soon he'd have his redheaded mate by his side, under him, and everywhere in between.

Soon.

Balin gripped Jamie's hand and never wanted to let go. That had been too close. He never wanted to see the fear and pain in his mate's eyes again. From the look of the storm around him, he had a feeling things were far from over.

He turned toward Ambrose and ran a hand along his angel's side. "Are you okay? I know we were focused on Becca back there, but are you still bleeding?"

Ambrose shook his head. "I'm fine. The bleeding has already stopped. Worry about protecting yourself and Jamie. Don't waste it on me."

Balin stopped where he was, forcing the others to do the same. "No, I get to worry about you and Jamie the same way. Do you understand me?"

"This isn't the best time for this," Dante said as the rain pelted them.

"Yes, as happy as I am my friend has found two loves, we can deal with the angst later," Shade said, and Balin wanted to deck him.

Yes, it wasn't the best time, but he needed to get his point across in case they didn't make it.

Something was off. Not just Kobal and the storm, but he could feel the presence of something else…something even more evil.

He had a feeling Pyro wasn't done with them.

The time had come, and Balin wasn't about to let the people he loved and cared for stand in the line of fire for him.

"We can talk about this when we finish this," Ambrose said as he leaned into Balin's touch. "We *will* win. And I love you, just so you know."

"Like there would ever be another outcome," Balin said, relieved that Ambrose seemed to understand that Balin loved him and Jamie with equal intensity.

"Yes, I'm glad that my two alpha men understand they love each other, but it's raining, and I want to get back to Becca. Meaning we need to go find Kobal now, okay?" Jamie said as she shivered in the rain.

Balin laughed despite the tension in the air. "True enough. Now, what's our plan?" He palmed the daggers at his hips, keeping them hidden just in case an unsuspecting human were to see them. With the way the storm raged around them, he was pretty sure that wouldn't be a problem.

It seemed the humans knew enough to fear what was outside their doors.

It might have been the djinn magic leading them to feel that way, and Balin was grateful. That meant they could use their own powers without having to worry about peering eyes.

They made their way to the place where Jamie was sure Kobal was and froze.

Hades.

Holy Hades.

Djinn and demons littered the abandoned streets of the warehouse district. Each were in their supernatural form, as if they didn't care about getting caught. Balin couldn't sense any humans around, but there had to be at least thirty djinn and twice as many demons.

To their left, a fire erupted from a warehouse. To the right, djinn in their supernatural forms crossed their arms over their chests, their magic pouring from their pores as they fueled the storm. In the center of the street, the demons stood with broadswords and glares.

"What the fuck is this?" Dante asked, smoke billowing out of his nose.

Damn, Balin didn't want to be there when Dante changed into his dragon form. That would mean death for too many to count if he became that enraged.

"If we don't stop them from raiding the streets of this city, they've declared war," Ambrose rumbled as he clenched his sword.

Jamie grabbed Balin's hand, the fear wafting off her in short bursts. "There's so many."

"We'll take them down," Shade growled. "We won't be able to take them all at once."

Dante grinned. "I'll take the peasants since I can take them more than one at a time."

Shade nodded. "I will help."

Ambrose looked off to the side. "Balin, do you feel that?"

He nodded, letting that familiar feeling of distrust and disappointment wash over him without leaving a mark like it had done so many times before.

Pyro.

"He's in the warehouse to the right. You know I cannot kill him," Balin spat, anger at Lucifer's curse rolling through him.

"It is long past time that I make Pyro pay for his mistakes," Ambrose said as he leaned down to kiss Balin then Jamie on their temples. "I will take that warehouse while Dante and Shade take the underlings. Jamie, I want you to stay up here and use your djinn powers against the storm. Stay out of the way of the fighting."

"I can help."

Ambrose nodded. "And you will, but not with the fighting. You're stronger with the magic within because you and only you can fix this. You're not trained in fighting, not yet."

"Something we will fix soon," Balin growled as he squeezed Jamie's hand. "I'll take the warehouse that's on fire. I have a feeling we'll find our djinn leader there."

Jamie nodded, worry on her features. "He's there. I can feel him. Be careful." She stood on her tiptoes and kissed Ambrose hard before turning to Balin. "Please." She pressed her lips to his, and he sank into the flavor of her kiss.

He wouldn't lose today—couldn't lose. He'd just found his mates, and he needed to stop the ones who wanted to kill them. It was past time.

Balin pulled back and nodded to the others. While Shade and Dante roared toward the masses, Balin ran off to the side toward the warehouse fire. He tried to put the fear for his mates and new friends out of his mind. They could take care of themselves.

He slid through the shadows, aware of the other demons and djinn around, but they weren't his priority. No, it was the leader of the attack—at least one of them.

Kobal had threatened Jamie, and for that alone, Balin wanted to kill the bastard, but now he'd taken it to a new level—endangering thousands of innocents all for his twisted game.

The roar of a dragon echoed in his bones, and he risked a look over his shoulder. Dante, still in human form, was on the attack. He sliced his way through the demons as though they were nothing but lower-level demons, not the high range Balin felt. Shade followed in the air, using his sword on the ones Dante hadn't reached.

Good, those two would be okay. He just had to pray Ambrose and Jamie would be the same.

The flames from the fire licked at his skin, the heat

reminding him of home. To a human, it would be too much, but for him, it was a welcome sight. He'd gain energy from the flame, much like a dragon.

He knew that wasn't the case for the djinn.

"I see your abomination found me," Kobal said from his place right outside the warehouse, his hands stretched out, palms up.

The djinn had to be using a lot of energy to keep the storm up, even with his other djinn, who at the moment were most likely dying at Dante's and Shade's hands.

"I'd quit talking about her like that if I were you," Balin warned as he palmed his daggers, ready to strike at any moment. "If you piss me off any more, I'll make you hurt before I kill you."

Kobal threw his head back and laughed. "You're just like your father said. Nothing."

Balin didn't let the taunt hurt him. He didn't care what his father said about him, not anymore.

"You do realize you're just the distraction in this game, don't you?" Balin asked as he moved closer, watching the sweat slowly drip down the djinn's temples. "Pyro's the main act while you're just here to distract us."

"You're lying, and I'm going to kill you for that. Pyro came to *me* because he couldn't get the job done. Who's the better man now?"

Neither of them in Balin's opinion, but he wasn't about to make an issue out of it.

"Pyro will be dealt with momentarily." He said a quick

prayer for Ambrose. "You're here because you're behind the times. The gods deemed these girls worthy, and all you've done is anger them."

"And you speak for the gods now, boy?" Kobal shook his head. "No, I don't think so."

Balin saw the djinn's arms straining as the power leached from him, the storm sucking him dry.

Maybe he wouldn't have to use his dagger after all.

He'd rather kill the bastard now, just to be sure.

Balin struck like a flash, embedding one dagger in Kobal's neck, the other sliding with ease under his ribcage, piercing his heart.

Kobal's eyes widened as he staggered. Blood gushed from both wounds, coating them both. Kobal lowered his hands, but the magic still poured from him, draining him of his life's energy.

"No..." the dying man gurgled.

"Sort of anti-climactic, isn't it?" Balin said as he pushed the man to the ground, watching him die. "You didn't have to take Pyro's taunts. You didn't have to die."

Kobal tried to murmur something but couldn't speak with the dagger in his neck.

Just as his eyes turned to glass, the djinn looked at the sky and smiled, taking his last labored breath.

Balin knelt to remove his daggers then followed the dead man's gaze.

Fuck.

The storm, without the djinn's power to control it, was

only getting worse. Dark black and gray clouds boiled. The wind howled through the streets, sweeping anything not nailed down in its path.

The storm wouldn't end on its own.

Another djinn would have to stop it…if they could.

He looked up the hill to where Jamie was hidden behind the trees and cursed.

She'd have to save them all.

Another demon roared, coming at him like a battering ram, and Balin focused on the battle at hand. He'd make it to Jamie's side one way or another, but first, he needed to make sure nothing could hurt her.

Then it would be up to her new powers to save them all.

AMBROSE LOOKED UP AT THE SKY AND CURSED. HE COULDN'T feel the magic from the other side of the street anymore, meaning Balin most likely had killed Kobal. From the look of things, it was far from over.

He couldn't deal with that right now. No, there was a demon waiting for him.

It had been a long time coming, and now he was going to do what he should have done ages ago on that battlefield.

He crept through the darkened alley, following the stench of the demon he should have killed. Ambrose cursed himself for not doing it before, for showing that mercy that had cost so many lives.

Without Pyro, would he have found Balin?

A slight pang echoed through him, but he pushed it down. There was no going back, no tempting fate. His happiness wasn't worth the dead that lay at his feet.

He *knew* that, even if he was grateful beyond measure for both Jamie and Balin.

Ambrose gripped the hilt of his sword and walked into the empty building—well, almost empty.

Pyro slouched in a chair a grin on his face. When Ambrose cleared his throat, Pyro faced him and chuckled.

"I knew it would be you. My bastard of a son can't try to kill me because of Lucifer's curse, but that's not the same with you, is it?"

"You shouldn't have come to the human realm. You've started a war."

Pyro shook his head and planted his feet firmly on the ground. "No, I don't believe I have. That fucking Kobal is a weakling, all that incestuous blood running through his veins. I'm sure my son has taken care of him if you're here."

"You've still brought human attention to yourself, Pyro. That cannot be tolerated. Our secrets cannot be revealed. None of us want a war with the humans, not even you."

He'd already stopped one calamity with Shade and Lily the previous year. He'd be dammed if Pyro threatened all supernatural kind just for revenge against the three of them.

"I couldn't care less about the humans. They're food for me anyway. All I want is for you and your precious *loved* ones to die. If I happen to start a war, and they blame it on you, all the better."

Pyro stood and stalked toward him, but Ambrose stood where he was, waiting for the perfect time to strike.

"You're not going to leave here alive," he said as he gripped his sword tighter.

"You're very sure of yourself. You couldn't kill me last time, and you won't this time. I was going to wait to kill you so you could watch me rape your bitch, but I don't care anymore. You're going to die, and then I'll get any one of my other demons to kill Balin."

"Cocky until the end, Pyro. That will be your downfall."

Pyro glared and lashed out with his claws, but Ambrose was faster. He turned on his heel, swinging his sword upward with all his strength.

Little resistance met his blade as he sliced through Pyro's neck, beheading the bastard in one swoop.

The demon's eyes widened as he reached up to the cut on his neck then fell to his knees, his head landing beside him.

Blood pooled around the body, and Ambrose let out a sigh.

He should have done that before. No, he'd thought he'd seen good in the man and let him live. He'd never been so wrong before, but through Pyro, he'd met his loves, his fate.

It was over.

It almost seemed too easy.

The wind slapped against the glass in the windows, shattering the one farthest away from him, and he cursed.

No, it hadn't been too easy.

The storm was out of control, and that meant Jamie was their only hope to stop it or all of this would be for nothing.

Without a djinn controlling it, the humans were at risk from the impact of the storm, as well as finding out supernaturals existed.

He gave one last look to the demon who'd plagued him for far too long and left the body where it lay. They'd clean up their messes once they were done.

Now he had a mate to help.

The mate who would help them all.

JAMIE FELL TO HER KNEES, THE WIND LASHING AT AND tangling her hair. She'd felt it when Kobal had died, her bones almost breaking under the strain of magic in the air. She couldn't see either of her men, but she had to pray they were okay.

She'd had the vague hope that once the djinn leader and his followers were dead, the storm would dissipate and it would all end.

Sadly, that wasn't the case.

There was no way she'd die on her knees though. No way, she'd go down fighting.

Using as much strength as she could, despite the roaring wind, she stood on her two legs, facing down the storm that wouldn't die. Another surge of rain and wind came at them and she stretched out her arm, palm up, to pull at the core of the storm.

As if she'd formed her own wave against it, her power clashed against the storm, sending it back into itself so it didn't attack the people below.

Her power waned, but she gritted her teeth.

There had to be something else she could do.

Before, it had taken all her strength to just keep the storm at bay, not letting it grow and move toward the unsuspecting areas of the city. As it was, she had no idea how they were going to explain this to the humans. The others had thousands of years of experience doing just that, so she'd leave it to them.

The storm brewing overhead, however, looked like it would be her problem.

Dante and Shade were finishing up the last of the demons and djinn. The pained screams as the enemies fell would forever echo in her mind, but it was better than the alternative.

If that made her cruel and callous, she didn't care.

She couldn't let her family die.

The rain fell hard, soaking her to the skin. She shivered, and her teeth chattered as the wind whipped across her, practically icing her bones.

It didn't matter. It couldn't.

The street filled with water as the rain dragged on, and she knew a flood was imminent. Damn it. There had to be something she could do. She couldn't last long like this, not when she didn't know the full extent of her powers. Instinctively, she knew how to stop the storm from moving on, but she couldn't stop it.

She didn't know how.

"Jamie!" Balin called as he ran to her, his chest heaving. His clothes held bloodstains.

"Oh, God, are you hurt?"

"I'm fine. It's not my blood." He stood beside her and gathered her into his arms.

Though she wanted to lean on him, she couldn't. She needed to do this on her own. She pulled back but gripped his hand.

"You need to stop the storm, baby," he said. "It's not something any of us can do. A djinn started it, so a djinn must stop it."

Her body shook as she kept that fragile hold on the cord the storm possessed. "I'm trying, but I don't think I'm powerful enough. At least on her own." A tear threatened to escape, and she cursed. She couldn't start crying because, once she did, she was afraid she'd never stop.

Balin ran a hand down her back and kissed the crown of her head. "You're stronger than you give yourself credit for."

"I can see the cord, or whatever it's called, that connects me and my magic to the storm. That's how I'm stopping its progress—or at least slowing it down. I don't know how to shut it down." She shuddered. "I don't know if I *can*. I'm going to find a way, damn it."

"If you can't stop it using your normal powers, you'll have to use our last wish, my love," Ambrose said as he came to her side. Though she'd been able to see him coming, she hadn't been able to focus on it, not when she had to use all her strength to deal with the storm.

Relief, sweet relief swept through her as he pulled her and Balin into his arms. It was short-lived however as she pulled back so she could stand between them.

"I need to focus on the storm and not fall into your arms right now. Are you okay?" she asked.

"I'm unhurt."

That didn't really answer the question, but she'd take it.

"Pyro?" Balin asked, and despite the pain radiating though her body as she fought the storm, she hurt even more for him.

"It's done," Ambrose said and leaned forward to place a soft kiss to Balin's lips.

As both men pulled back, she watched Balin's face for any hint of emotion but saw only the resigned expression that marked Ambrose's.

"I'm sorry you had to deal with something I should have been able to," Balin said, his voice low and barely audible over the raging wind.

"I would do anything for either of you," Ambrose said. "For now, we need to help Jamie. Love, if you can't stop the storm on your own, you'll need to use your wish. You saved Balin and Becca—both people you love. Now you need to save *everyone* you love."

Jamie nodded. "I had already figured that's what I'd have to do, but I needed to make sure. You know more about them." She turned to narrow her eyes. "Something we'll have to change. Soon."

Balin framed her face with his hands as the rain continued to pour down on them.

"You can do this. No matter what happens in the future, you'll always have us. We'll do all in our power to make sure you don't regret using up your wishes so early."

A gust of wind slapped at them, draining her energy just that much more.

"I'll never regret using the wishes as I have. Never."

She kissed him hard then moved to do the same to Ambrose.

"Hold me?" she asked, needing their strength.

"You should never have to ask," Ambrose said as she stood between her two men, yet also under her own power, ready to use her last wish as a djinn.

She closed her eyes, focusing on the storm, praying that this would work.

"I wish for this storm to end and the magic that came with it to cease, keeping the humans unaware."

She added the last part to keep Kobal's initial magic that had kept the humans away intact. She could only hope it worked.

Slowly, the wind died down, and the flooding receded. The rain became almost a drizzle, a soft memory of the storm that had raged with all its fury.

Shade and Dante walked toward them, their clothes wet and their bodies strong, but with each lagging step, she knew they had to be as tired as her.

She watched as a small sliver of moonlight cracked through the clouds, and she smiled.

"It worked," she rasped out.

Shade smiled, and Dante shook his head as if to clear it.

Her men held her closer, and she inhaled their heady scents, wanting to go home and never let them go.

"You're amazing, my djinn," Balin whispered.

"Our djinn," Ambrose corrected, and she laughed.

In the face of all that had happened, she laughed.

It would be okay.

They'd won.

CHAPTER 18

Ambrose settled his hand over Jamie's naked hip, loving the way her soft skin felt against his palm. They were in their bed in her home…no *their* home. He and Balin had tired her out the previous night showing her exactly how much they loved her, but he wanted her again.

And, his cock was ready to make that happen.

It had been almost a week since the storm had taken out the abandoned warehouse district. With the help of some of the supernaturals, the humans said it was a freak storm that had cleaned out the wasted area they'd been meaning to renovate anyway. The city would soon have parks and new business down there, replacing the seedy underbelly it had once been.

The blood and stench of death had been washed away, leaving no trace of what had happened that fateful night.

Kobal and Pyro were dead, and those who wanted the

triad's heads were gone. Though Jamie didn't have any more wishes up her sleeve, she still had the magic that ran through her veins, rendering her as long-lived as he and Balin. Balin would live as long as Ambrose and Jamie were alive thanks to their bond, and now Ambrose had something to live for besides being a warrior.

He had hope.

A future.

Despite the echo of pain he felt at the thought, they'd have children to raise. He would tell them of their lost half-siblings so those children would live on in memories.

It seemed as if they had a future to embrace. One with Jamie's parents. Through a lot of discussions, they'd decided to tell her parents about her new life. As no one had ever been through this type of situation before, they felt that they had a right to make their own progress and make sure that they could have the future they wanted. Though no one could become a supernatural without the gods' will—apparently—they could still make sure their connections to the human realm weren't burnt beyond recognition. They had a life here and would do anything they could to keep it.

Though they would never return to hell, they had a home in the human realm—and in the angelic one. The day before, his council had sent a missive saying that Balin would be an honorary angelic warrior—something that had never been done before.

Jamie had received the same honor.

It seemed that the council felt that anyone who could

protect the supernatural secret and save the angelic kind was deemed worthy in their book.

He'd take it, even if it felt high-handed.

They'd sent a third missive asking him to join their council—again.

And, like the previous times, he'd declined.

He had a family to enjoy, and he wanted them to be free in the angelic and human realms, and if the new djinn leader, Temperance, had anything to say about it, they'd have a place with the djinns as well. Though he knew Jamie already had plans to talk with Temperance about training so she could find the full extent of her powers and control. That would take time, but he knew she'd be happy. They all would be.

A far cry from where they'd stood before.

Jamie's lush bottom pressed against his groin, and he groaned, pulling himself out of his thoughts.

Balin chuckled and slid his hand between Jamie and Ambrose, cupping her ass and brushing against Ambrose's cock.

Ambrose groaned again, rocking into the both of them.

"I thought we were sleeping in," Jamie grumbled as she wrapped her leg around Balin's waist.

Their demon moaned as Ambrose was sure his cock was pressed against Jamie's soft pussy.

"From the feel of it, I don't think you want to sleep anymore," Balin said as he kissed her softly.

Ambrose watched his lovers kiss while he ran his hand over her stomach and lower to circle her clit.

Jamie whimpered, and he sank two fingers into her heat, brushing Balin's cock in the process.

"Fuck, that feels good," Balin said as he rocked against them both.

Ambrose worked her until she panted, her body blushing. Balin bent his head, sucking on her nipples, and she came against them.

He quickly reached back to get the lube from the nightstand drawer. They'd been preparing her for this, but now it was time.

"I'm going to sink into that sweet ass of yours, my love. And, while I do that, Balin's going to fill that pussy of yours. We're going to love you until you can't move."

"That sounds like the best morning ever," she said breathlessly.

"Hell yeah," Balin said.

Ambrose slowly worked her hole, preparing her for him. Her bottom pushed back, eager for his touch, and he chuckled.

"Wait, my love, it'll be better with anticipation."

"The hell with anticipation. I'd rather have you in me," Jamie said, her body writhing under her Balin and his touch.

They were all still on their sides, so it would be tricky, but well worth the wait. When she was ready, he positioned his cock at her puckered hole and held her hips.

"Push out, my love," he said as he gently rocked his cock past the tight ring of muscles. She moaned, and he stopped, letting her body get accustomed to his size. Then he slowly pumped his hips, letting his cock slide into her tight heat, her ass clenching around him.

Dear God. This was heaven.

Well, a part of heaven.

Sliding into her pussy or mouth, or Balin's ass or mouth, was just as heavenly.

Right now, right at this moment, he'd found perfection.

When he was fully seated, he gripped her hips and rocked a bit more.

"Ambrose, oh, God, yes," she said, her body flush against his.

"We're not done yet," he whispered into her ear then kissed behind her earlobe. "Balin, are you ready?"

He looked up at his demon lover who stared at them with dark eyes, his nostrils flaring as he inhaled their scents.

"Past ready." Balin carefully lifted Jamie's leg just a bit higher and slowly slid into her heat.

Ambrose felt his other lover's cock press against his through that thin layer of tissue and shuddered.

Fuck.

This had to be the best thing ever.

"I'm so full," Jamie whispered as both men lay still, waiting for her to acclimate.

"I love you," he whispered to them both then began to move.

Balin matched his rhythm, so they worked in and out of her in tandem, slowly rising to the crest that would surely break them all.

His balls clenched, and he reached around to massage

Jamie's breasts. She leaned into his touch, and he rolled her nipple.

"I'm going to…"

She didn't finish her sentence. She tightened her lower muscles around him as she came. He followed soon behind, his cum jetting within her, filling her up. Balin groaned as he did the same, their breaths in sync, their bodies entwined.

"We need to do this every morning," Jamie said once she could speak again.

Ambrose chuckled. "Anything you want, love."

Balin moved to get a wet towel then cleaned them up. Ambrose lay back with Jamie resting on his chest, her nipples hard against him.

"I know you haven't asked, but I'm okay if we don't get married the traditional way," Jamie said, and Ambrose froze.

He risked a glance up at Balin, who stood at the end of the bed, his eyes wide.

Ambrose cleared his throat. "Actually, Balin and I were discussing how we could do something along those lines."

Balin knelt on the bed between Ambrose's legs so he could be close to Jamie as well. She leaned on her arms and turned slightly, a frown on her face.

"How are we going to do that?"

"Well," Ambrose started, "if you want, one of us can marry you in the human realm. In any of the other realms, triads are acceptable, even cherished. So, yes, the three of us can be married in a traditional angel, djinn, or demon setting."

"Not demon," Balin said with a grin on his face, showing that he was okay with not including demons in their future beyond himself—and hopefully their children and Fawkes.

"So you're saying we can be husbands and wife?" She laughed. "That sounds weird, but I'll take it. We don't have to have a human marriage. We're already doing things differently by living like this. We don't have to prove anything to anyone."

Ambrose traced her face while Balin did the same to her side. "Are you sure?"

"Of course. I love you both. I don't want to deal with the humans and have to make a choice between the two of you. I'd rather do something that makes the three of us happy."

He kissed her softly then Balin did the same.

"How did we get so lucky?" Balin asked.

"I have no idea. You'll just have to prove you're worth it," she teased, and Ambrose growled, moving her to her back so he could tickle her.

"Oh, really?"

"Stop!" She gasped through laughter.

Balin attacked her other side, and she wiggled between them. "Fine, you win."

"Good. You should know I'm always right," Ambrose said, his voice as serious as he could make it.

"Sure, baby, anything you say," Jamie said. "Have you heard from Becca by the way?" she asked, her teeth biting into her lip.

"No, why?" Ambrose said as he ran a finger over the

indentions she made with her teeth. "Wouldn't she call you and not me?"

She shrugged, worry on her face. "She hasn't called me or anyone else. I thought maybe since she seemed to like you, she'd call to ask you about her true half or something."

Ambrose nodded, understanding. "You mean the fact that Hunter hasn't claimed her yet, though we all know she's his mate? Oh, and how since I left you for a year because I had to deal with my council that maybe she saw a similarity in her own situation?"

"Yes, that." She blushed under his gaze and he leaned to kiss her cheek.

"I don't know exactly what's going on, but I have a feeling that fate will help if needed."

"As long as you think you're right."

"You just said you'd listen to anything I say," he teased.

She slapped his side and laughed.

"Speaking of, I have an idea for your store," he said as she sat up.

"Really? I thought I'd have to close it and move to something different since it's not doing well in this market, and now that I'm not human, I'm going to have to figure out new things to do."

Balin ran a hand down her leg. "I don't have a job up here either, other than helping Ambrose and the angels if they need me."

Ambrose nodded. "And we'll need you both in the future, I'm sure. What I was thinking is that you can use your store for not only humans but supernaturals as well. You can open it up to fairy tales and histories of the supernaturals. We can have a wizard or witch ward off part of it so the humans don't go there, and then the supernaturals on the human plane will have somewhere to go to read subjects that humans wouldn't care about."

He'd been thinking about what to do for her since before he'd come back down from the angelic realm, and with all that had happened, he was just now able to voice his plans.

Jamie's eyes widened as a wide smile broke over her face.

"Oh, my God. I love it!" She wrapped her arms around him and hugged him hard. "It's perfect."

Balin smiled. "I could help with that, you know. It's something that could benefit everyone and will give you something that's still part of the realm you grew up in."

"I love you both so much. You're my mates, my lovers, and my warriors. I have to be the luckiest girl in the world."

"You two saved me. There's nothing I wouldn't do for you," Balin said.

Ambrose pulled her and Balin into his arms as they fell back on the bed, a tangle of limbs and breaths. "No, you two saved me. Or, maybe, we saved each other. Though we don't know yet what the future will bring, we have each other to lean on."

They had each other and their futures.

He didn't need five thousand years of history to tell him that his life had changed and only for the better.

They were his present and future and the saviors of his past.

They were his everything.

And, he hadn't needed any wishes to make it happen.

The End

Coming next in the Dante's Circle world, An Unlucky Moon where Hunter and Becca find out what it means to be different yet so alike they need each other.

Thank you so much for reading Her Warriors' Three Wishes I do hope if you liked this story, that you would please leave a review! Reviews help authors and readers.

Thank you so much for going on this journey with me and I do hope you enjoyed my Dante's Circle series. Without you readers, I wouldn't be where I am today.

If you want to make sure you know what's coming next from me, you can sign up for my newsletter at www.CarrieAnnRyan.com; follow me on twitter at @CarrieAnnRyan, or like my Facebook page. I also have a Facebook Fan Club where we have trivia, chats, and other goodies. You guys are the reason I get to do what I do and I thank you.

Make sure you're signed up for my MAILING LIST so you can know when the next releases are available as well as find giveaways and FREE READS.

Happy Reading!

Carrie Ann

Dante's Circle Series:

Book 1: <u>Dust of My Wings</u>

Book 2: <u>Her Warriors' Three Wishes</u>

Book 3: <u>An Unlucky Moon</u>

<u>The Dante's Circle Box Set</u> (Contains Books 1-3)

Book 3.5: <u>His Choice</u>

Book 4: <u>Tangled Innocence</u>

Book 5: <u>Fierce Enchantment</u>

Book 6: <u>An Immortal's Song</u>

Book 7: <u>Prowled Darkness</u>

<u>The Complete Dante's Circle Series</u> (Contains Books 1-7)

Carrie Ann Ryan is the New York Times and USA Today bestselling author of contemporary and paranormal romance. Her works include the Montgomery Ink, Redwood Pack, Talon Pack, and Gallagher Brothers series, which have sold over 2.0 million books worldwide. She started writing while in graduate school for her advanced degree in chemistry and hasn't stopped since. Carrie Ann has written over fifty novels and novellas with more in the works. When she's not writing about bearded tattooed men or alpha wolves that need to find their mates, she's reading as much as she can and exploring the world of baking and gourmet cooking.

www.CarrieAnnRyan.com

Montgomery Ink:

Book 0.5: Ink Inspired

Book 0.6: Ink Reunited

Book 1: Delicate Ink

Book 1.5: Forever Ink

Book 2: Tempting Boundaries

Book 3: Harder than Words

Book 4: Written in Ink

Book 4.5: Hidden Ink

Book 5: Ink Enduring

Book 6: Ink Exposed

Book 6.5: Adoring Ink

Book 6.6: Love, Honor, & Ink

Book 7: Inked Expressions

Book 7.3: Dropout

Book 7.5: Executive Ink
Book 8: Inked Memories
Book 8.5: Inked Nights
Book 8.7: Second Chance Ink

Montgomery Ink: Colorado Springs
Book 1: Fallen Ink
Book 2: Restless Ink
Book 3: Jagged Ink

The Gallagher Brothers Series:
A Montgomery Ink Spin Off Series
Book 1: Love Restored
Book 2: Passion Restored
Book 3: Hope Restored

The Whiskey and Lies Series:
A Montgomery Ink Spin Off Series
Book 1: Whiskey Secrets
Book 2: Whiskey Reveals
Book 3: Whiskey Undone

The Fractured Connections Series:
A Montgomery Ink Spin Off Series
Book 1: Breaking Without You

The Talon Pack:
Book 1: Tattered Loyalties

Book 2: <u>An Alpha's Choice</u>

Book 3: <u>Mated in Mist</u>

Book 4: <u>Wolf Betrayed</u>

Book 5: <u>Fractured Silence</u>

Book 6: <u>Destiny Disgraced</u>

Book 7: <u>Eternal Mourning</u>

Book 8: <u>Strength Enduring</u>

Book 9: <u>Forever Broken</u>

Redwood Pack Series:

Book 1: <u>An Alpha's Path</u>

Book 2: <u>A Taste for a Mate</u>

Book 3: <u>Trinity Bound</u>

<u>Redwood Pack Box Set</u> (Contains Books 1-3)

Book 3.5: <u>A Night Away</u>

Book 4: <u>Enforcer's Redemption</u>

Book 4.5: <u>Blurred Expectations</u>

Book 4.7: <u>Forgiveness</u>

Book 5: <u>Shattered Emotions</u>

Book 6: <u>Hidden Destiny</u>

Book 6.5: <u>A Beta's Haven</u>

Book 7: <u>Fighting Fate</u>

Book 7.5: <u>Loving the Omega</u>

Book 7.7: <u>The Hunted Heart</u>

Book 8: <u>Wicked Wolf</u>

<u>The Complete Redwood Pack Box Set</u> (Contains Books 1-7.7)

The Branded Pack Series:
(Written with Alexandra Ivy)
Book 1: Stolen and Forgiven
Book 2: Abandoned and Unseen
Book 3: Buried and Shadowed

Dante's Circle Series:
Book 1: Dust of My Wings
Book 2: Her Warriors' Three Wishes
Book 3: An Unlucky Moon
The Dante's Circle Box Set (Contains Books 1-3)
Book 3.5: His Choice
Book 4: Tangled Innocence
Book 5: Fierce Enchantment
Book 6: An Immortal's Song
Book 7: Prowled Darkness
The Complete Dante's Circle Series (Contains Books 1-7)

Holiday, Montana Series:
Book 1: Charmed Spirits
Book 2: Santa's Executive
Book 3: Finding Abigail
The Holiday, Montana Box Set (Contains Books 1-3)
Book 4: Her Lucky Love
Book 5: Dreams of Ivory
The Complete Holiday, Montana Box Set (Contains Books 1-5)

The Happy Ever After Series:
Flame and Ink
Ink Ever After

Single Title:
Finally Found You

EXCERPT: AN UNLUCKY MOON

Next From New York Times Bestselling Author Carrie Ann Ryan's Dante's Circle Series

The fiery depths of hell were a cool afterthought compared to the torment of what lay before him. Hunter Brooks ducked the punch aimed at his head and rolled to the ground, coming up on his feet a few yards away. He never let his gaze leave his opponent, even as he moved his arm to stop a kick to the neck.

The low roll of thunder in the distance set his wolf on edge, but he tamped it down. The rain would come eventually, and Hunter wanted to make sure he was done with this before then. The circle was already a mud pit, the wet sludge clinging to his torn jeans—he didn't want to deal with more of that.

His wolf brushed along the inside of his skin, an animalistic presence that wanted revenge, blood, and death.

The man within him wanted the same thing.

The other wolf came at him at his fastest speed, but Hunter was faster. His hands shifted to claws, and he slashed out, catching the other wolf along the shoulder. His opponent screamed as blood seeped from the deep wound, but Hunter didn't care. He squeezed his fingers together, cutting the other man deeper.

His opponent met his gaze, the anger all but lashing out at him.

Hunter had seen the depravity of a winged demon bent on quenching its thirst and lust on decaying corpses within the depths of the gladiator games.

This wolf had nothing on that.

His opponent slashed his claws down Hunter's side, but Hunter moved too fast for the other wolf to break the skin.

He'd spent enough time playing around with this wolf, allowing him to think he actually had a chance. Hunter lifted a lip and showed fang, growling deep within his chest. The air around him seemed to freeze, and time stood still.

Hunter cocked his head to the side as fear seeped into the other wolf's eyes. Finally, the other wolf knew its life relied on Hunter's mercy.

The others called Hunter an animal.

They called him depraved.

Soulless.

Yes, this wolf had something to fear, but death would not be among them.

Not today.

Hunter kicked out then twisted, causing the other wolf to fall to his knees in pain. He gripped the bastard by the neck and squeezed.

"Forfeit," Hunter growled, his voice scraping against his throat from lack of use.

The other wolf's eyes rolled back, and then he slammed his hand to the ground twice.

The murmurs and howls around them forced Hunter to look at the crowd. He and the other wolf stood in the center of the Nocturne Pack circle, blood and mud covering their bodies and worn jeans. Other members of his Pack growled around them. Some had looks of relief on their faces. Others held a bit of fear…or anger.

The latter would have to be dealt with soon.

"Matthew calls forfeit," Liam Murray, council member and one-time friend, called out. "It is up to Hunter whether to call death, but the circle has chosen. Hunter is our Beta."

"As it should have been in the first place," Josiah, their Alpha, spat. "I have spoken and the circle has agreed. My choice reigns."

"For now," Dorian Masterson whispered, though Hunter wasn't sure if anyone else had heard the bastard.

Hunter had keener senses than most wolves due to his bloodline and destiny. His stint in the gladiator games of hell had only honed them stronger. He'd been back only a month, and he still didn't feel as though he fit in his skin. Everything had changed in his absence.

The council had grown with more power. His Alpha had

grown weaker without Hunter there to protect him. Josiah's last protector had perished

Samuel…Samuel, Hunter's brother, had died protecting the Alpha when the council had tried to take over.

None of it made sense to Hunter. He'd fought for his life countless times and killed so many demons and other supernaturals that he wasn't sure the blood would ever leave his hands, yet when he'd returned to the human realm, he'd faced another battle.

His own Pack.

Hunter rolled his shoulders then stalked toward his Alpha, who stood surrounded by the five council members. That alone pissed him off to no end. The council should have no place near the Alpha. There were only advisors on good days and whispers on bad ones.

Yet they stood there and had demanded a fight to the death to secure the position of Beta.

A position that Samuel had held.

A position Hunter had held before he'd been taken by the demons and forced to serve.

He knelt in front of his alpha, glaring at the others as he did so.

"My Alpha," Hunter grumbled then turned his head to the side to bare his neck. Others gasped around him, but he ignored them. They should have been the ones to bare their necks, but they'd become lax in their duties and rituals.

They'd thought the Pack was a democracy.

They would soon be proven wrong.

Josiah put his hand on Hunter's shoulder and nodded.

"You're a fine Beta, Hunter. You will make me proud. You make me proud."

Something warm started to fill him, piercing through the ice at his Alpha's words, then dissipated. His wolf howled within him and hardened against the intrusion. No, it wouldn't do any good to warm at his Alpha's words.

Hunter wasn't a warm man. He was a killer—his Alpha's killer. He'd been raised to be that wolf, and he'd fulfilled that promise in hell. Now he was back within the confines of his Pack and ready to kill again.

Or at least that's what he told himself.

"Hunter, good fight," Alec Brennan, another of Hunter's one-time friends and council member, said as he slapped his shoulder. "You almost killed that Lloyd wolf." A vicious gleam entered Alec's eyes, and Hunter grunted.

"Let the wolf live in his memory of defeat," Hunter growled. "I'm not in the mood to kill a useless slug who isn't worthy of the title Beta."

"Watch what you say about my son," Gregory Lloyd snarled. The older council member tried to come at him, his teeth bared, but Alistair Jacobs—the remaining council member—held him back.

"It would do no good to fight like animals," Alistair drawled. "We might have the wolves at our beck and call, but we will remain civilized."

Hunter snorted at that. There had to be over a hundred wolves surrounding them in human form, each shirtless, ready to shift if necessary. Each adult male—and some of the juveniles—were marred with scars and tattoos that celebrated their victories in battle.

At any moment, since the circle was over, they could break out in brawls to release the tension.

There were only two ways to release the tension riding through their bodies—fighting and sex. As wolves, they didn't care about privacy and modesty. If there was a woman—or a man, if that was their inclination—in front of them, they'd fuck them hard, letting the stress and worries from the day seep away.

Since there were no willing partners at the moment, Hunter was sure a fight would break out soon. Blood and sweat would soon permeate through the air, filling Hunter's nostrils to override the stench of betrayal and anger that poured from the wolves that had lost their hope today.

Today, like most other days, fighting would rule over sex.

The females were back in their homes—what few females they had. Wolves were born, not bitten, in their world, unlike what the fandoms believed. Though it was easy to get pregnant, it was hard as hell to keep that baby and even harder to produce a girl.

Their absence at the circle meeting had been the council's decision, not the Alpha's. Their history had always held their women in deep respect. Not only were they wolves in their own right, but strong fighters as well. They were feared among the men if someone threatened their pup.

Yet the council had declared them weak in Hunter's four-year absence. Apparently the women—and men—who had fought back against the council taking over had been beaten or killed.

Nothing was right in the Nocturne Pack.

Hunter kept blaming the council for all of it, but he knew it wasn't the five of them. No, it was three of them who held the power—or at least thought they did.

For now.

"Come on," Liam whispered. "Let's look at those cuts of yours at my place. It will rain soon anyway. I'd prefer not to get my hair wet." He grinned at his last remark, but Hunter didn't respond. Unspoken was their need to talk about the undercurrents within the circle.

Hunter had been back in the human realm for a full month, yet change took time. After Ambrose, Jamie, and Balin—and of course the young demon, Fawkes—had rescued him from the depths of hell, he'd returned to the realm he'd grown up in.

Unlike most supernaturals, wolf shifters and some other types of shifters lived within the human realm but were hidden deep within the forests. Their own magic kept the humans away and their secrets buried. Other supernaturals lived in other realms that were accessible through only the human realm. It was as if the humans themselves were the glue that held everyone together.

Fitting considering the humans weren't really humans at all but merely diluted down versions of supernaturals themselves. They didn't know the things that went bump in the night were real and had no idea that, within themselves, they held the ability to change into another being…if something were to alter their course, that is.

Hunter had grown up with the humans around him and his Pack at his side. They might be dark and depraved in the best of times, but he'd loved them like his own.

He'd thought he'd return to the Pack he'd known, but that had not been the case.

Four years was a long time to be gone.

Everything had changed and not for the better. Though one thing might offer the light on his horizon.

He'd left her alone so he could find his place and be better for her. Now it was time.

He'd find her soon. His Becca.

"You must be thinking about a woman," Alec teased as they made their way back to Liam's home. "You're smiling."

Hunter grunted then walked inside the place with Liam and Alec following. He turned on the lights and stretched his arms over his head. He was damned tired after that run even though he still felt a bit on edge since he hadn't hunted big game.

"I don't smile," Hunter growled.

Alec just shook his head and stole a beer from Liam's fridge. Liam scowled and slapped the back of Alec's head.

"You never ask to take my shit," Liam snapped.

Alec frowned. "I didn't think I had to, Murray," he drawled.

Hunter blinked at the two of them, their tension different than it had been before he'd been gone. While before the two had always bickered and annoyed each other, this felt different. Before they'd always smile and get over it, the tension dissipating after a few moments. Now, though, there seemed to be an underlying current between the two that Hunter couldn't quite put his finger on.

"Guys? It's beer. Get over it."

The two men swiveled their heads at him and glared. They might have looked nothing alike, Liam with his dark looks and blue eyes, Alec with his brown hair and green eyes, but right then, they had the same expression.

Hunger, anger, and confusion all rolled into one.

What the hell?

Looking at Liam, Alec twisted off the beer cap then took a long swig. Liam's jaw clenched as he ground his teeth together, and then he handed Hunter a bottle.

Hunter looked between the two men but put his questions aside. He had enough to deal with without delving into whatever drama they had.

"Tell me about what I missed," he said after a minute of awkward silence.

"Everything, Hunter," Liam said.

"No shit," Hunter snapped. "Give me specifics."

"When you left—" Alec began then cut himself off. The other man clenched his jaw then took a deep breath. "No, when you were taken, things went to shit. We still don't know how you were taken to the demons, Hunter. You have to believe that."

Hunter nodded and meant that. He knew the two men in this room wouldn't have sold him to the demons. That was all he knew though. He had his ideas of what had happened, but no proof.

Finding out how he'd been sold as a slave to the highest demon bidder was high on his list of priorities.

Liam cleared his throat then put his hand on Alec's shoulder before sitting down on the couch. Alec shot him a look, and Liam pulled his arm away.

"When you left, Masterson, Lloyd, and Jacobs thought they found an opening for their plan," Liam continued. "They've never hidden from those who've looked as though they want to take over the Pack. They want to bring the wolves into the twenty-first century, as they put it, and force a democracy."

Hunter cursed. "We're wolves. That cannot happen. None of the other Packs who have tried that have survived. We're not humans. We have wolves wrapped around us, deep within the very aspects of our souls and beings. Denying an Alpha should hurt."

Liam nodded. "You're not telling us anything Alec and I haven't said before. The amount of pain, though, depends on the Alpha."

Hunter held back a grimace. "Josiah is getting older, but we don't age like humans. His power should only increase with age."

Alec shook his head. "Not without a Beta who can support him or without the magics that got him the position anyway. An Alpha can't survive without a Beta. Josiah holds all the magic and strength of the entire Pack on his shoulders, but he can't rule and be himself without another to lean on."

Hunter nodded. "He would have been fine if he hadn't lost Clara."

Liam ran a hand through his hair. "She's been gone for a decade, Hunter. Josiah is stronger than he gives himself credit for, but he can't do it alone. He shouldn't have to do it alone."

"And Samuel, may he rest in peace, wasn't strong enough to protect him," Alec whispered.

Hunter didn't wince or move at the mention of his late brother's failures. No, that wasn't quite right. He couldn't call his brother's decision a failure since the boy had done all in his power to protect the Pack. It just hadn't been good enough. There had never been any question that Samuel hadn't been strong enough for the position, but the kid should never have been put in harm's way to begin with. If Hunter had been there, Samuel would be alive.

That above all else would be something that would haunt Hunter until the day he died.

"Have you found his killer?" Hunter asked, his voice low, deadly.

Alec shook his head. "No, but we can make guesses."

"The three bastards who think they can take over the Pack." Hunter clenched his fists, his fury riding him hard.

"You're here now and named Beta in truth," Liam said. "We couldn't do it alone, not and keep our families alive and the Pack fluid, but we'll be by your side, Hunter."

Hunter nodded but stayed silent.

"The struggle has only just started, Hunter," Alec put in. "We don't know what the others have in store, and we don't know exactly what they've done in the past. All we know is that we'll protect Josiah and you with our lives."

Hunter inclined his head at the two men who had been his best friends since they were pups. The three of them had always been thick as thieves, and when they'd grown into adult wolves, they'd taken their positions as council members and Beta in stride.

Alone they were strong.

Together they were stronger.

"This will cause a war if we're not careful," Liam murmured.

"We're already in a war," Hunter said flatly. "We just need to make sure it's contained."

The last thing he wanted was to bring their conflict into the other realms and hurt the humans.

Especially one particular human. She'd already been hurt once from a supernatural battle, and he'd be damned if he'd let another touch her.

He'd walked away from her once to ensure her safety.

He wouldn't do it again.

Find out more in <u>An Unlucky Moon</u>. Out Now.
To make sure you're up to date on all of Carrie Ann's
releases, sign up for her mailing list <u>HERE</u>.